COLOR OF AUTHORITY

WHEN TAKING A KNEE BECOMES TAKING A STAND

BRUCE CARLETON FISHER

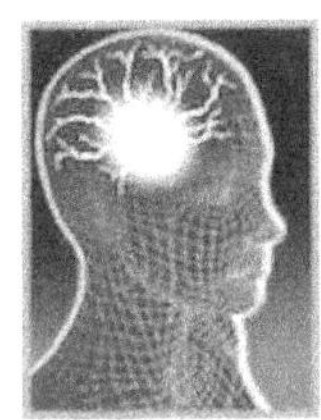

To The
Orishas
Ancestors
and
Paternal Grandmother, Julia Freeland Fisher Martin Robison Delany,
Malcolm X, Marcus Garvey, Fannie Lou Hamer,
Steven Biko, Patrice Lumumba, Dr. King, Louis Farrakhan, Muhammad
Ali, Clarence Avant, Sam Cooke, Harry Belafonte, Nelson Mandela,
Angela Davis, Fred Hampton, Huey P. Newton, James Brown, Toussaint
L'Ouverture, Gordon E. Fisher, their Loved ones, Mothers and Widows

CONTENTS

1

HAPPY LANDINGS

Lt Colonel Jesse Hawkins, United States Marine Air Corps, looked down on the flight deck of the USS Theodore Roosevelt then checked the heads up display.

Air speed, three hundred knots. Altitude, eight hundred feet. Perfect.

He lowered the tail hook on the F/A 18E Super Hornet and prepared for a fifty degree left bank turn.

Extending the speed brake and setting the throttle to idle, he began interval air braking. He was about to engage the auto pilot but suddenly changed his mind.

After establishing U.S. freedom of navigation rights, in the South China Sea, the Nimitz-class nuclear powered super- carrier, had made San Diego, California its new home port. That deployment had been Hawk's last and it had taken him, literally, around the world.

As part of Operation Fisted Glove, the carrier had launched 1,800 sorties against Al Qeada in Iraq and Syria.

The strikes totaled more than 10,618 flight hours, and delivered over a million pounds of ordnance.

Hawk had flown more than a hundred of those sorties.

Sitting behind the stick of 44,000 pounds of super turbofan thrust, he'd directed massive air strikes on people he'd never seen.

He was glad he'd never seen them.

He didn't allow himself to even think about them. He was carrying out his orders. And the number one thing Hawk Hawkins always did, was carry out an order.

Bottom line; Nobody could ever say that Lt. Col. Jesse Hawkins didn't have the right stuff. But occasionally, in the quiet of the wee hours, he sometimes worried for his immortal soul.

But none of that was on his mind right now.

He hadn't flown combat in years. These days he was enjoying the relative peace and quiet of the Miramar headquarter squadron.

He was at a point where he wasn't interested in a higher command. At this stage of the game all he wanted was to finish his bit and retire with benefits.

He'd been promoted to Lieutenant Colonel only a year ago and even if he stayed in, he didn't like his chances of ever making full Colonel. He knew he could keep jockeying for another ten years if he wanted to, but he was ready to go.

It had been one helluva ride, but it was over.

This was the last time he'd land one of the fiercest combat fighter jets ever made, on the deck of the "Big Stick". That's why he hadn't engaged the auto-pilot. He wanted to be personally involved with every moment of this final approach.

As he extended the slats and and slowed the fighter further he remembered the days when he'd been terrified of this maneuver.

Especially at night.

The thought of planting a jet plane on a skinny, rolling, pitching, 500 foot strip of paint, in the middle of the ocean, at 130 knots, in the dark, was scary.

It still was, but nothing like it used to be.

He checked his air speed again as he headed into a ninety degree donut on final approach.

As the jet dropped to four hundred fifty feet he eyed the glide slope on the Optical Landing System. Trajectory was good.

The meatball was on the line and he was on speed.

He suddenly called out,

"324 Hornet, ball nine point one."

The system responded,

'Ball Ball Ball.'

Moments later the tail hook snatched the high tinsel steel cable stretched across the flight deck and the jet slowed from 130 knots to 0 in two seconds.

It never got old. Like a base runner trying to beat the throw; You never knew if you were safe until it was over.

2

WHO'S YOUR FRIEND?

You wanted to see me sir?"

VMFA Commanding Officer Colonel Titus Jaworski, returned Hawk's salute.

"Howdy Hawk" he said.

At ease."

The head honcho of Hawks's Marine Air Group, grinned while stretching a long arm over his desk.

Hawk shook his hand and waited to learn why he was here. Jaworski didn't keep him waiting long.

"Before you leave us" he said,

I wanted to personally thank you for your service and extend my best wishes for your future.

Gonna miss you Hawk. You're one of the good ones."

'Did he mean a good officer or good nigga?' Hawk thought but said instead.

"Thank you sir."

Over the years Hawk had mastered the lessons taught by his mother from the age of understanding.

From day one she'd drilled three things into his head; Don't make no trouble. When they say what, don't ask why, and most important, survival beats all.

To that end, Lt. Col. Jesse Hawkins, was adept at being an Uncle Tom.

Not a true Uncle Tom in the accepted sense.

Although he usually said what he knew was wanting to be heard, he was never psychologically subservient.

"Sit down, sit down" Jaworski entreated while dropping back into his own chair.

"Really sorry to see you go" he said again.

"What'd you put in, twenty years?"

"Twenty-two" Hawk answered.

"Twenty-two years" Jaworski repeated as he flipped through a folder on his desk.

You look too young for that.

Guess it's true, Black really don't crack."

"Yes sir. No sir" Hawk stumbled.

The reference sounded and felt condescending but he responded without guile.

Came in when I was twenty-one.

Graduated college early."

"Yeah you're plenty smart alright" Jaworski agreed.

Says here you were commissioned out of USC, via their NROTC program. Bachelors in Civil Engineering. That's quite a program they run. No dummies coming out of there."

"No sir."

Jaworski continued studying the folder's contents.

"Not only did you graduate in the top percentile, but you led the PAC 10 in rushing your last two years.

That's some superman shit son."

Hawk lowered his eyes and voice.

"Had an All-American line both years sir."

"Just what I'd expect you to say" Jaworski replied.

But it wasn't the line breaking tackles and stutter-stepping'. That was you."

Hawk didn't like discussing his athletic abilities with his superiors.

He'd always suspected that his fellow officers were more comfortable accepting him as a physical superior more so than an equal officer.

Some had convinced themselves it was only his physical prowess that allowed for his presence among them. Nothing at all to do with anything else.

He'd learned to be okay with allowing them their pacifier.

"Guess I'm blessed sir" he said.

"I'll say."

Jaworski put his elbows on the desk and leaned forward.

"So what are you going to do now?" he asked.

Jaworski had never shown any personal interest in him before. Instead of asking 'Why now?' he said,

"Probably find a place in the old neighborhood.

Settle back in. Maybe teach, coach a bit. "

Jaworski adjusted his seat.

"Yeah, I expect you could do those things" he said.

His jovial demeanor turned suddenly serious.

"But really,

including all your allowances, you're pulling down what?; Around a hundred twenty K?"

Hawk's antennae shot up.

You're used to a decent standard of living" Jaworski said.

How're you going to get along on only half your base pay?"

'Now I know you ain't worried about my money' Hawk thought but said instead,

"I'll be all right. I managed to put away a little something over the years."

"Good for you, glad to hear it.

You'd be surprised how many don't.

But I'll bet you could use a little buffer yeah?"

Hawk shrugged.

"Depends on what we're talking about."

Jaworski's mood lightened.

"I was talking with a friend the other day and your name came up."

'Who you talking to about me'? Hawk thought but asked instead,

"How's that?"

"You ever think about going into politics Hawk?"

The question was out of left field.

Hawk answered with a well-trained neutral expression.

"Can't say that I have sir."

"Well you should. You'd be a natural at it."

"If I may sir. What's this about?"

"My friend is a close associate of Edric Everhart.

You know who that is?"

'Hell' Hawk thought, 'if you know, everybody knows'

but he said instead,

"The preacher presidential candidate, yes sir."

"That's right. The thing is, if he wins, he's going to name my friend to head the DNI."

Hawk waited for the punchline but his boss followed up with,

"The campaign is looking for men who can follow orders." 'Yeah so, Hawk thought before answering,

"A lot of men can follow orders sir."

"They're wanting you" Jaworski replied.

"Why me sir?"

Jaworski leaned back and folded his arms across his chest.

"Drop the sir" he said. Do yourself a favor.

Go see my friend."

Hawk had been invited to ignore rank. A foundational tenet fundamental to a functioning military had been waved.

He didn't want another mission. He'd looked forward to retiring while he was still young enough to enjoy it.

But ultimately it was an easy decision. Today he was still a Marine, and he did what he always did.

He looked his commanding officer in the eye and said,

"Who's your friend?"

3
THE BIG BOYS

Why are we even discussing budget at this point?

Rule one; Never count your chickens. Quickest way to lose."

Four star General Angus Kellogg, (U.S.Army ret.) two hundred sixty pounds of crusty sledgehammer addressed a gathering in a Los Angeles penthouse.

He was talking to the Republican party presidential candidate, who was present as the subject of the meeting.

Hawk sat on a blue velvet Nico couch intently listening to the conversation. He found the entire scenario surreal.

He was meeting with the most influential men in the country and he could see no logical reason for his being here.

"There's one inescapable fact" Kellogg was declaring.

We've got to expand the party's perimeters."

The sound of Kellogg's voice made Hawk uncomfortable. It was phlegm garbled ugly. He sounded like he was strangling, like his neck was chocked with slime and gravel.

If a talking frog had pneumonia it would sound like Kellogg. Hawk wanted to clear his throat.

"Frankly" Kellogg announced,

We can't put this country on a path to global Christian dominance until we win this election."

The statement was so odd that Hawk wasn't sure he'd heard it right. He looked around the room. None of the others seemed surprised by the declaration.

"It's a new day" Kellogg said.

There was a time when this conversation would've been absurd. But times have changed. The key to winning is winning. Nothing succeeds like success."

Kellogg seemed to be ranting, but his redundant cliches perfectly exemplified his future plans.

Today, winning simply means securing the Black female vote. Getting that vote is the whole ball-a-wax".

That's when Hawk realized why he was there.

They needed the decorated Black Marine to parade around in the upcoming campaign.

'Okay' Hawk thought,

That accounts for me but what about the Hispanics? They're the fastest growing demographic and there isn't a Hispanic anywhere in the room.'

Kellogg seemed to read his mind.

"Most of the Mexicans are too scared to vote" he declared.

They know ICE will be waiting for them.

But these church going Black gals are a different story.

We need to get on them right away."

Everhart off-handedly proffered a preference for old school voter suppression to which Kellogg replied,

"If I had my druthers that'd be how I'd play it too. And if this approach falls short that's what we'll do, but Like we said. Times have changed."

Kellogg looked to Hawk, who met his gaze with a blank canvass.

"But fortunately for us" Kellogg continued, Most Black voters are Christians.

And who's got the greatest Christian ticket of all time?"

He paused as a seldom seen grin spread over his face.

"We do." he exploded.

All we need is the right point person to carry the message to the Black community."

Hawk listened poker faced but Everhart seemed uncharacteristically vulnerable.

The candidate was as transfixed by the occasion as Hawk, and for many of the same reasons.

He was rich and successful now, but he'd started life in a lowly Texas trailer park.

"A vote for Everhart is a vote for Jesus Christ Himself" Kellogg proclaimed.

The audacity of the statement embarrassed Everhart but it only spurred Kellogg on.

"And any vote against him" he shook his fist overhead,

Is a vote for the Devil in hell."

He raised both arms overhead and made the victory sign.

"If you love Jesus, you'll vote for Edric Everhart.

That's the message we're going to pound and pound and pound" Kellogg insisted.

If you love Jesus, if you love Jesus, if you love Jesus.

And nobody, and I mean nobody, loves their Jesus more than these African American gals."

The old General had given it his best. His face had turned a soft pink and tiny beads of sweat glistened on his forehead.

Dressed in his usual black vestments, Father Will Guillory, grinned profusely. The U.S. Superior of the Society of Jesus, stuffed both hands in his pockets and rocked back on his heels.

Guillory had received special dispensation from the Vatican to act as Everhart's Secretary of the Treasury, should he win.

Unlike Kellogg, Guillory's voice was soothing. His dulcet tones and choice of words generally had a calming effect.

"Relax Angus" he said.

Don't discount the entirety of the Hispanic Catholics. Remember, they're the only ones who actually name their children after Jesus. Those who do venture out to the polls will certainly have some inclination toward our ticket.

And you've seen the polls. The numbers get better every day. Internal projections suggest we're making inroads with independents as well as conservative minorities.

It'll be close but if we shave a few more Black and Brown votes in the big cities we're in there."

Guillory took a sip from a handblown Baccarat cognac glass before directing a confirming glance to Hawk.

"We don't have to worry about the Blacks" he said.

Given the proper use of our resources, I don't see any reason to panic."

Despite Guillory's manner and tone, he'd rightfully earned the nickname, 'The Black Pope'. But Everhart wasn't convinced.

He got up from the overstuffed Nu buck leather chair and meandered over to the window.

Looking down on the Century City streets below, he was circumspect.

"Angus might be right Will" he said.

The polls are encouraging, but they're not foolproof. There's many a slip between the cup and the lip. Times are indeed changing. If we're going to be in for the long run we need those fresh votes."

Everhart didn't know much about politics but he did know human nature. He'd fed his flock a steady diet of, we're better than them, and he knew it wouldn't be easy to substitute the menu.

Speaking to Guillory's reflection in the window pane he asked,

"How're we looking out here?"

Carter Boatwright, partner at Vinson and Elkins, Huston's largest law firm, joined the conversation.

"We have no chance to win California" was his matter of fact reply.

Boatwright, was a thirty five year old wunderkind with noble ambitions and angular good looks.

His successful strategies representing clients before the Texas supreme court in corporate patent infringement cases, had resulted in his becoming the youngest partner in the firm's history.

It wasn't only Boatwright's legal mind that convinced Guillory to bring him aboard the campaign. Boatwright was also a fellow Jesuit.

"No point wasting resources here" Boatwright said.

With his back to the room, Everhart interjected.

"Depends on how you define resources."

Father Guillory suddenly broke in.

"Find a running mate from California" he said.

Somebody not too flashy.

We still won't win the state but we can imply inclusion."

Something about the moment stirred Hawk to speak.

Shifting in his seat he ventured,

"Excuse me gentlemen but just to be clear; what exactly is my involvement?"

He instantly regretted it. He didn't want to look pushy. Everhart turned around,

"That Black female vote" he said.

Surely you know that."

Hawk did know that but the naked frankness of Everhart's response caused him to cough.

"Something stuck in your craw?" Everhart asked but didn't wait for a reply.

Been looking forward to meeting you.

You come highly recommended. General Kellogg tells me Colonel Jaworski has nothing but the highest regard for you.

He says you're a patriot who never fails to carry out an order."

Hawk was wondering what Jaworski was getting out of this when Angus Kellogg asked,

"Is Jaworski right?"

Angus Kellogg served thirty years in the Army.

The last ten had been attached to the Special Activities Division of the C.I.A.

He'd made his bones in SAD where he was part of two separate groups. SAD/SOG for tactical paramilitary operations, and SAD/PAG for covert political action.

Kellogg gave Hawk the once over.

"Your former C.O. says you're a fella who knows how to play ball.

He says you know what to say and how to say it. That right?"

Before Hawk could answer Kellogg continued.

Cause I'll tell you before we get too deep into this;

If I thought you didn't understand the game, I'd a-never agreed to you being on the team."

All eyes trained on Hawk.

For the first in a long time he didn't have a ready tongue. Kellogg wasn't keen on his silence.

"We don't wanna keep you if you don't wanna stay so,

you staying on the field or you hitting the showers?"

This wasn't a hard question. Hawk straightened up.

"I've always been a team player sir."

"Alright then." Kellogg leaned forward in his chair.

Now let's get one thing straight. Whenever we're talking about Blacks around here, we're not talking about you. I understand you're one of the good ones."

Carter Boatwright instantly objected to the characterization.

"You can't say that" he said.

Kellogg wasn't a man to be challenged by what he considered to be a snot nosed white shoe.

"Can't say what?" he demanded.

"That he's one of the good ones" Boatwright replied.

You're implying that he's an exception, the rule being, that the majority of his race are not good."

Kellogg exploded.

"Got-dammit Carter, you know what the fuck I mean."

Spinning back to Hawk, Kellogg insisted.

"You know too."

For a brief second it appeared that Kellogg was apologetic.

"You've made considerable contributions to the country. You pulled your weight. But not everybody's like you. Understand?"

Hawk did understand. He understood that he was what was known hereto-fore as an 'acceptable negro'. A non-threatening, compliant, social eunuch.

When compared to the stereo-typical angry, lazy, uneducated scary Black, Hawk was indeed, an exception to the conventional rule.

He'd worked long and hard to cultivate the distinction and he wasn't ashamed of it.

A chuckle suddenly escaped Guillory.

"I was thinking about what Angus said" he explained.

You're one of the good ones. It reminded me of the parable of The Good Samaritan." His shoulders shimmied slightly in silent mirth.

Those Samaritans must have been an absolutely abhorrent bunch, he said. Imagine. Out of all the Samaritans, in the whole of the land, there wasn't but one, one good one." He chuckled again.

Even though it hadn't been that funny, the mood lightened. Hawk took advantage of the moment to ingratiate himself.

"I could show up when you needed me, and stay away when you didn't" he offered.

To see what else he might learn he asked,

Is there any particular talking point you'd like me to advance?"

"You can sell them anything you like" Everhart answered.

His famous smile finally made its grand entrance.

"That's your job."

Pouring cognac from a crystal Decanter he added,

"But whatever you say, whatever you do; Bottom line, we need their confidence, and I'm counting on you to deliver it."

'You'll never have their confidence' Hawk thought but said instead,

"Yes sir."

Suddenly effervescent, Everhart spouted.

"Let me state the obvious. You're our black face. You'll deal with the usual suspects; civil rights organizations, academics, religious leaders et al. Start by making inroads with the big churches. The bigger the better".

"Go after the TV preachers first" Guillory laughed sarcastically .

They make the best persuaders." Covering his smile with well manicured fingers Guillory again chuckled at his own joke.

"Just make them understand" Everhart insisted,

It's in their best interests to support this campaign."

"Because it is" Guillory added.

Hawk understood this was the same election season soup warmed over. 'But you never know' he thought. Maybe I could actually influence policy.' What did he have to lose? He wasn't sure.

"Yes sir, no problem sir" he promised, trying to find non-committal phrases to follow up with.

"I could be your man" he hesitated. If you think we might all benefit?"

Angus Kellogg lost it.

"In case you didn't notice" he gurgled. It's a dog fuck dog world out here. And unless you got a hankering to be stank-ass canine cunt, you best forget about everybody else and worry about yourself".

'Just checking' Hawk thought.

Kellogg wouldn't know it but he was Hawk's favorite kind of guy. A man who spoke his true mind. 'Kiss my ass' Hawk thought but said instead,

"I've no cunt hankerings of any kind sir."

Guillory rested his glass on the African Blackwood table.

"Now now Angus" he said.

Lt. Col. Hawkins will be working with us, and we don't want him to feel unappreciated."

"Damn right we don't" Everhart echoed.

Look at this guy. Big, strong, handsome, military. He's exactly what we need."

Everhart grinned and snapped his fingers.

You've got to wear the uniform" he said.

Hawk heard 'Sold'.

Unsure how he wanted to proceed, Hawk took the measure of the moment before answering.

"Thank you sir.

You'll forgive me but, this is all a bit sudden.

It's an honor to be asked to serve. It's a great opportunity but it's also a tremendous responsibility.

You're aware that I'm recently retired after more than twenty years of service. I hope you'll understand that I need a little time for consideration."

"Take all the time you need" Everhart replied.

We won't be ramping up for a couple of months but I'll need to know soon enough."

4
HOME COMING

Inglewood Park cemetery was still the same as he remembered.

With its infinitely flowing fountains, lush foliage and grand monuments, it felt more like a palatial estate than a burial ground.

Everybody from Billy Preston, to Billie 'Buckwheat' Thomas was buried here. Lots of famous White folk too.

It was also notorious for being haunted, but Hawk thought it was the perfect final resting place for his mother.

He'd been especially happy to see that her grave had been meticulously cared for. He'd be sure to write the administration office a letter of gratitude.

Taking a last look around he whispered, "I love you momma" as he passed between the towering wrought iron gates.

It had been a long time since he'd been home and L.A. felt both familiar and strange. While the mountains still imposed themselves majestically against the powder blue skies, palm trees still bowed gracefully with the many winds and freeways still snaked along like celebrity funeral processions, something felt different.

The giant green letters of Susan Miller Dorsey's name stood out against the white field of the High School sign.

The first glimpse of his Alma Mater instantly transported him to back in the day.

He automatically saluted the flag that still flew in front of the outdated stucco exterior.

The craggy grass creeping over the edges of the cracked sidewalk felt like the perfect welcome mat.

As soon as he saw the front steps of the school, the old R&B hit, "Whomp There It Is" instantly popped into his head.

This was where he'd first run into Loretha Moton.

Loretha, with her skinny legs and almond eyes, had dropped her lunch when he'd stumbled into her.

'Man was I nervous' he thought, as he remembered that first day of school.

While standing in front of the building, he'd panicked after seeing the sea of red handkerchiefs visible in every direction.

'Aw hell no' he'd thought. I'm wading ass deep in Bloods and me in my blue Dockers.'

He was new to the area. When his Mother had gotten a house-keeping job at a large hotel for more money than she'd ever made, the first thing she'd done was move out of Pacoima.

All he'd wanted was to play football here, but now he wondered if he'd made a mistake.

He'd planned to go straight to the lost and found and get some pants, any pants, to change into.

That's why he hadn't seen Loretha.

He'd been looking past her into the school's interior, wondering which way to go once he got inside.

To make matters worse, they'd bumped heads when he'd bent down to help pick up her lunch.

After that, she'd turned her head whenever they'd passed in the halls. He wondered where she was now.

Was she married? Did she have kids?

He bitterly remembered Vernon Howard, the gangbanger who'd also had a thing for her. He'd been the first person to ever pull a gun on Hawk. Vernon had also been the first guy Hawk knew to get killed in a drive-by.

He slowed the car down as he soaked in every curve and contour of the buildings. He thought about going inside to relive the sights and smells of hallways and class rooms but decided against it. Too many security hoops to jump through now-a-days.

He'd heard of plans to give the place a facelift.

The faded modular buildings could definitely use some renovation, but that was a concern for older heads.

As he cruised down Farmdale Avenue remembering first kisses and rivalries, he was just a sixteen year old kid.

When he turned onto Constitution Avenue and saw Jackie Robinson Stadium, it was like seeing Holy ground.

Memories of the stadium locker room where he'd laced up for the Dorsey Dons, came flooding back.

This was where his transformation from introverted momma's boy to star athlete had begun.

In the beginning things had been sketchy with his new team mates. They hadn't known what to make of the quiet nerd who didn't hang with the usual crowd. Did he think he was better than them? They didn't know that his momma just wouldn't let him run the streets.

Early on, they'd called him chicken hawk but he never flinched. At scrimmages when they'd tried to put a hurt on him, he always gave as good as he got. Often as not, he was the one bringing the pain.

It wasn't long before it became obvious what he could do on the field. He never argued with coaches or players; He always let his game do the talking.

Gradually, grudgingly, his teammates started to respect him, then accept him. In short order they dropped the chicken and just started calling him Hawk. Yet, for as much of a team player as he was, he never fully trusted anybody. Friends turned deadly around here real fast.

It was during this time that he started to master the philosophy of 'Go along to get along.'

His BMOC status solidified on a November Friday evening in the fall of '91. The night of the big game.

Nothing in the high school sports universe was bigger than a Dorsey, Crenshaw football game.

Even though he was only a freshman, Hawk had managed to make varsity as a third string tail back.

The Dons had kicked the Cougar's ass the last time they'd played and added injury to insult when they'd won the after game fight as well.

On this night the Cougars showed up like they always had; Ready to play.

After a back and forth battle with several lead changes, the endgame went from tense to straight Hollywood.

It was fourth and goal, with three seconds left on the clock and the Dons were down by four.

More by luck than design, the Dons had driven eighty yards in the final minute of the game but they'd stalled at the Cougar three.

Dorsey's All American tail back Sharmon Shaw, was out of the game thanks to Crenshaw D-Backs, Kaleon Green and Demetrius Henderson, viciously converging on him and ending his night.

To make matters worse Dorsey had lost their full back to an unsportsmanlike conduct call. A field goal was useless, so out of pure desperation, Coach Paul Knox, put Hawk in.

Hawk was supposed to seal the edge on an option play but when the quarterback muffed the snap the ball ended up on the ground. Hawk snatched it up, but instead of running, he'd flicked it to the tight-end who made a finger tip catch in the end zone as time ran out.

That's when the shooting started.

. . .

Most of the Crenshaw Cougars were Crips. A lot of them were from Hawk's neighborhood. Some of them were people he was cool with. But not tonight.

Humiliated by the last second loss, the Crips in the stands took revenge on the crowd.

Everybody was scrambling for cover when Hawk saw Loretha, frozen with fear, standing on the sideline totally exposed.

Two people got shot that October Friday night.

Neither was Loretha.

In the midst of the chaos, she'd found herself safely sheltered beneath the protective shoulder pads of trusty number thirty two.

After that night she'd never ignored him again.

They went together for two years before her family moved to Oakland.

He was reliving the bitter-sweet pain of first love lost when he heard his name called.

"Hawk? Jesse Hawkins?"

He turned to see the smiling familiar face of his old friend Dennis Cox.

"I thought that was you" Dennis laughed.

Got-damn! When you get back?"

As the men walked toward each other there was the sense that not a day had passed unseen between them.

"Den? Ain't this a bitch" Hawk chortled as he hugged his old best friend.

After a second they stepped back to take each other's measure.

Dennis was wearing work clothes. His olive green cotton tee shirt had the word 'Supervisor' printed in a semi-circle over his heart. He looked good. Healthy. A far cry from the last time Hawk had seen him.

Dennis had gone from being a well dressed street hustler, to a raggedy-ass crack casualty in the blink of an eye. By the time Hawk headed off to preflight indoctrination, Dennis was locked up.

. . .

"I heard you were dead" Hawk said, relieved that the rumors weren't true.

"Shit nigga" Dennis laughed.

Extending his arms out to his sides he made a whooshing sound like a jet engine. Then he made some jerking motions like he was crashing and his rotund body shuddered when he shouted,

"BAM! I heard *you* was dead!"

Their laughter was deep and real.

When he finally caught his breath Dennis said,

" Sho am glad you ain't dead."

"You too" Hawk answered.

"How long you been back? Where you stayin' at?"

"I got a spot over round Tenth and Adams" Hawk grinned.

Dennis nodded his approval.

"Cool, I'm still out in Pacoima. Got a little three bedroom, married a lil Mexican shortie, twin girls."

Hawk grinned so hard his face hurt.

"Look at you" he said. I never thought I'd see you holdin' down a square job, let alone wife and kids."

A look of quiet pride settled on Dennis' face.

"Learned groundskeeping up at Wayside" he said.

Worked a bit on the fire line too.

When I applied here I put it all down as my work experience."

Hawk shook his head.

"I can't believe these people hired a convict."

Dennis laughed.

"Me neither but it's been twenty years."

"You been here that long?"

"What I said. Drive in from Pacoima every morning. First one here everyday, 5:00am.

Look at these hands."

Dennis held out calloused gnarled fingers for Hawk's inspection.

"Damn."

This was a whole new Dennis. Back in the day, the aspiration of most young men in the hood was to be a player. The mark of a true player was the fact that he had soft hands. Soft hands meant you made your money with your mind, not your back. In those days Dennis' hands were as soft as butter. Now they were harder than petrified wood.

A glint of sunlight flashing off Dennis' wrist caught Hawk's eye.

He looked down to see that Dennis was wearing a beautiful heavy yellow gold watch.

Now this was the Dennis he remembered.

Glancing at Dennis' feet he half expected to see a pair of hand crafted Italian cap-toes. But no, Dennis was wearing work boots.

Nodding at the watch Hawk asked,

"They paying you right or you got a side hustle?"

"Oh you best believe they payin' me right" Dennis beamed. <u>And</u> I got a side hustle."

Seeing a trace of disappointment in Hawk's face, Dennis quickly added,

"No, nothing like that.

I quit the dumb shit a long time ago. Totally legit. I'm Head groundskeeper here, plus, I work ground maintenance over at Inglewood Park Cemetery, on the weekends."

Hawk's smile broadened.

"I just left there. You the one taking care of momma's grave?"

"You know that" Dennis smiled back.

Yo momma more my momma than my momma.

I think bout Miss Hawkins er' time I go over that side".

Hawk felt the bond only lifelong friends experience.

Dennis had been taking care of his mother's grave even though he'd thought Hawk was dead. That's a good friend. Dennis' eyes suddenly shone with the memory of the good ole days.

"I member she pick us up after school" he said.

Take us to Micky Dees. The movies. Ya'll had that pool at ya'll apartment. Summer come, she bringing out lemonade, yellin' at us,

'Ya'll stop that runnin and keep yo voices down.' All the time she making more noise than all us put together."

Dennis suddenly snapped his fingers, pointed at Hawk and laughed.

"And that time Dicky Washington almost drowned. Don't be for Miss Hawkins he'd a died sho".

"Dicky Washington" Hawk sighed.

Haven't heard that name in years. How Dicky doing?"

"Oh Dicky dead."

"Serious?"

"HIV, pneumonia, some shit. Dicky been dead".

The look on Hawk's face triggered Dennis to add,

"Dude, damn near er'body we know either dead or in jail."

"Terry Pedigree?"

"Dead."

"LuBop?"

"Dead."

"Toy Tommy?"

"Ain't nobody seen Tommy in years.

I'm tellin' you son, niggas all fucked up round here."

"What about our boy Jilly Jill?"

"Oh, he work for the city," Dennis nodded.

He aw-ite. We bout the only two niggas I know got jobs.

So what about you? What you gone do? He asked.

"I'm thinking about going sky diving" Hawk announced, smiling in Dennis' face before he could react.

"Nigga, you got a serious death wish" Dennis snapped.

The fuck you tryin' to prove?"

"Nothing" Hawk's eyes cast a rakish glint.

I'm alive. That's all."

"You gone get enough of that white boy shit" Dennis chided.

"It's not white boy shit."

"Fuck if it ain't. What other nigga you know, flyin' jets, jumpin' out airplanes?"

Hawk smiled. "I know a couple."

"You would" Dennis laughed.

Then Hawk got serious.

"I got a offer to work with the Everhart campaign."

Dennis' head snapped back.

"Nigga. Look at you" he said.

His happiness for his friend was suddenly interrupted.

"That's good for you personally" he said.

But Everhart ain't gone do nothin' for niggas in general.

Why you ain't workin' for Booker?"

Hawk shrugged.

"Booker didn't ask" he said.

Plus you know I'm Republican right?"

"Nah, I ain't know that. But I ain't surprised."

5

SHOULD I STAY OR GO?

Hawk looked over the equipment laying on the field and asked,

"What's happening here?"

Dennis pointed a gnarled finger and answered with authority.

"Them lawn and leaf rakes. Straight edge and sweep. Sweep rakes kinda like a broom. They the ones shaped like fans. Good ones got spring-steel teeth. The length is graduated so you get a straight leadin' edge. Some got rounded leadin' edges too."

Dennis indicated a particular rake.

This rake here is for scraping just the top of the grass. Just a little bit. You can see the way the teeth designed. It pulls just enough so you don't get into the dirt."

He walked over and picked up a different rake.

"We got a rock rake here. It's a straight edge. Use it to dig below the surface.

Straight edge for heavier shit. Rocks, sticks and shit. Right rake for the right job."

The conversation momentarily paused before Dennis asked,

"So, you the right rake for Everhart?"

"I haven't decided."

"Ain't decided?"

"I need time to regroup. I've been doing what other people want me to do all my life. I'm gonna do what I wanna do for a minute."

Dennis smirked. "Sky dive?"

"Damn straight."

Dennis suddenly shouted.

"Boy yo momma would-a been proud as fuck. I can see her now. Ya'll wouldn't need no press people and shit. Yo momma be like, 'That's my boy, he can fix it, move out the way, let him work.' She done told the whole world by three o'clock. Man. So proud."

But then Dennis asked again.

"No shit, what you gone do?"

"They want me to head the federal prison system."

When he got over the initial shock Dennis questioned what he'd heard.

"That's a straight come up fo sho but we could use you mo' better round here."

"I am here. I live here."

"Yeah but livin' here don't really mean nothin. You sayin' you be dealin' with these boys after they in prison. They gotta be dealt with before that. These boys seeds.

Listen to me. You Listening?

They got everything they need already inside them, but some-body got to bring it out.

They ain't planted in fertile ground. Hood need tillin', people need cultivatin',

otherwise they just be weeds."

After studying Hawk for a moment he asked,

"Tell the truth. What they got in mind for us?"

Everhart's words came back,' Sell them anything you want.'

"You know the answer to that" Hawk said.

"Okay then, so what people like us sposed to do?"

"What people, Black people?"

"Nah, law abiding people.

Used to be if a nigga did the right thing he might stand a chance out here. It ain't even like that no more.

Take you. You spent your whole life tryin' to fit in. Basically you cooned you way up."

"Fuck you talking about?" Hawk snapped.

"I worked my ass off for everything I got."

"Nigga I know that, but you ain't wearing no uniform no more. If shit go left on yo ass now, ain't nobody know nothing bout you a fighter pilot; work for rich muhfukkas, educated and shit.

You just another nigga in the street. And they killing niggas in the street all day long.

So when a nigga with a square ass job, doin' all the right shit, ain't no different than a fucked up crack head nigga, what we spose to fuckin' do?"

Hawk sought to stay inside his conservative boundaries and went with a neutral response.

"Come on Dennis man. This shit's been going on way before you and me came along.

It's going to take a minute to turn it around.

If Black people would stop blaming white people for everything bad that happens and get our shit together "

Before he could finish Dennis started laughing.

"Who you think you talkin' to nigga?

I knew you when your nose was snotty. Everybody wanna make it out of the hood, but nobody tryin' to make it in the hood."

"Hey, I'm here!"

"Yeah, you here, but what you doin'. How you helpin'?"

"Nigga I ain't superman and I don't wanna be."

"Ain't nobody ask for superman. These people wanna put us in our place once and forever. That's why they kill us like they do."

Dennis pointed to the athletic field.

"Don's already lost three this year. It's terrorism."

"Cops aren't terrorists."

"What is it then?"

"You gotta have law and order."

"Can you hear yourself?"

"Yes I hear myself. You can't just let people run wild."

Dennis squared his shoulders.

"And when they use the law to beat you down?"

Hawk didn't flinch.

"We have protections against things like that."

"Aw nah. You really believe that pledge allegiance bullshit. You actually think this your country. What happened to you?"

Dennis' sudden passion surprised Hawk. He'd never thought of Dennis as politically inclined.

I know you always been a go along to get along kind-a nigga" Dennis said,

But when they wrote that 'all men equal' shit, they wasn't talkin' bout you.

I don't care how many wars you fight or how much taxes you pay. This ain't your country."

Hawk wondered where Dennis was headed.

Dennis was all too ready to show him.

"You did alright and ain't nobody gave you nothing, right?"

Hawk's jaw jutted forward.

"Right."

"So if you can do it why can't everybody else?"

Hawk folded his arms across his chest and held his position.

"That's right."

"You got skills, I'll give you that, but some of your skills is bullshit."

Hawk raised a quizzical brow.

"Look man" Dennis continued,

Everybody can't be no fighter pilot. We need down to earth help round here. We need trade schools and shit."

"Why you tellin' me?"

"Cause you the nigga with the hook up."

Hawk sidestepped the issue and asked instead,

"What bullshit skills?"

"Com-on man, the way you played your way through classes when you really should-a at least been on probation; not cause you couldn't do the work but cause you ain't half try.

And fakin' your way off the IR when you wasn't all the way right, just so's you could add to your numbers. Bowing and scrapping to Principle Wells and Coach Knox to stay in they good graces."

Hawk smiled involuntarily.

"And I know you wasn't no different when you got to S.C. or them Marines neither. I don't know many black folk with the gift of the Blarney stone, but you; Man you something else."

"Blarney stone?" Jesse snickered,

What you know about the Blarney stone?"

Dennis took umbrage at the inference.

"I can't know about the Blarney stone nigga"?

"I'm just surprised."

"Fuck yo surprised. I might not a went to college or nothin' but I got internet and I can read muthafukka."

Hawk postured to soothe Dennis out but instead of calming down, Dennis persisted.

"And I'ma tell you again, he insisted,

Stead-a helpin' them snakes in D.C. you need to be teaching these young brothers here how to do the shit you did. Without all the coonin'."

This time the inference proved too much and the oft restrained 'hood' Hawk entered the conversation.

"Nigga I don't know what the fuck you think you talking about, but ain't no shame in my game" he said.

I didn't coon my way to Lieutenant Colonel in the United States Marine Air Corps.

I didn't coon my way to squadron leader in the United States Marine Air Corps.

I might have made some strategic choices to ensure a relationship here and there but so what? It's called tact, diplomacy."

"That's what it's called when white boys do it" Dennis replied.

"Whatever"Hawk answered. He wasn't apologetic or defensive.

"I did what I had to do" he said.

Whether it was on the ground or in the sky. When I went on a hop and things got hot, ain't no such thing as coonin'.

When Bubba got a boogie padlocked on his six and about to catch a heater up his blower and I got to pull some circus shit to keep him from punching out, or me from bustin' the deck; When it come to that shit, Ain't no such thing as coonin'. Bet your ass on that."

"Yeah" Dennis laughed. Whatever the fuck that means.

Like I said, you got skills. But, we both know;

If some coonin' had-a been called for..."

Hawk grinned in spite of himself.

"Fuck you" he smiled.

Dennis was almost sheepish.

"I'm just sayin' cause I love you."

Hawk appreciated his friend's considerations but remained comfortable with his decisions.

"If I decide to take that job" he said,

I can do more for us from inside the system than outside."

Dennis looked momentarily puzzled.

"Listen to me. You listening?" he said.

We all inside the system."

6

AMERICA'S PREACHER

Edric Everhart, a forty five year old, boyishly handsome man of slender build, had through luck and circumstance become the man of the hour.

His thick black hair and engaging smile had helped make him a triple threat of media, church and politics.

His mega church, aptly called 'Fort Jesus', comprised a sixty-thousand-member congregation just outside of Dallas.

Every Sunday he broadcast live from Fort Jesus to fifty million viewers. Because his audience stretched from the Atlantic to the Pacific, he 'd become known as, America's Preacher.

When he'd first begun his ministry he'd preached a populist prosperity gospel. Every man a king, every woman a queen. His pitch had been; Everything was possible according to one's level of faith in Santa God.

In recent years however, many Whites across the country had become so discontented with their societal condition, that he'd changed course.

His majority White audience, increasingly believed minorities were gaining too many advantages under the present system.

If things kept going the way they were headed they feared they'd soon lose their ruling majority.

As a result, a fierce White nationalism had spread across the country.

Everhart recognized a trend when he saw one and modified his message accordingly.

Claiming that God had given him a vision for the future, he'd transformed from a Shepard into a Pied piper.His revamped theology combined a new age prosperity doctrine with old testament racist dogma. The blending of old-time religion with pride and country proved an exceedingly potent elixir.

When mixed with Everhart's unique ability to deliver the message, the dogma had a most desirous effect.

Extolling the virtues of biblical bondage not only served to intoxicate the flock, it also made him the undisputed champ of the discontented.

Thanks to his folksy demeanor and good looks he'd become a TV star while social media had transformed him into both the messenger and the message.

In addition to the new approach gaining him a multitude of new adherents, it also garnered the attention of political Right-wing think tanks.

Chief among these was the Conservative Washington D.C. based, C street group, or as it's known among its members, 'the Family'.

The primary purpose of this invisible cadre of powerful government movers and shakers was to establish their agenda of Christian dominance among the highest placed rulers in all the world.

Recognizing Everhart's immense popularity, they'd solicited him to enter the upcoming Presidential primaries as the Republican candidate.

Everhart had never actually aspired to political office. But because he suffered from chronic vanity syndrome, the idea of being President appealed to him.

. . .

Edric Everhart had a high opinion of himself despite his hardscrabble beginnings.

His mother, Lily, hailed from a lower middle-class Texas family and had conceived him at 17.

His father, a career soldier, had been killed in action before they could marry.

Delta Force Sergeant Major, Billy Simmons Everhart, had been training Salvadorian government troops in counter-insurgency when his position was overrun by the FMLN.

When her parents learned the Sergeant Major was dead, they'd insisted Lily put the baby up for adoption. When she'd refused they'd kicked her out of the house.

Luckily, or so it seemed at the time, her father's sister, took her in. The aunt, a retired elementary school teacher, lived in a trailer park in nearby Irving Texas. On the surface she appeared charitable, but behind closed doors she treated Lily like a bondservant.

The only reason she'd let Lily and the baby live with her was to claim them as dependents for tax and social security purposes.

When Lily turned 21 she'd taken a waitressing job at a bar in nearby Oak Cliff.

Edric was five years old the night she'd kissed him on the forehead, told him she loved him and left.

He'd never seen her again.

Anty, as Edric called his great aunt, rarely spoke of Lily. Whenever the subject came up she'd only say that Lily'd run off and wasn't coming back.

Rumor had it she'd been murdered by a trick in a West Dallas motel.

Years later at Anty's funeral, a woman whom Edric had never seen before, sidled up next to him at the grave site.

As Anty's casket was being lowered into the ground, the woman cupped her hand to her mouth and half whispered,

"Your mother was a whore" and walked away.

· · ·

After that he'd never gone back to Irving, but he'd always acknowledged it as the place he got his start.

Rather than enroll young Edric in the public school system she knew so well, Anty instead home schooled him.

But his real education had come in the form of Christian television.

Every day Anty did three things. Gossip, complain and watch Christian TV.

Edric's earliest memories were of shouters, pleaders, and people who babbled incoherently. As a toddler he'd thought preachers had magic hands that could make people stand, sit or fall over, just by waving them.

When he got older Edric noticed that preachers never seemed to have any money.

They talked nonstop about how God could do anything but apparently the one thing God couldn't do, was give them money. People had to do that. And they did.

Cash was scarce around the trailer. There wasn't much available for new toys or clothes, but Anty could always manage to scrap together something for her favorite preachers. The trailer was a menagerie of cheap trinkets, sent by grateful ministries in return for her 'love' offerings. Over the years she'd donated thousands of dollars to their ministries, yet all the trinkets combined weren't worth a hundred bucks.

But Anty didn't care. She considered the joy she got from her 'programs' to be priceless. She knew just about every Anglo Christian song ever written. And even though she sounded like a wounded wildebeest, she sang along with all of them, all day, everyday.

Young Edric started joining in when he was still in diapers.

Then one Sunday, when he was around 7 years old, Anty took him to an actual church.

.   .   .

Faith Temple, Four Square Pentecostal Church, was led by Pastor Bill Fredericks.

Fredericks was a dynamic man who preached in the classic Pentecostal charismatic style. He had a flare for the dramatic and was sometimes more than a little animated.

Edric was sitting in the front pews when the choir started singing 'Onward Christian Soldiers'.

When Pastor Bill strode into the pulpit, he looked more like a GQ model than a preacher.

Dressed in a white polo shirt and beige chinos, he'd faced the congregation and raised his arms.

Anty fairly floated out of her seat. Edric's little feet didn't reach the floor and he'd hopped down as the congregation stood, and began enthusiastically singing along.

Edric was so impressed by the singing that years later, he would adopt 'Christian Soldiers' as his Fort Jesus TV theme song.

Pastor Bill noticed little Edric's enthusiastic singing right away but it was the seven year old's correcting him that really got his attention.

Pastor Bill was teaching on the subject of healing when he stated,

"As Jesus was returning from Judea, two blind men called out to him."

Suddenly a tiny voice rang out.

"Jericho" it chimed authoritatively.

"Jesus was coming from Jericho when he healed the blind men."

Pastor Bill stopped mid sentence. After a moment he started to laugh.

Although embarrassed, the Pastor recovered gracefully and extolled the congregation,

"Alright church, say it with me" he said.

The congregation responded in unison,

"Out of the mouths of babes."

. . .

That morning, Faith Temple fell in love with Edric and from then on Anty brought him to church every Sunday. Pastor Bill instantly recognized the precocious progeny's potential and took him under his wing.

By the time Edric was nine years old he was teaching Sunday school and leading youth services.

Anty reveled in the reflected attention and treated Edric like a prince from then on.Then one Sunday things took a seminal turn.

After serving the church for more the fifty years, the beloved Deacon Cheeks, died. He'd been a member of the church since long before Bill Fredericks ever came along.

Every Sunday, rain or shine, he'd stood in the vestibule's wide cedar doors greeting congregants while issuing orders to all the ushers.

His passing had marked an end to an era and cast a visceral pall over the assembly.

Pastor Bill thought young Edric might be just the thing to brighten the church's mood.

So it was that eight year old Edric Everhart came to preach his first Sunday morning sermon.

He'd captured their hearts the moment he stepped up on the milk crate placed behind the lectern. Peeking over the rostrum, he barely reached the microphone. Choosing his text from the book of Ecclesiastes, he spoke loud and clear.

"To every thing there is a season" he began.

And a time to every purpose unto heaven."

He took the mic from its stand and stepped off the crate. His Squeaky voice sounding ever more endearing as he regaled the congregation.

"A time to be born, and a time to die."

He strode back and forth in the pulpit, his little head bobbing like a baby chick. Peering into the pews, he'd enchanted the church with visions of Deacon Cheeks.

He reminded them that they shouldn't be sad because the

Deacon had been a good and faithful servant who'd gone home to his reward.

"Can't you see him?", he asked pointing skyward.

There he is.

Surrounded by the Shekinah. Bright shining as the sun.

He's up there in heaven right now, looking down on us. And oh he's smiling.

He's smiling because he's wrapped in the warm loving arms of Jesus."

By the time he'd finished, the entire church was on its feet. Hands stretched up, tears fell down, all while joy and praise rose to heaven.

After that people came from all over whenever he spoke.

He proved especially effective at raising money.

As the choir would softly sing "Bringing in the Sheaves"

He'd strut to the front of the pulpit and call for the ushers to prepare the baskets.

Raising his little hands over his head, a smile beaming from his cherubic baby face, he'd sing.

"We will Come Rejoicing bringing in the Sheaves".

As the baskets passed among the pews he'd repeat,

"Will a man rob God?

Will a man rob God, Hallelujah."

He'd go on like that until the collection was finished.

The tactic proved so effective that he'd used it long after he'd stopped believing in God.

7
BACK IN THE SKY

The Elsinore Jump Club was just 70 miles Southeast of Los Angeles, but it was light years from the stagnation Hawk sought to escape.

Although it consisted of little more than Flatlands encircled by foothills on one side and a dense wooded area on the other, it had the distinction of representing the gateway to the supreme rush.

As Hawk pulled up to the pier at the club's small man made lake, he got a closer look at the property.

It wasn't much. Only a faded office bungalow, a couple of small hangers, one twin engine, two single engine Cessnas and little else.

Watching the heat waves wriggle up from the worn asphalt runways, he was glad he'd rented the air conditioned three person sleeper RV for the trip.

This environment was subject to extreme temperature swings. Hot as hell in the day, cold as hell at night. Since there were no motels for miles and sleeping in a tent for the month he'd be here had been out of the question, the RV was on point.

The barren surroundings were in stark contrast to the fertile hospitality he'd just experienced.

He'd spent the past weekend with Dennis' family and had found them to be everything he'd never thought they'd be.

The twins, Veronica and Vanessa, were truly adorable. Identical snaggle toothed smiles, simultaneously appeared when they'd shown off their art work and test scores. But they were most excited to introduce 'Bobby', their clumsy, spotted brown mongrel puppy.

Hawk reveled in their closeness as they romped through the house, singing off key and giggling over secrets only they understood.

But most of all he marveled over the lady of the house. He shook his head when he thought of Sylvia. To him she was all a man could want in a woman.

She possessed earthy good looks that she wore with unassuming dignity. Her personality was affable with no hint of falseness. She was your big sister's best friend who you'd always had a crush on.

When it came to the twins, she was attentive without being strict, reprimanding them when needed but otherwise letting them develop their own sense of self.

Quietly humming to herself, she'd moved effortlessly around the kitchen. Darting from burner to burner, she'd flitted like a humming bird between dishes. As she flicked dashes of this into pans of that, it looked to Hawk almost as if she were dancing.

Her constant attention to Dennis left no doubt how much she loved him.Dennis always had a way with the ladies, but this one was special. He'd really lucked out this time.'There's only one way to get and keep a good woman like that' Hawk thought. 'You had to be a good man.' Dwelling on the attributes he admired in his friend's wife, it occurred to Hawk that he might be a chauvinist.

He readily accepted the designation.

After almost no consideration at all, he'd concluded that regular sky diving just wasn't going to cut it. He was going to fly the wing-suit.

He didn't just want to free fall. He wanted to sail through the skies like a bird. Like a hawk.

But in order to even take wing-suit lessons, he first had to qualify with a certified advanced free fall instructor.

The whole deal would take the entire month.

The receptionist smiled as she greeted him.

Her large blue eyes were unable to mask her surprise when she'd looked up from her cell to see a Black man.

Hawk was used to it. Whites were always surprised when he showed up in traditionally non-Black situations. Dennis was right. On a basic level this sky diving thing was totally some white boy shit.

"Hi. Sharla Thorell" she said, blithely extending a sturdy yet feminine hand. Hawk took it and introduced himself.

"What can I help you with?" she asked. She couldn't have been more than twenty two.

"I reserved a couple of packages" Hawk replied.

I want to fly the suit."

She smiled condescendingly,"Good choice, she said.

Do you have any skydiving experience?"

Her quizzical expression belied her actual belief that she already knew the answer.

"Not really" Hawk said nonchalantly.

She nodded knowingly and was checking the computer for his reservation when he casually added,

"I flew fighter jets for the Marines but I never had to get out of one." He didn't have time to fully appreciate her reaction before a couple of guys came through the door.

"Marc, Jodi" Sharla called as the duo entered the office.

"This is Jesse Hawkins. Jesse, These are the club's other instructors."The guys were also young but Hawk knew youth was no impediment to jumping out of airplanes.

"Pleasure" he said, extending his hand to the closest of the pair.

My friends call me Hawk."

"Hawk wants to fly" Sharla chirped in a tone too chipper to

inspire confidence. Hawk had no intention of being Sharla Thorell's student.

As soon as he'd reached out to Marc Thaggerly, before the six foot tall, bronzed mop head could release his hand, the words

"So I'll be training with you guys" were already out of Hawk's mouth. Jodi offered a wide grin. Marc, not so much.

Hawk didn't think Sharla was incapable of instructing him. In fact, he thought she was probably more than competent. He didn't want to train with her because she was gorgeous. Her oval face and full lips could easily be featured in any beauty magazine. Her crystal eyes shone with the kind of optimism that was reserved solely for young white females. Her athletic build was completely feminine while her well tanned skin was perfectly complimented by her pale yellow hair. He couldn't help noticing the fabric of her tee shirt straining against the unharnessed flesh pushing relentlessly beneath it.

Hawk didn't take up with beautiful white women. This training would call for close physical contact. He'd seen how she'd looked at him, ever so fleetingly, when he'd said he'd been a fighter pilot. He'd seen that look thousands of times. It started with cheerleaders and co-eds in his football days. Eventually even S.C. faculty, had looked at him that way.

To Hawk, white women meant trouble. He didn't want any trouble, especially thousands of feet in the air. He'd never been with a white woman. Not in high school, college; or even Europe. Part of his reasoning, if it could be called that, stemmed from a long ago admonition from his mother.

When he'd been in high school he'd had an after school job at Miller's Hardware, a mom and pop operation in mid-Los Angeles. One dayhe'd told his mother that the owner's teenage daughter, had asked him if he wanted to go to a movie or something sometime.

He'd never forgotten her reaction.

He could almost smell Lysol and ammonia as he remembered standing over the kitchen sink in their tiny apartment.

Shaking a potato peeler inches from his face, she'd soberly rebuked him,

'Don't be no fool' she'd said.

Her button nose crinkled into her coffee brown face almost disappearing as she'd warned, 'Nothin' in this world get you kilt faster than messin' with a white woman.'

It wasn't what she'd said so much as how she'd said it.

Not a trace of doubt nowhere.

The RV proved to have more room than he actually needed. Still, he was grateful for the extra space even if he didn't use it.He appreciated it because of all the nights he'd spent at sea sleeping in bunks only a bit larger than caskets. But even given the excess space, at times it felt more comfortable just to be outside. Some evenings he'd sit by the R.V. wrapped in a blanket and just space out.

One night, after doing double jump duty, he'd been so tired that he'd dozed off outside. He was resting comfortably when he suddenly jerked awake. He'd opened his eyes in time to see a jetliner roaring directly overhead. For an instant he was paralyzed. He imagined how it must have felt to those who'd looked up when he'd flown over.

The days passed with Hawk taking classes at an accelerated pace. He was up at six, making sure to be on every available jump from the first one at daybreak to the last at sundown.

Being in the air again made him realize how much he missed flying. The experience of looking down on the world as it passed beneath him was a feeling unmatched in the physical world.

Jumping was far different than piloting. In the past, being in the air without a plane wrapped around him was something he'd avoided like herpes. Now he was exposing himself just because the action gave him the juice he craved. He jumped with both Marc and Jodi until he was certifiable. It took two weeks.

But as exciting as jumping was, it proved down right bland compared to the suit.

Wing-suiting was far more intricate than parachuting. To do it well, body placement was paramount. The slightest movement of the head or shoulders made a big difference in trajectory and speed.

The pilot manipulated flight characteristics by changing the shape of the torso, de-arching, rolling the shoulders, and adjusting the tension of the suit fabric. Hawk's advantage was his excellent body awareness. He fell instantly and totally in love with the suit.

Slipping through the sky under his own command, free of any rigging restraints, gave Hawk a feeling only a junkie could appreciate. As silly as it was, every time he flew, at some point, he'd pretend to be Superman. He was sure everybody did it. Jodi had admitted as much.

Jodi Nugent left his Marcus, Iowa home at 18. He'd done it the old fashioned way. He'd quit his wet-milling job at Little Sioux corn processing plant and hitched cross country. He supported himself by doing odd jobs along the way. If he liked a place he'd stay a week or two. The trip to California had taken three months.

Professionally, he was a stuntman when he could get work.He enjoyed falling off high rises and sprinting in and out of burning structures.

Hawk got on better with Jodi than Marc. It would be disingenuous to say that Jodi didn't see color. He did. Everybody does. It just wasn't a factor in his dealings with Hawk.

Not that Marc was in any way overtly unfriendly. He was just more circumspect in their nonprofessional exchanges.

Hawk sensed that he'd done too well, too quickly, too easily, for Marc's liking. But Marc's attitude didn't affect Hawk's concentration. He'd dealt with people who couldn't clean his cleats for as long as he could remember.

He knew Marc was aware of his military background and suspected he got a kick out of giving him orders. But even if that were true, he couldn't have gotten much satisfaction from seeing his instructions executed almost effortlessly.

It's generally accepted that wing-suiting adds an advanced degree of complexity to skydiving but Hawk was a natural. He'd perfected maneuvers in days that had taken others months to master. At certification, Marc Thaggerly's congratulations were accompanied by a smile that never quite reached his eyes.

The month had passed quicker than Hawk had realized and even though he wasn't ready, it was time to get back to the real world. It was just past sun up as he checked the RV's fluids, when he heard a commotion down by the pier.

A small group was watching a man, standing on what looked like a flying skate board, glide above the lake from one to the other. Hawk drunk ran to the pier.

"What in the world?" he panted to a fudgey man in a floppy hat.

"It's called Fly Board Air" the man answered.

Read about it in PolitiFact. Didn't believe it."

The pilot, who wore only a small pack on his back and a helmet, was using a single visible control to manipulate the platform.

He slowly spun the board 360 degrees while making an arching 45 degree bank turn. As he came out of the turn he leaned backward, pushing the board out in front of himself, bringing the craft to a stop.

For a moment he hovered in place.

From a height of 20 feet, the device's miniature turbojets caused the lake below to swirl in tiny rotor-wash eddies. Adjusting the controls, the pilot spiraled upward to 40 feet before leaning forward on the platform and throttling up. He effortlessly reached 35 knots before braking again.

Noting the ease of the craft's acceleration, Hawk figured it could go much faster.

As the pilot landed vertically on a platform fixed to the pier, Hawk spotted Jodi leaning against a long sleek white trailer. The words ZAPATA RACING were emblazoned on its side.

He sprinted to him.

"You see that?" He asked.

"It's something right?" Jodi laughed, pointing to the lettering on the trailer.

Guy's name is Franky Zapata. French dude. He's training to set an altitude record. Thought he could keep a lower profile by practicing here."

"Judging by all these people I'd say his profile is pretty high" Hawk offered.

"You can't keep something like this a complete secret" Jodi Shrugged. "

Plus, he wants a few people to see it because It's so unbelievable that most people think it's fake."

"You know this guy?" Hawk asked.

"Met him when he came here a couple of years ago to promote his first invention. Kinda the same thing only much more rudimentary.

The old one used water shot out of high pressure nozzles. The water would lift you a few feet in the air but it was nothing like this.You had to be attached to a boat or something in the water for it to work."

"Well this ain't that" Jesse agreed.

How does it work?"

"It has six engines. Four turbo-reactors inside the platform put out 250 horses each. There're two more on the sides for stabilization. There's a logic board inside that uses electronics similar to those used to stabilize drones."

Hawk was mesmerized.

"What's he use for fuel?"

"Plain kerosene. That's what's in that pack on his back."

Hawk's eyes glowed like candles on Methuselah's birthday cake.

"You wanna fly it don't you?" Jodi teased.

"I can't even tell you. If there's ever a way. Please, please."

Jodi suggested he stick around a day or two.

"You never know" he said.

8

FORT JESUS

When the campaign called, Hawk was ready.

He didn't know what was coming next but it would be hard to top the Fly Board Air.

Surprisingly, Frankie Zapata had graciously allowed him to fly the board and had even personally instructed him.

He didn't have time to fully master it but, because so much of its's operation depended on balance, he'd done surprisingly well in a very short time.

But there was something else Frankie mentioned that he couldn't get out of his mind. Something called the carbon fiber jet pack. A jet you could strap to your back.

He was just outside of Dallas when he drove up to the entrance and saluted the gigantic flag flying at the access gates of Fort Jesus. The beautifully landscaped compound sitting on 650 acres of undulating sylvan terrain was a mighty testament to the faith Christians had in Jesus.

· · ·

In addition to the 35,000 seat main sanctuary, the compound boasted a 4000 seat theatre, a massive full service gym, 2 olympic size pools, 50,000 square foot overflow building, state of the art television broadcast studio, a two story book store/gift shop and a pharmacy.

The crowning jewel of the complex, apart from the sanctuary itself, was to be Faith Academy. The church's twenty five acre academic campus was currently still under construction.

The compound wasn't just a series of buildings, it was a community.

No sooner had Hawk entered the opulently appointed inner-office, with its elaborate renderings of iconic Christian images, than Everhart went straight to business.

If I win this thing, law and order will be your given name" he declared by way of greeting.

"Any public relations problems arising from my policies, will be yours to address."

Everhart's tone bore no angst. He was strictly matter of fact.

Under my administration there won't be any coddling of criminals. If they weren't criminals they wouldn't be in the system" he said. His smile was cordial, as though he'd been talking about an elementary school field trip.

Do we understand one another?" he asked.

"I always carry out my orders sir."

"That's what I want to hear."

It was quick and to the point, the way Hawk liked it.No disingenuous word waltzing. Everhart made clear that his policies would be harsh on minorities, and Hawk's job was to publicly dilute and de-racialize them by virtue of his blackness.

It should have been a job for the State Department or Justice but Hawk accepted it for what it was.

Everhart visibly relaxed while retrieving a bottle from the built in bar secreted in the mahogany book shelf. He poured a balloon glass of Remy, Louis XIII cognac and offered it to Hawk.

"You'll be your own man regarding how you handle your affairs" he lied. Hawk didn't want a drink but when it appeared that he'd demur, Everhart insisted.

"It's three thousand dollars a bottle." Hawk accepted the glass and settled into his seat.

You'll have all the resources you need and full discretion as to utilization. As head of the BOP you'll report directly to me."

"Not DOJ?" Hawk asked.

He'd spoken before he'd thought. This couldn't become a habit.

"Me" Everhart repeated. Until I say different.

I've got things to do and I don't want Justice slowing me down."

'I know that's right' Hawk thought as Everhart's usually affable eyes narrowed.

I won't micro manage you but I'm letting you know, I'm a hands on type of guy." Hawk could feel Kellogg and Guillory in the room.

"Yes sir" he answered and let it go at that.Everhart's boyish smile returned.

"I don't have to tell you what this is going to mean to your personal life" he said.

You'll be an instant V.I.P. Not a bank in the country will refuse you a loan."

Hawk considered the assumption. 'Me getting a bank loan ain't the most ludicrous part of this scenario' he thought. Everhart remained upbeat while extolling the benefits of office.

"You'll have access to every amenity befitting a man of your position. All the things a man desires will be at your finger tips."

If Hawk remembered his Sunday school correctly, these were the same words the devil spoke to Jesus in the wilderness. These were words he'd never imagined would be said to him. These were words he liked.

He knew he wouldn't have any real power. 'So what. I get the perks without the responsibility' he reasoned. He didn't see a down side. The ship was going to sail with or without him, so why not?

"You're not married?" Everhart asked.

The question brought Hawk back to the moment.

"No."

"Good. Because women are going to throw themselves at you like rocks at a rattle snake."

Everhart's uncharacteristically gritty laughter inferred he knew that of which he spoke.

"I don't care what you do on your personal time" he said.

But your public image has to remain pristine. Your reputation must be beyond reproach."

"No problem sir."

Everhart disregarded the response.

"I'm going to do things that some people may have a problem with."

"By some people; you mean Black people?"

Everhart answered without contrition.

"Among others" he said.

Too little education among all the poor, not just Blacks. Most people don't have the necessary skills for future jobs."

He took a reflective sip of cognac before adding,

"We need monumental mass production if we're going to remain competitive in the global marketplace. You know what that means?"

"Beat the Chinese?"

"Bingo. But how do we do that if the re-education process takes so long?"

"I don't know sir, how do we?"

Everhart threw his hands up.

"What can I tell you? I'm an old fashioned guy."

He suddenly sat up straight.

What I'm about to say doesn't leave the room."

Everhart's crystal blue eyes turned a gun metal grey as he semi-whispered.

"We're exponentially expanding the private prison enterprise system. We have international cooperative participation agreements as regards our global aspirations.

'No wonder he's whispering' Hawk thought.

'He knows this is bullshit.' But Hawk listened silently, agreeably nodding from time to time as Everhart laid out his intentions.

"Kellogg and Guillory have secured certain of our allies to production coalition trade agreements for the manufacture and distribution of goods and services.

By utilizing our available resources we'll be able to provide those goods and services at a cost nobody can beat."

Hawk silently absorbed what he'd always known but willfully ignored. The slave trade in the USA had changed over the years, but it was still alive and it was thriving.

"We're going to mass produce everything from diapers to cheap electronics" Everhart continued.

When I say cheap, I don't mean inferior. We'll have the best of everything, at absolutely the lowest prices in the world."

Drawing on his recently acquired compunction for candor Hawk inquired,

"May I speak freely sir?"

"Haven't you been?"

"Yes sir but, don't the Chinese have more workers than we do?"

"Yes" Everhart agreed, But we have prisoners in ally countries too. We can draw labor from them as well. China only uses their own people. Yeah there's a billion of them but they still have to export in order to beat us. Our allies trade policies will favor us over them."

Hawk wanted to know why he was being told this.

"Because you're on the team now. You need to know the play book. Seeing as how you'll be in charge of Federal prisons; When the press asks you my position on private prisons, what do you say?"

"That's not our job. We represent federal institutions. You don't have a position."

"How do you answer concerning federal prison camps that mass produce products on a global scale?"

"I'm not aware of any places like that" Hawk said as he raised his glass.

9
CAMPAIGN

The next few months proved as hectic as any of his combat days. He hadn't realized campaigning would be so physically demanding. Neither had he considered the monotony, the hurry up and wait, last minute location changes, security checks, and endless lines. It was a lot like the Marines.

He was constantly moving from backwater boon-docks to skyscraper skylines and everyplace in between. Not only was it tedious, repetitive and time consuming, but he almost never got enough sleep.

There was nothing spectacular in the way the campaign conducted its business. They stuck to the message and they pounded it over and over. Everhart considered his campaign speeches as sermons, and he delivered them with the same aplomb that had successfully endeared him to millions.

Everhart's unlikely recruitment was due to the untimely death of the Democratic incumbent. In the later part of his first term, while gearing up for re-election, the late Commander in Chief found himself embroiled in a major scandal.

The allegations against him were that he'd compromised

national security, by illegally negotiating secret peace agreements, with terms favorable to Islamic nations.

It wasn't true, but that didn't matter.

While he certainly hadn't made any secret deals, the President was in fact interested in what he called 'fair' solutions to the Mid East challenge. This position didn't suit the plans of his advisories.

They'd initially thought it would be easy to get rid of him. He wasn't particularly popular. He'd presided over a basically flat economy at home, and he hadn't been particularly successful in advancing U.S. interests abroad.

The peace and prosperity sentiments that had brought him to the Whitehouse, had settled into the malaise of routine, and the public tired of social protests that faded out due to their own fatigue.

Without serious popular support, the President's enemies thought the allegations of appeasement would be enough to ruin his re-election bid.

But the President proved more resilient than expected. Even though he was under constant accusation and threat of impeachment, he'd refused to resign.

He had good reason to fight back. He could prove that his adversaries had helped facilitate the sale of banned technologies to the very States he was accused of appeasing.

He'd scheduled a press conference to reveal their subterfuge, but hours before the broadcast, he'd suffered a fatal heart attack. Conspiracy theories flourished but nothing could be proved and nothing gained traction.

In the madness that followed, Reid Parker, an Independent Senator out of New Mexico, eeked out a victory in the Democratic primary, over California Governor, John T. Booker.

Parker, owed his razor thin victory more to Angus Kellogg's proficiency in dirty tricks, than to the public's acceptance of his quasi progressive politics.

The Republican strategy had been simple. In a general election, they'd rather face an Independent, from a small population state, rather than a popular Governor, from a financial juggernaut.

To that end, Kellogg resorted to chicanery to undermine Booker's aspirations.

He began by disseminating disinformation that named the pro Israel group AIPAC, as the main financial and strategic backers behind Booker's candidacy.

Despite denials by all concerned, a lot f people believed it.

At every rally Everhart baited his supporters with rants of,

"The Governor of California will turn the entire United States government into a Jew-town Bazaar.

He'll put every office in the federal system on the block. Whatever office you want, he can get it for you."

'Wholesale!' The crowds roared.

Playing to the lowest human instincts was Kellogg's most potent weapon.

He understood that when it came to believing the worst about people the masses were most readily persuaded.

Outlandish stories flooded social media, supermarket checkout lines and certain news outlets.

The most outrageous attack was an internet hyped series of stories accusing Booker of necrophilia with the corpses of Hollywood celebrities.

One tale had him in the city morgue, dressed in drag, holding a decapitated head in his lap.

The caption described him as singing both parts to the Dolly Parton, Kenny Rogers hit, 'Islands In the Stream'.

The more outrageous the claim, the more it circulated.

The camel's back broke late in the primaries when an audiotape purporting to be Booker, mysteriously surfaced at major news outlets across the country.

In nationally aired newscasts, Booker, supposedly in a private conversation with a staffer, was clearly heard to say,

"These niggers and fence fairies are a cancer spreading everywhere. They're like locust, eating up the land and leaving nothing behind."

At a hastily convened news conference Booker emphatically denied it was him on the tape. He'd insisted that it was a clever impersonation meant to discredit him.

But the die was cast. Minority support dried up over night.

Later analysis proved the tape was indeed a fake but by then the primaries were over.

Parker then protested to the FCC that Everhart had an unfair TV advantage due to his televised sermons.

He demanded the FCC grant him equal air time.

To squash the dispute, the FCC requested, not required, Everhart give up his Sunday morning broadcast.

He didn't want to do it, but rather than risk appearing churlish to an adoring public, Everhart agreed.

In order to get the biggest bang for his buck, he used the occasion of his well advertised 'Last sermon' to formerly introduce Lieutenant Colonel Jesse Hawkins to the nation.

An estimated 100 million people tuned in to the celebrity studded extravaganza that Everhart produced to showcase the event.

———

In the midst of a rousing oration, in which he'd invoked the majesty of God's purpose, Everhart ushered Hawk onto the stage.

As soon as Hawk walked across the platform, a roar went up. Everhart held Hawk's hand in the air and strode around the stage. Fist pumping and smiles all around welcomed the masquerade to the party.

From then on, wherever Everhart appeared, whether unannounced at a local baby christening, or at a jam packed NASCAR event, William Guillory, Angus Kellogg and Hawk Hawkins were always by his side.

The candidate made sure everybody knew he was irrevocably

committed to faith, military might and law and order. And of course, diversity.

After Hawk's debut and the appearances that followed, he did indeed become the official black face of the campaign.

But the jury was still out regarding the Black female response to Hawk Hawkins.

The lack of response was because he seldom spoke more than a few predictable words.

His chief role, as he understood it, was to stand in close proximity to Edric Everhart and be Black.

As far as the campaign was concerned he played his role perfectly. But despite Everhart's prediction of acceptance, much of the Black community dissed and dismissed Hawk. Either through disdain or disinterest, most Blacks accepted that he was an Uncle Tom, who was either too stupid to know he was being used or too Tom to care.

Given those parameters, it was totally the latter.

He was aware that some people saw him as a sell-out but his feeling was; 'Them niggas ain't paying my bills.'

Hawk, like most people, had multiple personalities.

There was the Lt. Col Hawkins persona, whose military image was meticulously crafted. That guy would never publicly utter the N-word.

Another personality was homeboy Pacoima Hawk, to whom the designation nigga, came second nature and commonly without malice. Homeboy Hawk generally only came out around other home boys.

Then there was Hawk, the confident, steadfast rock, who always did the right thing. This was his go to entity, his home page. But last and also least was the real Jesse. The guy he barely knew.

He hadn't spent a lot of time deeply analyzing himself. He'd never asked himself the existential questions concerning his deepest desires, what he wanted to leave behind, how he wanted to be remembered. A lot of what he did, he'd done for two basic reasons. Because it was expected, and because he could.

He'd been many things to many people for many reasons, but they weren't his reasons. He'd primarily acted out of a sense of duty; First to his mother, then his team mates, and finally the Marines.

His personal ambitions were basic. He didn't want to rule the world or be the richest man in it.

He was just a regular Joe with reasonable mental, and exceptional physical skills. All he really wanted was to find a girl, and live in peace.

His mother was the primary reason he was the way he was. With no man in the house, he'd been her primary emotional support. Because he knew how much she depended on him he never wanted to disappoint her.

He'd felt the same way about his team mates, and later his comrades in arms. Whoever he was involved with could always count on him to hold it down.

But even though he'd always set his own goals, they'd always been within someone else's parameters.

Subtleties, like examining the rational of compartmentalizing the N-word, had been one of the many areas his schizo personality board of governors had left unexplored. Within the tightly knit community of his personas, there were still some vacant lots.

He found campaigning in the Northeastern states to be the most taxing. New Hampshire, Maine and the like, had presented formidable challenges to his considerable ability to affably bullshit. Luckily, Everhart didn't require him to attend private fundraisers. Those wealthy donors didn't need to be persuaded by delusions of diversity in order to hitch their wagons to Everhart's star.

Hawk was most at ease when they'd stomped in the South because he was able to blend in. After making his obligatory appearances he'd fade into some hole in the wall Black establishment where he became invisible once the uniform came off.

At least in the Southern states the race card lay more openly on the table. He preferred the direct approach over experiences like Concord.

The pharmacist wasn't behind the counter when he'd walked in, so he'd waited. While he stood there, a White patron entered and stepped up to the counter. When the pharmacist returned, the guy ordered ahead of Hawk.

"I think I was first" Hawk said.

The pharmacist continued to wait on the other guy.

"Be right with you" he'd said without looking up.

Hawk left.

Walking back to the hotel he'd run into a guy on the street who lowered his head and hocked a loogie at his feet when they'd passed.

Hawk kept walking. Incidents like the pharmacy thing happened all the time, but It'd been a while since he'd encountered vulgarity like the spitter's. Then as he crossed the intersection, he heard the click of a locking car door.

Whoever locked that door did it so he'd hear it.

He hadn't been approaching any car. He wasn't dressed like a thug. They weren't afraid of him. They did it to race-light him. To insidiously insinuate that no matter what he wore, or how he appeared, he was still a nigger; And all niggers were pieces of shit to be guarded against; Unless of course, you needed their vote.

Because of his preaching prowess, Everhart was able to enamor Black listeners all across the South.

Instead of appearing at the more prominent established Black churches, Everhart reversed his approach and made the rounds at lesser known houses of worship. He thought he'd play against type by appealing to the grassiest of roots.

With the help of local clergy, the campaign gained traction by simply making the same tired promises they'd made for decades.

The fact that being a liberal only meant handing out liberal amounts of walking around money, didn't hurt.

Taking full advantage of the Black communities's penchant for forgiveness, combined with the incessant use of the name of Jesus, Everhart was able to make considerably more in-roads with Blacks than had initially been thought possible.

Yet underneath all the acceptance, it seemed to Hawk that the Black Southerners were just happy to be getting attention from an important White man. Any important White man.

'The force is strong in these ones' he silently mocked.

To him, the so called Southern Black 'leaders' were no more than toadies who carried the establishment's water.

'Their agenda is the same as everyone else's' he thought.

In the game of political musical chairs, keeping a seat at the table was all that mattered.

These guys accepted the shiny object and sold their people down the river, just like always. He identified.

By mid October the constant traipsing from city to city, eating little and sleeping less, had taken its toll.

With Everhart gaining in the polls Hawk requested and received a few days R and R.

He was exhausted when he got to the apartment.

It was after midnight and he wondered how Everhart managed to stay so up. 'He can't be in better shape than I am' he thought. But no matter about Everhart, Hawk needed a break. He fell across the bed fully dressed, and passed out.

It was early afternoon when he finally stirred.

When he stepped out of the shower, the mirror ridiculed him. He needed a haircut. Knowing there was only beer in the fridge, he decided to walk the few blocks to Johnnie's Pastrami before heading to the barbershop. The thought of the neighborhood staple brought a smile to his face.

Strolling down West Adams Boulevard his heart dropped as he

approached Johnnie's walkup service window. It was covered with plywood. Johnie's was out of business.

This was where he'd had his first au jus' dipped pastrami sandwich. As a boy he'd stood on his tip toes, peering through the window to watch the server pile heaps of steaming hot strips of meat onto soft French rolls. The top half of the bun was then dipped in the au jus before wrapping the dripping delicacy in yellow wax paper. Hot crispy onion rings greased up a brown paper bag to top it all off.

He couldn't understand how the popular eatery had disappeared while the demographic of the hood had stayed basically the same. 'What? People don't eat pastrami no more?' He swore he smelled fries and onions as he kept walking towards Blue's barbershop. Albeit with less bounce in his step.

Even though it was a Thursday afternoon, the shop was full.

Black men in barbershops behaved in much the same way as Black women in beauty shops. Always a lot of gossip. But there was also a lot of politics. Blue's would be the perfect place to check out the pulse of the community.

The Black barbershop was also like the Black church in that it was a social equalizer. Not only could you hear varying viewpoints, but you might also run into just about anybody there.

Blue's was generally a lively place but as Hawk entered the brightly lit, tidy workplace, he found it unusually quiet. The customary cacophony of music, laughter and verbosity was conspicuously absent.

The entire shop was focused on a TV news report of a man killed by police.

A patron indignantly blurted, "Nigga was on the phone."

Blue Johnson, the shop's owner explained.

"He was talking to his girlfriend. She heard him get killed. Few days later she was dead too.'

Cynical grunts percolated through the shop.

Brownlee, a skeletal snaggle-toothed, West Indian, stopped sweeping the shop floor and leaned on the long handle of a wide brush broom. His lower jaw slowly rotated like a cow chewing cud as his sunken eyes squinted toward the door.

"Ain't you Selma Hawkins boy, Jesse?" he asked.

Brownlee had haunted the neighborhood since the late fifties. Even though he was most times drunk, he generally always made common sense. Hawk looked skeptically around the room before admitting,

"Yeah, that's me."

"Humph." Brownlee grunted and returned to sweeping up the puffy clumps scattered between the barber chairs.

Blue motioned Hawk into his chair. Other than Brownlee's short commentary Hawk couldn't read the room. Everybody in the shop had a poker face. He acknowledged their blank stares with a quick nod and pinched smile.

Blue crisply snapped a barber apron in the air and Brownlee wheezed at Hawk,

"Boy, you left here a hero and come back a busta."

Everybody, including Hawk, laughed.

"Got-damn Brownlee, what I ever do to you?"

Hawk's forced jocularity was designed to prolong the fake levity as long as possible.

Blue, a rotund six footer with the tapered fingers of an artist, draped the apron around Hawk's neck and deftly fastened it in one fell swoop.

"Don't pay Brownlee no mind" he said. Blue's melodious baritone resonated like a church bell.

"He don't know his own name half the time." Brownlee stopped sweeping again and turned to Blue. His face conveyed no malice but also no surrender.

"I know more '*n*' you think I know" he said. Pointing a bony finger at Hawk he huffed,

I know this boy ran away with the PAC 10 when he played for SC.

and I know he ran away from us when he signed on with that fake-ass preacher. I know that much."

When it came to disrespect, Concord New Hampshire ain't had nothing on Blue's Barber Shop. Hawk straightened in the chair.

"What's fake about him?"he asked.

Hawk was certain that the old wino would say something inconsequential that he could quickly dismiss. But Brownlee didn't get a chance to say anything before a middle-aged man in a faded green track suit interjected.

"When I first seed you on TV my wife said you was from round here. I said no, couldn't be. Wouldn't nobody from round here be for no publikins".

Now Hawk was in familiar territory.

All his life, when he wasn't telling White folk what they wanted to hear, he was telling Black folk what they didn't.

"Listen man" His timbre was slightly apologetic bordering on piteous.

I'm a Marine. And the way I see it, Republicans care more about both the troops and Black people than Democrats do."

Hawk hurried the conversation along less anyone challenge him. For familiarity sake he allowed his dialect to conform to local cultural norms.

They good for jobs too. The reason a lot of us can't find work is because the Democrats got so many rules that business' can't afford to hire people."

Over in the corner from behind the cover of a girlie magazine, a voice arose.

"If you gone start with that bullshit you might's well stop talking right now."

The voice was familiar but Hawk couldn't quite place it.

"How's that?" he said.

The magazine lowered, revealing the dark lean features of T. Edmond Longstreet.

T. Edmond hosted a radio program that boasted the largest Black audience in the country. His influential drive time program 'Street Signs' was syndicated in every major media market on the map. That's why he'd sounded familiar.

Longstreet's on air personality was that of a socially conscious shock jock. Every day, five days a week on his broadcast, he extolled listeners coast to coast to take responsibility for themselves.

'Vote your own best interests' was a mantra he repeated daily. He advised Blacks to 'Run your own political candidates, bank with Black banks' and such. 'Education, not integration' was his motto.

His rhythmic chatter patter cadence made him a hit with a wide demographic. He was cajoling by nature yet consistently upbeat, always promoting self reliance.

Sponsors coveted him vastly more than anything that was thy neighbor's, and he worked all that magic between playing and making the hits.

"Republicans ain't done nothing for Black folk since Abraham Lincoln" T. Edmond declared.

His blunt delivery was contrary to the smooth tenor he presented on air.

The reason there's so many regulations is because without them Republicans would work poor people to death. And not pay em' shit. You make it sound like regulations are the reason jobs don't get created. Jobs do get created; just not here."

T. Edmond carried a lot of weight in the community. He had a reputation for straight talk while Hawk's credibility was suspect. If he took a position against T. Edmond it'd better be strong.

"Hey T. Edmond. Didn't expect to see you here" he said.

"Neither I you" T. Edmond shot back.

But tell me more about how Republicans care so much about us?"

Longstreet wasn't your average adversary but Hawk had done this a million times. Mustering his most poker face he went on auto-pilot.

"Well one of the first things we're going to do is get out of any trade deal that screws over American workers."

Before he could get up a head of steam T. Edmond interrupted. Laying the magazine aside he slouched back in his seat.

"Listen my friend" he said,

I watched you. We watched you, from the moment Everhart first spoke your name. We see you on TV skinnin' and grinnin' with a man we know is not our friend. He knows we know he's not our friend and he's sent you into the fold to convince us otherwise. Now in order to do that, you gotta do better than trade deals."

The interruption threw Hawk off his stride. He was used to flowing unimpeded through his schtick. He usually spoke in places where no one dared interrupt the Black guy singing the praises of the Republican party. This was his first experience with a hostile, savvy opponent. Before he could regroup T. Edmond asked.

"Didn't I read somewhere that you said white people were better than us?"

Hawk's demeanor immediately changed. The apologetic tone gave way to somber gravity as he pushed Blue's clipper hand away and sat forward in the chair.

"That's not what I said" he parried.

What I said was, they believe they are. They believe they have the right to rule by virtue of their inherent superiority."

In response to the churlish shroud that blanketed the shop Hawk coaxed,

Stay with me here.

Put yourself in their shoes for a minute.

Imagine that your race had made the most extreme societal advances in the history of humanity. In industry, science, medicine, government, philosophy, whatever.

You've achieved accomplishments in areas that other races haven't even wondered about."

He looked around to make sure the environment wasn't turning ugly. So far so good.

For example, how many of us know what the Large Hedron Collider is?"

He quickly added, Not you T. Edmond."

When not a trace of recognition appeared on any other face, he explained.

The Large Hadron Collider is a particle accelerator.

It speeds up photons and neutrons to damn near the speed of light, then smashes them into each other."

"What it do that for?" Brownlee asked belligerently, as though there could be no earthly good reason for such nonsense.

Hawk slammed his fist into his palm declaring,

"It makes tremendous energy, he said. Some people think it might even alter time."

T. Edmond added,

"Who thinks they'll use it to make a weapon?"

"That's the point, Hawk exclaimed.

They're the ones who dreamt it up, so they can do whatever they want to with it. It's the largest, most complex single machine in the entire world, and you never even heard of it."

"Where is it?" Blue asked.

"Switzerland" T. Edmond answered. Whitest country on earth."

"Now consider this" Hawk urged.

If the scientists are right, and the human species began in Africa, then that means white folk made all their strides long after other humans; Us, had thousands of years head start on them.

And even still, they went on to create, and dominate, the modern world. And and and... they did it while they were the what? The minority people."

He paused to let the thought take hold.

Now if you're doing all these exceptional things, and other people; Us, ain't doing shit, what would you think?

Now I ain't saying if you can't beat em' join em'.

But I am saying, don't be no fool. And before you judge me, ask yourself, if they have a point."

The rational only served to further exasperate T. Edmond.

"Black people have contributed to the advancement of the planet on every level since time immemorial" he proclaimed.

Tell me of Tariq Ibn Ziyad?"

"Who?" Hawk asked.

"Exactly."

The Moorish General who crossed the straits of Gibraltar in 711 AD to conquer the Visigoths of Spain. His cities boasted raised sidewalks and paved streets hundreds of years before Paris had them.

These Moors, these sons of Ishmael, these Muslims, who ruled the most sophisticated society in Europe for almost a thousand years, came from Northern Africa.

Son, you may know their history but you don't know yours."

The man in the green track suit was impatient.

"Plus, we ain't got time to be worrin' bout partrika beams and shit. We too busy tryin' to make rent."

"So say what now?" T. Edmond added.

Hawk recognized he was dealing with 'hood' T. Edmond.

What he didn't know was that the private T. Edmond had secrets he couldn't begin to imagine. He ignored track suit man and sarcastically addressed T. Edmond.

"You got rent problems Longstreet?"

"I'm not like you" T. Edmond answered.

His manor turned inexplicably congenial, but his words retained an edge.

"I'm not just lookin' out for myself here."

"Neither am I" Hawk protested.

"Well I ain't hear you ask any of these good people what they care about."

Hawk looked around the shop.

"That's why I'm here" he said.

To find out what's on people's minds."

A wry smile stretched T. Edmond's narrow lips.

"That's easy" he said.

The number one thing on people's minds now-days is the murder of unarmed Black people by police. That and the fact that for the most part not a got-damn thing happens to them because of it."

Hawk knew to be careful. These men weren't going to listen to any bullshit on this subject. The problem was, all he had to offer was bullshit.

He had to play the cards he held so he just went with it.

"That's because the shootings fell within departmental guide-lines." He didn't expect it to fly, but at least it wasn't a lie.

A burrow wrinkled T. Edmond's otherwise smooth brow.

"Well tell me this" he said.

What guidelines got to do with Black activists turning up dead in burnt out cars in Ferguson? Or Black judges turning up dead in the Hudson river? Turning up dead on their front doorsteps in Chicago? What guidelines got to do with Black women being hung in jail cells? If those are the guidelines, what's your boy going to do about changing the guidance?"

Hawk attempted to project a confidence he didn't have.

"I have his ear" he said. He'll listen to me."

"No, he won't" T. Edmond replied. But tell him this anyway.

We done. We ain't taking it no more."

10

GHOST POSSE

Monte Cristo, a slender athletically built Black man of strong convictions and few words, peered out the rear double door window of a service van.

The van was parked curbside in a quiet middle class neighborhood in suburban Cleveland Ohio. Zorro, a dark skinned bearded bowling ball of a man, crouched next to Monte Christo. His raspy whisper broke the silence.

"What kinda dog you say?"

"Saint Bernard" Monte Cristo said.

Don Quixote, a fair complected Black man, sat in the driver's seat. His latex gloved fingers played anxiously over the plastic wrapped steering wheel as they waited.

None of the men in the van, knew the other's true identity. It was a strategy straight out of Hollywood but it was a good idea, so they'd used it.

Zorro nodded in the direction of a man being pulled along the sidewalk by a massive shaggy dog.

"That him?"

Monte Cristo reached for the van's sliding side door.

"That's him."

Don Quixote remotely adjusted the passenger's sideview mirror to get a better look.

When the man was close enough, the side door suddenly slid open.

Monte Cristo and Zorro stepped out and stood directly in the path of,

"Officer Lockmann?" Monte Cristo asked.

When he'd heard his name, off duty police officer Jim Lockmann, stopped so suddenly he choked the dog.

Lockmann didn't know what these guys wanted but he quickly regained his composure and assumed an authoritarian tone.

"Yeah I'm Lockmann"he answered defiantly.

"What do you want?"

Monte Cristo's eyes momentarily softened as he offered a disingenuous smile.

"Tommy Rice says hello" he said.

Zorro fired first, discharging the fifty caliber Smith and Wesson Magnum from inside his coat pocket.

The round slammed through Lockmann's chest opening a grapefruit size hole in his back.

Almost simultaneously the charge from Monte Cristo's Ruger Bowen .500 Maximum, blew off the top half of Lockmann's skull, spraying a pink mist through the air.

Still holding the leash, Lockmann bowled over backward.

What remained of his head thwauked off the pavement like a hollowed out pumpkin.

The van was already moving when Monte Cristo slipped back in. Zorro slammed the door as they picked up speed. Gazing in the rearview, Don Quixote announced,

"Dog's dragging him down the sidewalk."

Zorro looked back. Monte Cristo didn't.

They cruised casually through light traffic, making sure to obey all laws. Monte Cristo checked his watch.

"Four minutes" he announced as they stripped off their outer clothes.

They stuffed the clothing into a plastic lawn bag and a few moments later Don Quixote called out,

"Homeless."

A tent city appeared on the sidewalk beneath an overpass.

The van door opened and Monte Cristo tossed the plastic bag into the camp.

Minutes later Monte Cristo checked his cell map.

"Turn right at the light."

As the van entered West Liberty street, Monte Cristo and Zorro each placed a hand on Don Quixote's shoulders and spoke in unison.

"Vengeance is mine, so too recompense; The day of their calamity is at hand."

After a moment the van suddenly rang out in laughter. Quixote shook so hard the van wriggled a little. Monte Cristo made a stern face,

"Yeah, I'm Lockmann" he mocked.

"What do you want?"

Zorro yelled,

"Justice Muhthafukka"

Blam! Blam! Justice."

They laughed again.

A short distance later they drove into a self-service carwash.

Don Quixote pulled into an empty wash station and ripped the plastic off the steering wheel.

They abandoned the van and made their way to a nondescript sedan parked in a corner of the lot.

Don Quixote and Zorro slid in the front while Monte Cristo climbed in back. Don Quixote fished a key from under the floor-mat and thirty seconds after arriving at the wash, the avengers drove away.

Nobody spoke as they turned off Western Avenue onto Dalton, just a block from Union Terminal.

Don Quixote could barely bring the sedan to a full stop before Monte Cristo and Zorro were on the sidewalk.

Don Quixote removed the latex gloves and dropped them in a public trashcan. The men staggered their distance from each other as they made their way to the train station.

Once inside the terminal they split up.

Within minutes, each arrived at a different platform and boarded a different train, bound for a different destination.

11

JEZEBEL'S PRIESTS

That November Edric Everhart was elected President of the United States of America.

At the popular Texas sponsored Black Tie & Boot Inaugural Ball, Guillory had become so uncharacteristically drunk that Kellogg had to have him escorted back to his hotel.

Otherwise the Inauguration was both a political and social success.

But the event proved most enchanting in one particular respect. For the first time, the public was introduced to the rarely seen new First Lady.

'Nell' Thompson, a thirty eight year old, svelte vision with a blazing intellect, was the daughter of Huston's largest cattle rancher. She'd been introduced to Everhart following a speaking engagement and although there'd been an immediate attraction between them, at the time both were involved with other people.

Adding to the complication was the fact that, Nell's upbringing had been much more privileged than Everhart's. In light of this, her father had strongly objected to the courtship.

Nevertheless, Everhart pursued and eventually married the one he considered to be 'the girl of my dreams'.

When asked how he'd won her over he'd said, "I don't know, but I think it was my honesty. Her daddy was a cattleman and she could smell B.S. a mile away."

Someone once wanted to know if he'd have given Nell a second look if she had been Catholic. He'd grinned slyly saying, "I'm glad she was Evangelical but If she'd a been Catholic, I'd been Catholic, because I was hot on the tail of Nell." The public was equally smitten.

But beneath the euphoria of victory lay the reality of the new administration's biggest challenge.

While he may have been a lucky husband and a most effective speaker, Edric Everhart didn't know the first thing about governing a nation.

This wasn't a problem for Guillory or Kellogg. Their first order of business was to mold the newly elected President in their image. Given his Christian bona fides, he was the perfect frontman for their vision.

Despite his proclivity for spotting ulterior motives, Everhart was oblivious to Guillory or Kellogg having any. After all, they'd come to him via the same conservative think tanks that had drafted him in the first place.

He never imagined that his advisors would be operatives of an international coterie of one world government promoters.

And yet. Not only were the usual suspects like the Bilderburg group and Trilateral commission, included in their number, but occult and fraternal secret societies were represented as well.

The Goal of the transglobal cartel was two fold; Take control of the world's energy resources and put an end to the spread of Islam.

Their first gambit was to install their guy in the Whitehouse.

In the first oval office meeting, Angus Kellogg, empowered by the courage of his convictions, had thrown himself headlong into his pitch to Everhart.

"The Chinese aren't the problem" he'd declared.

They're political atheists for Christ's sake."

While the analogy drew a wry smile from Everhart, it garnered a twinge from Guillory. Undaunted by their silent commentary, Kellogg soldiered on.

Theologically speaking, they're not out to utterly destroy us. But those goddamn Muslims are fucking kamikazes."

This time the dichotomous analogy caused Guillory to peek over the top of his glasses in mock incredulity. In response Kellogg snapped,

"You know what the fuck I mean. Whether they're Kamikazes or vest bomb wearing rag heads, it's hard to discourage a man who don't mind dying."

Intermeshing his manicured fingers across his slightly protruding belly, Guillory slumped back in his chair.

"He's right Edric."

Guillory's manner was more tranquil than his message.

Machiavelli held that of all possible governments, the best was a theocracy. Why? Because you don't need an army to control the people, and most importantly, they freely give you their money."

Everhart listened quietly. Fully aware he lacked all knowledge of the levers of government, he'd given these men his full confidence.

"That's why we're at a disadvantage vis-a-vis the Muslims" Guillory pressed.

In the Islamic world the Imams have absolute power. Why? Because when they speak, they're speaking the word of God Himself.

Consequently, the law is whatever they say it is.

The Buddhists on the other hand, don't have policy making power in China."

When he declared,

"And the Russians worship the Kremlin for God's sake"

Guillory winced again.

He and the retired General were on the same page ideologically, but they were polar opposites in terms of civility. Although he'd never shown Kellogg disrespect, Guillory privately considered him the Yogi Berra of policy makers.

"The Chinese may want to dominate us in the global market place" Guillory continued,

But at least we're playing the same game.

With these Muslims it's a different game all together.

Their game is zero sum. In order for Muslims to win Christians have to die. Period."

Guillory finally arrived at the heart of the matter.

Our only defense is for you to wield the same power in this country, as the Imams wield in theirs.

Your word must be the word of God just like their's is.

And as such, your word, and your word alone, must be the irrefutable law of the land.

Don't worry about the constitution. The courts will interpret the limits of your authority."

Guillory took Everhart by the elbow and leaned in close.

Clenching his fist for emphasis he insisted,

The point is, God has chosen you, at this precise moment in history, for one purpose only. To preserve and protect the White race and promulgate the rule of Christ over a civilized world. God has ordained you as the Protestant Pope, to lead the White race into the future."

Settling into a somber temper, Guillory asserted,

Now this is the important part.

In order to be successful, you need only be skilled in two things; Iron will and Romanita."

Everhart nodded in agreement even though he had no idea what Romanita was. Guillory instinctively explained.

Romanita is a doctrine practiced by the most successful Popes. It rests upon one basic principle.

Cunctanda regitur mundus.

If you can out-wait all, you can rule all.

Essential to its working are three vital tenets.

A sense of timing reamed with patience.

A ruthlessness that excludes emotion, and a messianic expectation of success."

It was an easy sell.

After announcing the head of a Conservative Christian group as Secretary of State, Everhart's worldview was firmly established. From there, every top government post went to clergy or laymen who were selected and vetted by the leadership of the Christian right.

Main stream media concerns over the establishing of a theocracy fell on apathetic public ears. Scores of Jewish and other non-Christian organizations, flocked to federal courts to challenge the constitutionality of the appointments. Citing U.S. Constitution, Article VI, clause 3.

'No religious test shall ever be required as a Qualification to any Office or public Trust under the United States' were filed in courts everywhere.

But due to the outstanding groundwork of conservative state legislators and private sector representatives, who'd drafted state-level legislation, the state supreme court rulings went in Everhart's favor. The motto of state law maker's became,

'Praise the lord and pass the legislation.'

In order to win public favor Guillory had the treasury department direct deposit $1500 to the bank accounts of every federal tax payer on record.

They kicked started the scheme with a nationally televised ad campaign in which Everhart was featured at a podium amid a backdrop of flags and the Statue of Liberty, saying,

'We servants of your government are not just hearers of the word, but doers also.

Proverbs 3:27 tells us, Do not withhold good from those to whom it is due, when it is in your power to act.

Accept this reward as a token of your government's appreciation of your faithfulness.'

Once the deposits hit the banks, public support was a done deal.

But the public's sense of well being was short lived.

A succession of economic disasters soon followed.

The administration's lynchpin strategy to world wide economic supremacy was to secure the cheapest labor possible. In order for their plan to succeed the minimum wage had to be just that.

To keep shipping costs down, manufacturing also needed to be localized.

Banning abortion, eliminating pell grants and outlawing unions would produce poor, uneducated workers with no representation.

Without a social safety net to fall back on they'd be forced to work for whatever wages employers would pay.

But if the economy continued on an upward trajectory Everhart's plan would fail. Nobody wants change when things are good. To that end, the administration engineered a massive economic collapse.

The meltdown occurred when the country awoke to reports that the accounts of every major bank and credit agency had been hacked.

While deletions of data had been coded in such a way as to keep international markets as stable as possible, trillions had disappeared from domestic financial institution records.

The panic tsunami that swept the country carried frantic crowds into the streets. In an attempt to calm the hysteria the Fed made an unprecedented move. Instead of tightening credit requirements, to guard against further loss and fraud, the Fed wildly loosened regulations.

In what was billed as an effort to win back consumer confidence, trillions of dollars in unsecured low interest loans were made available by the banks.

Government sponsored infrastructure projects created tens of thousands of steady jobs, stabilizing the economy almost as quickly as it had failed.

Having averted their self made disaster in this way meant, it wouldn't be long before massive deregulation, cheap money, hyper consumerism and low unemployment would overheat the economy.

But rather than raise interest rates to slow the economy and guard against inflation, Guillory instructed the Fed to keep rates low.

As a result of the cheap money, personal debt exploded. Then as quickly as the flood gates had opened, they closed. Guillory shut off the spigot. The Fed tripled the borrowing rate and banks called in loans. Defaults went through the roof. Businesses evaporated as inventories gathered dust, suppliers went belly up and the unemployment rate ballooned to Great Depression levels.

As a result the homeless population mushroomed. Shelters were overrun and entire communities devolved into squalor when city services evaporated.

This was the environment when Everhart delivered the State of the Union address.

Hawk, Kellogg and Guillory were already in place when Everhart strode into the recently replanted Rose Garden.

The press and the nation anxiously waited Everhart's vision for the way out of the economic collapse.

Flashing his celebrated smile he stepped smartly to the podium, opening his remarks with the customary greeting,

"Good afternoon my fellow Americans."

It was the only traditional thing he'd say that day.

I know you're wondering how we're going to get out of this mess, so I'll get straight to it" he began.

He suddenly stretched his arms out toward the cameras as if to embrace the viewing nation.

My fellow citizens, I say to you today, in front of almighty God and all mortal men;

Let this hour mark the beginning of a new era; A new direction in the foreign and domestic policy of the United States of America.

As God is my witness, if you'll listen to your President, do what I say and trust me, I promise not only to lead you out of this desert of despair, but I will lead you into the oasis of a future that few have had the courage to envision."

He paused while taking a panoramic scan of the press corp. When he spoke again he picked up the energy.

"This will be an historic era" he exclaimed.

The era that claims the right, no, the duty, to govern this great nation, by the wisdom and authority of almighty God."

The audacity of the statement paralyzed the press who sat in stunned disbelief.

"Since the foundation of this grand democratic experiment, we've abided by the doctrine of separation of church and state. It was a good idea for its time. Yet today, when I consider the state of the union, the way of the world and the hearts of men, I'm led to the inescapable conclusion, that the only way out of this mess, is to bring the hallowed name of Jesus into these hallowed halls of government."

A rustling tide of clicking shutters clattered through a press corp of confusion as Everhart changed gears again.

You've heard it said that history repeats itself.

Well it does.

At this very moment we are experiencing the repetition of the exact same circumstance that challenged the prophet Elijah during the time of Jezebel's priests.

Like the faithful of old, we today, find ourselves in the midst of a holy war.

Nobody wants to call it that, but that's what it is.

And the same question that confronted Elijah way back then, is challenging us here today.

The question was and is,

Who's God Is God?

Let me ask that again.

I said, Who's God is God?"

Everhart paused, scanning the audience once more from end to end. An expression of moral superiority nestled stoically on his face as he stepped from behind the podium and paced to and fro.

"Jezebel's priests say that Ba'al is God" he declared.

I, like Elijah before me, proclaim that Yahweh, Jehovah is God almighty.

You may not realize it but the new Jezebel's priests are these present day Muslims, straight out of the heart of Babylon.

And the new Ba'al is none other than Allah Himself.

That's right! Allah."

The press rumblings became more pronounced causing Everhart to raise a quieting hand.

"Now I want you to remember how God sent forth a fire that burned not only Ba'al's altar, but also everything around it."

Peering solemnly into the cameras he intoned,

"Well that's what Jehovah Yahweh God is going to do again in these times.

These people who want to destroy our way of life;

These Muslims who hate us because of our freedom;

I'm telling you today that God is going to utterly destroy them.

Destroy them to a point where there's nothing left but ashes.

And He's going to use us to do it.

The time of kowtowing to the blasphemers is over.

It's time to finally let the Islamic world know again and forevermore, Who's God is God."

Throwing his arms skyward he exclaimed,

"For I the Lord thy God am a jealous God,

Thou shall have no other gods before me."

Lowering his arms and snapping back to the cameras, he cautioned,

"And I give you fair warning. I come as a thief in the night. Blessed is he who keeps watch."

Then suddenly, without taking a single question, he announced a final,

"God bless you and God bless the United States of America."

And just like that, he stepped away.

Media criticism was swift and brutal. The press accused the President of unnecessarily and recklessly inciting war. But while there were plenty of distractors, there were also many who agreed with the President.

Everhart used the ensuing political chaos as cover to implement additional draconian domestic policies. While Islamic saber rattling commanded all the headlines, behind the scenes Kellogg was assembling his workforce.

In quick succession banks foreclosed on minority homes, personal property and businesses.

Minority, as well as progressive White media outlets, were subjected to insurmountable regulatory requirements. Many had their licenses revoked or suspended as major sponsor accounts dried up.

Once their fiscal objectives were comfortably underway, Everhart had to figure out what to do about the unintended victims of his manipulations, i.e. broke Whites.

The solution was proposed by Vice President Oliver Greathouse, the little known Congressman from Kern County, California.

Having formally represented agriculture interests in his district, Greathouse introduced a novel proposal.

In order to relieve Whites burdens, Greathouse suggested creating the "Colonist Relief Act".

The government grant was established to provide financial assistance to qualified applicants.

The grant was based on the premise that, in order to establish a solid new foundation, the government had to restore certain historic property rights and losses.

To qualify for relief, the applicant had to prove they were descended from, or related by marriage to, settlers of the original colonies or territories.

Grants were provided on a sliding scale. Whatever the taxpayer had claimed the last year they'd filed, plus a calculated monthly stipend, was what the government granted.

The agency set up to handle the millions of claims that poured in, routinely approved White applications regardless of documentation.

Any Black applicant who filed and was mistakenly approved, was later arrested and charged with fraud.

Almost immediately White America got back on its feet.

But with minority conditions worsening, repercussions followed. Some Black pro athletes refused to take the field. Without their star players some major league teams dissolved. Many Black businesses were seized by the government on allegations of funneling funds to terrorist organizations. The NAACP was on the terrorist list.

In response, millions of minorities had fled West. The problem was, policy was the same everywhere. The administration's plan to secure labor for their agenda coincided with their sub rosa designs on racial supremacy. A lot of Blacks were going to jail, and as is always true, everything went smoothly until it didn't.

The back breaker came in the form of an elderly Flint Michigan woman being manhandled by police during a routine traffic stop.

In a cataclysmic eruption of collective fuck this shit, citizens spontaneously poured into the streets and did what angry mobs do.

Within hours the Michigan National Guard showed up and blockaded the city. They did what they were ordered to do. There was no curfew declared or orders to disperse given.

When the armored personnel carriers arrived on Saginaw street in downtown Flint, the Guard started shooting as soon as boots hit the ground.

The event was reported as mild civil disobedience when it was reported at all.

Hawk had just bought a replica 1966 AC Cobra when he got the news.

———

Mashing the accelerator a little harder, he further loosened the reigns on the 425 horses stampeding under the snubby hood. The melodious grumble of the Borla exhaust system was music in his ears as the surging raw power pumped through the 427 cubic inch power plant.

His own heart surged as well. This was what he lived for. Powerful machines that went fast.

Just last year he'd been a retired jet jockey;

Now he was the Director of the Federal Bureau of Prisons.

He hadn't looked for it or even dreamed about it, but here it was.

Lompoc Federal Correctional Complex, is a low-security federal prison 175 miles North of Los Angeles. Everhart had personally called and directed him to meet the bureau's Regional Director. He wasn't sure why and he'd puzzled over Everhart's insistence that,

'We're going to put your civil engineering skills to work.'

Despite Hawk's protests that he'd never employed those skills Everhart had simply ignored him.

'I'm going to bring a lot of opportunity to the state of California' Everhart had insisted.

'Governor Booker needs to know that this administration will be a good business partner. After all, It's the native state of the Vice President.'

Considering the President's priorities, Hawk figured Everhart would cultivate an alignment with the Governor if he could, but if he couldn't, he'd just steamroll him.

Everhart intended to create a mammoth federal detention network in California. In an effort to establish good will in the historically liberal state, he'd named the project Camp Edmond G Brown, after the state's popular former governor.

'It'll be the largest and finest of its type' Everhart promised while instructing Hawk.

'See to it I don't get bogged down in red tape. I don't care what it costs. Make it work. That's an order.'

Hawk had responded automatically.

"Yes sir."

He drove hard along U.S. Hwy 1. The Cobra's coil over spring suspension hugged the coastal curves tighter than Big Momma after Sunday service as the highway took a northernly heading just west of the coastal town of Santa Barbara.

Thundering up the scenic ribbon of asphalt, headed toward the start of a different type of mission, Hawk suddenly wondered if he should really be in such a hurry to get there.

The fudge brown officer at the guard station looked up from the credentials he held and smiled. Returning Hawk's ID, the guard pointed to the nearby administration building.

"Right over there sir" he said.

Trying and failing to conceal his pride he offered,

Sir, if you ever need anything, anything at all, you just let me know."

Easing his foot off the clutch Hawk asked,

"What's your name bruh?"

Startled by the unexpected familiarity, the guard stammered.

"Wesley, Wesley Painter sir."

"Thanks Wesley" Hawk called over the rumble of the engine.

I won't forget."

Looking over the interior of the office suite, Hawk found the place much fancier than he'd thought it'd be.

The receptionist showed him through the wide, linseed oiled, oak doors into the inner office.

It looked more like a corporate executive suite than a prison administrative office.

The doors closed and Hawk was immediately greeted by the gregarious Regional Director.

"Good afternoon sir" the man said.

Pleasure to meet you. Gary Walters"

the Director beamed while pumping Hawk's hand.

Walters, 60-ish, with dyed blond hair, was an 18 year veteran of the California penal system.

"Thanks Gary. Can't wait to get started" Hawk answered.

He sized Walters up by the strength of his grip. It was firm enough but his tailored Italian suit and tan complexion made him appear more Hollywood impresario than federal prison administrator.

"I'm proud to work for you sir" Walters said too enthusiastically to suit Hawk.

You'll have all my best efforts."

Something about his words didn't feel quite as right as they sounded. For one thing Hawk wasn't used to civilians calling him sir. Especially executive level White civilians. He wasn't sure what the other thing was. He just knew there was another thing.

I'll be your liaison with Federal Prison Industries operations" Walters said with a smile that reminded Hawk of Marc Thaggerly.

"I didn't know there was a Federal Prison Industries" Hawk said.

Is it what it sounds like?"

"Yes sir it is" Walter's perked up.

Federal Prison Industries, also known as UNICOR, is a wholly owned United States government corporation."

Hawk was slightly taken aback by Walters satisfied tone.

"It started in 1934" Walters said.

As a prison labor program for federal inmates."

'Of course' Hawk thought. That was the height of the Great Depression.'

From 1925 to 1939 the nation's rate of incarceration had gone from 79 per 100,000 residents, to 137. Mostly because of the greater incarceration of Blacks. Hawk masked his distaste as Walters went on.

"Last year, UNICOR generated $2.8 Billion in sales" he said.

He sounded prideful as though he'd been personally responsible for the bottom line.

"Doing what?" Hawk asked.

"Everything. From agribusiness, clothing, and textiles, [Walters raised a finger to emphasize each enterprise] to Electronics, Office Furniture, Recycling, and Services".

"Ball park" Hawk asked,

What are the margins?"

"Depends" Walters replied.

Last year we paid labor 5% of net receipts, 15-30 percent went to materials, the rest profits."

"Impressive" Hawk deadpanned.

Where do we start?"

"I thought we'd begin with a comprehensive assessment of operations. Purchasing, logistics, manufacturing, global supply, things like that."

The receptionist's voice came over the intercom.

"Director Hawkins, Angus Kellogg on line two."

Walters pressed the intercom button and the unmistakable garble of Angus Kellogg spilled into the room.

"Hawkins" he trumpeted,

Pay close attention to what Walters says.

Don't fuck this up."

Hawk was used to asinine colleagues, but it was different this time. This time they needed him. At least for now.

"Thanks for the vote of confidence" he answered.

But what's this have to do Flint?

I thought we were dealing with an emergency."

"That's not your concern" Kellogg replied.

We're expanding the camp system to include private correctional institutions. We're starting right there in Lompoc. You're going to oversee the expansion. Don't ask questions, just listen. Walters will fill you in on the details."

Hawk tried to remember why he'd taken this job but then gave his pat answer.

"No problem. Anything else?"

Kellogg repeated don't fuck it up and the line went dead. Almost immediately the receptionist's voice came back over the system.

"Mister Nick Carlsen is here to see you Director Hawkins."

Hawk's quizzical expression prompted Walter's explanation.

"He's your right hand man" Walters said as he held down the intercom button again and instructed the receptionist to,

"Show him in."

The doors opened and six feet three inches of heavyset grim entered the room. The dark brown suit he wore fit his robust frame well enough, but Hawk saw a roll up your sleeves kind of guy.

With quick determinative steps the balding, mustachioed hulk strode across the room and stuck out a meaty hand.

Walters made the introductions.

The men silently assessed each other as they took their seats.

"Carlsen represents our management arm" Walters explained.

He'll be your point man during the expansion."

The intercom buzzed again.

Walters reached for it but this time Hawk covered the buttons with his outstretched fingers. His unflinching gaze told Walters this was Hawk's watch. As Walters slid his hand away Hawk pressed the button.

"Hold all calls" he said.

Carlsen broke the ensuing silence.

"Management Training Corporation is the third largest operator of correctional facilities in the United States" he announced.

We're responsible for more than 330,000 offenders."

Carlsen's ruddy complexion and worn countenance were accentuated by cheeks lined with deep creases that resembled ruts in a dirt road after a hard rain. His voice conveyed years of unassailable authority.

You'll call the shots of course, but MTC will be managing all the facilities in the system.

I'll be your man for purchasing, production, distribution, and the like. We have tons of experience and we know how to get the most out of our resources.

Our main thing is"

Hawk suddenly cut in.

"What's your background Mister Carlsen?"

The question caught Carlsen off guard and he reacted with almost imperceptible indignation at being interrupted.

"Twenty five years in corrections. New Mexico" he said.

A subdued umbrage colored his tone. He didn't like being questioned by anybody, let alone Hawk.

"Ten as Otero County Prison Warden, and fifteen running Otero County Immigration Processing Center" he said.

"Are those MTC managed facilities?" Hawk asked.

"Yes."

Carlsen wondered why he'd been asked.

"Good" Hawk said.

His face stayed blank.

You've got the kind of experience I need."

Carlsen appeared relieved by the response and replied affably.

"You're going to need all the help you can get.

We're integrating all California's immigration detention centers into the program as well. It's a massive project. All federal, private and immigration facilities will be merged under one umbrella."

"That's massive alright" Hawk agreed.

"That's us" Carlsen nodded,

World wide. We manage facilities as far flung as Puerto Rico and Egypt."

His description of MTC's human resources had been as droll as if he'd been describing the production quotas for hand soap.

A folder pressed under Carlsen's hefty forearm caught Hawk's attention.

Curious about the heading, 'Camp Reagan' he asked,

"What's that?"

Carlsen hastily removed the folder and shuffled it back into his briefcase.

"It has nothing to do with these discussions" he huffed as he slid the attache' under the table.

On instinct Hawk asked if there were separate camps for White detainees.

Carlsen's answer was unapologetic.

He said detainees were assigned to camps according to which district court heard their case.

Hawk instantly understood.

White offenders were being assigned to appear in district courts that sent them to white only camps.

The camp expansion wasn't being named for former Governor Edmond G. Brown. It was dubbed Camp 'Brown' because that's who was going to fill it.

12

RUN

Danny Ortiz peered down the hood of the Peterbuilt 579 into the darkness ahead. He was driving north through the city of Fairfield Village, along Clifford Street just east of Flint Michigan.

He wasn't a trucker by trade. He'd been driving for hours and his shoulders hurt.

Danny was on his way to pick up Flint refugees who'd eluded the barricades and escaped the city.

A few miles up the road, where interstate 475 and Hwy 69 intersected, was a Michigan National Guard checkpoint.

He was supposed to intercept the refugees in the vicinity of Clifford and 12th, just east of the 475 and south of the checkpoint.

He didn't know how many there'd be, but he figured the fifty foot trailer he was hauling would accommodate whoever showed up. There was no moon and he strained to see in the low light.

Danny was associated with an ad hoc activist clique made up of techie and barista types from in and around the Austin Texas area where he lived.

They weren't a group who'd generally be described as revolutionaries. They were merely like minded people who were connected through social media and flash meetings.

It was at one of these impromptu gatherings that the group happened across a random post on a dark website.

The message, posted by somebody calling themselves John Brown, told of a band of Flint escapees, who were traveling along Thread Creek, trying to put some distance between themselves and the city. The group pooled their money to rent the truck and Danny'd volunteered to go get the refugees.

It had been two months since Martial law had been declared over Flint. Since then the city had become a closed ghetto in the strictest Warsaw sense. Barbed wire and hedge hogs completely sealed off the city and the perimeter was under constant patrol.

No media of any kind was allowed beyond the barricades. Inside the city, all communications were cut. Cell phones and computers were impounded and all personal identification was confiscated.

A dusk to dawn curfew was in effect and store shelves were empty. Government issued rations were less than 300 calories a day and municipal services were nonexistent.

The few brave journalists who'd initially covered the quarantine had been quickly and violently dispatched. If Danny were caught helping the escapees, he'd suffer their same fate.

He thought about all the people who'd willfully ignored the warning signs. Everybody witnessed what was happening but no-one wanted to believe it. Not here. This was a government ruled by law, not men.

It had been precisely this kind of head in the sand denial that had allowed the present cancer the time to spread.

The total news blackout had worked. After a few news cycles, that gave disproportionate national attention to random celebrity escapades or star athlete's numbers, the country forgot about Flint.

Anxious out of state relatives, concerned about loved ones, were given a number to call. Once connected, a recording instructed the caller to leave a message. That would be the end of it.

The administration's original stated objective in occupying Flint was to restore order. The actual objective was to gain compliance through suppression and intimidation.

Any suspicious behavior inside the ghetto resulted in immediate arrest.

Hundreds of Flintonians were charged with sedition.

Cases, ranging from unlawful assembly to unauthorized dissemination of information, were heard by military courts set up inside the ghetto.

Tribunals, appointed by Kellogg, tried the cases. The three judge panels constituted the final word on all matters and there were no appeals.

The legality of the actions was challenged by a plethora of organizations including the Civil Liberties Union, to no avail. The courts either upheld the government's positions or delayed rulings that would have prohibited their going forward.

To safeguard his personal security the President relied on a reservoir of select shock troops known as 'The Order of the Guardian Keep'.

This private army was administered by specially trained, highly disciplined Jesuit monks who oversaw the most ruthless of recruits.

The monks reported directly to Father Will Guillory.

It was the 'Keepers', dressed in their immaculate white uniforms, trimmed in gold braid pipping, who served as the Gospel Gestapo.

On Saturdays, out of public view, prisoners were brought into Northwestern High School's gym where they heard the charges and pleaded their defense. No lawyers were allowed.

On Sundays, convicted prisoners were bussed to the Genesee Valley Center Mall where sentences were carried out.

With no witnesses present, the condemned were lined up along the brick wall at the mall entrance.

At high noon a near-by church bell would toll.

At the sound of the last knell the Master Keeper would step forward and announce,

"And fire came forth from the presence of the LORD and consumed them, and they died before the presence of the LORD."

The Master Keeper would then give the order to Ready, Aim, Fire.

The corpses were later collected by garbage trucks.

The few accounts of atrocities that made it out to the world, were so inconceivably inhumane that noone believed them.

The rendezvous point should be close Danny thought.

He was sure to see something soon. Reaching for the gear shift he flicked the splitter down and the 18 wheeler slid into the lower gears. As the 500 horse power diesel down shifted, he sniffed under his arm.

The tattered flannel shirt he wore was almost as pungent as the highway's ever present road kill.

'He was longing for a bath when a shadowy figure suddenly appeared by the side of the road.

The absurdity of a Mexican smuggling Blacks inside the U.S.A. still seemed ludicrous but when additional shapes appeared he hit the brakes.

He eased the truck over to the shoulder and leapt from the cab. Racing to open the trailer doors he suddenly heard popping sounds. When he felt a buzz zip past his ear he realized he was under fire. He didn't know who was shooting at him but It didn't matter. He kept running.

The side of the freeway embankment proved steeper than he'd realized and he lost his footing. Tumbling headlong into a gulley he felt a series of dirt clods pop up around his head as bullets peppered the ground. Laying on his belly in the tall Black Medic weeds he was afraid to move and afraid not to.

The gunfire was coming from across Clifford Street to the west about 50 yards away. 200 feet to the north he heard somebody yelling "Run run run". He inched on his belly deeper into the weeds. It took all his resolve not to get up and run.

The sound of many boots rapidly clopping across Clifford Street froze him in place. It was the Guard alright. They must have been on patrol and lucked into the rendezvous. He held his breath as the shooting continued. Finally the footsteps faded to the north. He didn't know if any of the escapees had been hit but if they had, they were keeping quiet about it.

He remained stone still. He wasn't sure who might still be around. After an hour or so he was about to move on when he heard a Guard detail returning. He curled into a ball.

He instantly regretted not running when he'd had the chance.

But the Guard only concerned themselves with the truck.

Listening to the semi being chained up and hauled away, he knew they wouldn't find his prints inside the cab.

He didn't care if they did, just so long as they didn't find him right now. Hours after the Guard had gone he still waited in place. He wouldn't raise his head until daylight.

When the sun finally inched into the sky he cautiously periscoped up from the weeds. No sign of the Guard, but as depressing as it was, he knew his best bet was to stay put until it was dark again. He spent the day alternately napping and startling awake. He didn't have a clue what to do next. All he knew was the boots had gone North so he was going South.

Laying in the tall grass, staring up at the clouds, a bottle, carelessly tossed from a passing car, barely missed his face. When the sun finally set, he started walking.

He figured it was about 30 miles to the next town. If he only walked at night he'd get about 18 miles in six hours of darkness. He walked in the ditches following the road, ducking out of sight whenever headlights appeared.

Tripping over debris, stumbling through ruts while trying to stay out of harm's way, made for slower going than he'd calculated. His filthy clothes and dark skin made it clear he wasn't a property owner around here. He didn't want to answer any questions and the best way to do that was to stay out of sight.

As daylight approached, a nearby Bur Oak tree looked like the safest place to spend the day. Hoisting himself up into the cover of the branches, he heard his stomach gurgle. He was so hungry he felt hollow. From his vantage point in the tree he could see a MacDonald's in the distance. It might as well have been on the moon.

After a few tortuous hours, his leafy accommodations got the best of him. Finding comfort in an oak tree was like finding chitlins in a mosque. His legs kept falling asleep and ants kept him constantly scratching.

Before twilight had turned fully into night, he loosened the knot he'd tied with his shirt sleeve to keep himself from falling in his sleep, and let himself to the ground. Brushing himself off he set out into the dusk.

All he could think about was getting to a city where a dirty Mexican milling the streets was invisible.

He got as far as Island Lake Recreational Area, a wooded reserve on the outskirts of Green Oaks Township, before the it got light. As the sun came up he made his way off McCabe Road and into the forest. He felt like a vampire.

By the time it got dark again he was so hungry he almost didn't care if he got caught. Almost. Thank God for the reserve's visiting litterbugs. After inhaling the few scraps he'd stumbled across at a deserted campsite, he headed Southwest looking to follow a major thoroughfare.

The next dawn found him trudging along U.S. Hwy 23. With blistered feet and a fatigue that bore testament to the journey, he discovered he was just north of Ann Arbor.

He was relieved to see a Lowe's Home Improvement sign a half mile or so ahead. When he reached the center's parking lot he found hopeful day laborers already gathered there.

Danny sat down on a concrete parking stop next to a small group of men. The men weren't particularly friendly and greeted him with suspicion. 'Parking lot xenophobia' Danny thought, but he understood. Some of them had families, work was scarce and competition wasn't something they welcomed.

'You don't have to like me' he mused, I just want to blend in long enough to get back to Austin.'

He wondered what happened to the escapees. Did they make it? He hadn't seen or read any news reports for a couple of days. He wasn't sure if something like an escape would even be reported.

He was staring in the trash at a half eaten hotdog when a stubby man in new work boots handed him a paper plate wrapped in cellophane. A profuse "Gracias" was all he could manage. Not waiting for the offered plastic fork, he fumbled frantically with the wrapping.

Using his fingers to wolf down the rice and beans he never noticed the van pulling into the lot.

Suddenly somebody yelled,

"Todo el mundo congelar".

Everybody Freeze!

13
ICE COLD

When they'd heard the order to freeze the Braceros had scattered like buckshot.

They'd known exactly what to do but Danny had been caught flat footed. ICE had been the last thing on his mind. The agents who'd leapt from the van and knocked him to the ground, brought him to the County Jail.

The 100 year old jail in downtown Ann Arbor was located on the top floor of a two story rustic brick building.

It was built to hold 150 people and it was full.

Over half its detainees were being held on immigration charges. Almost 70 percent of the population of Ann Arbor was White but the jail held a majority of Hispanics and Middle Easterners.

The Hispanics faced mainly deportation charges but the Middle Easterner's interrogations had a national security bent.

It stank in here. Danny was sure it was the desperation.

As depressing as the jail was, he took comfort in knowing he'd most likely be deported.

ICE assumed he was an illegal day laborer and they'd charged him with "Removability from the United States of America." More than happy to play along, Danny hadn't spoken a word of English since the moment he'd been arrested.

Waiting was the only thing that happened in a holding cell.

"What's going to happen now?" he asked a leather faced man who shared the crowded cell.

The man, who looked to be in his mid forties, showed no signs of anxiety or depression when he casually answered,

"In a week or two they will take you to a room where you will see a judge on a TV.

The judge will say that you got to leave. They will ask you about your home country. Just say Mexico."

"Anybody ever get out of here?"

Danny knew full well the answer didn't matter.

The corners of the man's mouth strayed downward and his head slowly shook.

"ICE won't set bail, he shrugged.

Even if they did; No money."

Leather-man said that some of the detainees would be sent to detention centers in other states and from there to wherever.

Because of his experience at Stratfor, Danny knew more about the situation than he'd let on.

The Department of Homeland Security Appropriations Act of 2010 made funding available for not less than 33,400 detention beds.

This directive established a policy, interpreted by ICE as a mandate, to contract for, and fill, 34,000 detention beds on a daily basis. The directive would come to be known as the "immigrant detention quota" or, the bed mandate.

The Bed Mandate was unprecedented. No other law enforcement agency operated under a detention quota mandated by Congress. But the men sitting in these cells holding their heads in their hands, didn't know anything about any of it.

At least Danny didn't have to worry about getting out of town anymore. ICE would take care of that for him. He leaned back against the wall. Compared to a charge of sedition, deportation was a pretty sweet deal.

14
BARN DOOR OPEN

Hawk eased the Cobra into the West Adams apartment garage.

'Why do I keep this place?' he wondered as he lowered the garage door and padded up the back stairs.

'I'm never here.'

Letting himself in through the rear kitchen door, he went around the apartment opening windows to air the place out.

With all that was happening in the neighborhood he was pleasantly surprised to find the place unmolested. Mail had piled up on the floor beneath the slot in the front door. All junk.

Hawk had unofficially moved his offices to Camp Brown.

Head MTC honcho Nick Carlsen, was interloping on his authority and Hawk meant to show him what was what.

He didn't really care if Carlsen made an imprint on the project, he just liked being able to push back for once.

But the truth was, he found his responsibilities daunting and unrewarding. He'd thought he'd be sitting in an air conditioned office rubber stamping department decisions, not stuck in a real construction job.

Now he really wished he hadn't taken the job.

But he had, and he'd see the project through because that's how he rolled.

Over the last three years, more than 74,000 immigrant detainees from over 150 countries had been held at California's 10 public and private detention centers. That number was about to quadruple and it was up to him to make sure things went smoothly. He had his orders and he'd carry them out, even if he had to live in jail to do it.

With everything he had on his plate, he hadn't wanted to take the time to come back to L.A. but Dennis had insisted.

Dennis sounded disconnected when he'd called. Whatever the problem was, he wouldn't talk about it over the phone

Hawk pondered how to balance his old life with his new responsibilities. He couldn't keep doing things like this. On the other hand, Dennis was his friend and he wasn't about to forget where he came from.

Before he could get the beer out of the fridge there was a knock.

No sooner had the door opened than he knew it was bad.

"They took Sylvie and the girls" Dennis said pushing past him and flopping on the couch.

Hawk instantly knew what he meant.

"Where are they?"he asked.

"I don't know" Dennis stressed.

I came home and they was gone. The front door was open and they wasn't there."

Dennis' eyes bulged like golf balls and he ejected words like a jack hammer.

"They shot Bobby."

"Your dog?"

"They killed my fuckin' dog. Shot him on the kitchen floor.

Ain't nobody called. I ain't heard nothin'. You gotta find them."

"I will, I will" Hawk promised as calmly as he could.

Her papers in order?"

"Everything. We married. The girls born here. They ain't got no papers."

Hawk went to the kitchen and rummaged through a junk drawer. He came back with a pad and pen and handed them to Dennis.

"Write down their full names, birth dates and social security numbers."

Dennis grabbed the pen and paper and started writing.

"Ahma need to get back to you on the social security" he mumbled.

Hawk went into the bedroom and came out with a blunt. Dennis waved him off.

I would-a thought you wasn't doing that no more" he said.

This really was a different Dennis.

One of the ladies left it" Hawk answered.

He stubbed the blunt out. Suddenly Dennis blurted,

"And it ain't just me.

I had to hire damn near a whole new ground crew.

Braceros disappearin' like a Mexican rapture."

"I'll take care of it" Hawk reiterated as he couldn't think of anything else to say.

Dennis abruptly stood up.

"This shit got to stop"he said.

Hawk had never seen Dennis cry. Even in 2nd grade when he'd fallen off the jungle gym and broken his arm, he'd moaned and groaned but he'd never cried. These weren't tears of pain or sadness. Dennis was mad.

Hawk felt impotent.

"I'll get it in the system first thing in the morning" he offered.

Dennis didn't hear him.

"The girls don't even speak Spanish" he blurted.

They straight kidnapped my people."

Hawk mustered a mouthful of what he hoped came off as confidence.

"I'll get Homeland to issue emergency sweeps on family detention camps in the morning."

He was surprised when Dennis said,

"First camp you ought-a check is Brown."

"We don't have kids at Brown."

"If you don't, you will" Dennis said.

I know you know what's goin' on in Flint."

Hawk looked at the floor and Dennis suddenly asked,

"And what about Baltimore?"

"Where you hear about Baltimore?"

"So it's true?"

Hawk leaned back into the couch.

"It's supposed to be blacked out" he admitted.

"Nigga you can't black no shit like that out.

That shit's true?"

"Yeah."

"I told you these muhfukkas was bringing slavery back. How the fuck you work for these people?"

"Keep it down nigga. If I didn't work for them, where exactly would you go right now?"

Dennis glared back defiantly.

"So what you gone do?"

"I'll do whatever. I'll find them and get them released."

"Not them" Dennis exclaimed,

You just gonna sit by and watch this shit go down?"

"What shit?"

"All this shit."

"What you want me to do?"

"Something."

"I told you, I ain't superman."

"Listen to me. You listening?

This ain't about you. This about all us."

Hawk shook his head.

"Oh no" he scoffed,

You wouldn't be here if you didn't have a dog in this fight. You not here for us; You here for *you*."

Dennis glanced askance as he struggled to find words ugly enough to express himself.

"I can't go back inside" he said.

You don't understand. I wanna kill these people. They lockin' muhfukkas up like they was made a gold. Somebody like me get outta line and bam, I'm done. But you; You on the inside. You can do things other people can't."

"Like what?"

Dennis peeked over his shoulder as if to make sure no one else was listening. Leaning in he half whispered.

"Nigga you got any idea what a army of Black people could do?"

Hawk sat up straight.

"Nigga you got any idea how crazy you sound?"

Dennis shook his head.

"I don't know. Do I?"

Hawk couldn't allow the conversation to go on.

"I know you messed up right now man, but you should really stop talking."

His sober delivery had no like effect on Dennis who remained adamant.

"Listen to me. Sooner or later, Flint, Baltimore, gonna happen right here in L.A. Right or wrong?"

While Hawk searched for a response that had teeth, Dennis filled in the pause.

"You know I'm right. You listening?"

"No."

"You betta be. It's down to we gotta make our own justice."

"You ain't talking justice, you talking treason."

"What you call what they doin' to us?

This the kinda shit make a hard workin', law abidin' nigga just say fuck it."

Hawk dismissed the statement.

"When you see your people again you won't feel that way" he said.

"Yeah you right" Dennis agreed.

If they walked through that door right now that'd be all I care about. But what about the next man?"

"Better worry about you" Hawk answered.

Suddenly Dennis asked,

"You heard about ghost posse?"

"Ghost Posse?"

Dennis looked over his shoulder again.

"You heard about them police that kilt Tommy Rice and Mookie Brown, gettin' kilt right?"

"Yeah?"

"And that Ziderman nigga too."

"Yeah, what about it?"

"Ghost posse nigga."

"You saying there's an organized vigilante group killing cops?"

"Not just cops."

"Who are they?"

"Nigga I don't know, they ghosts.

What I'm sayin' is, niggas through waitin' on white people to do the right thing. It's some eye for a eye shit goin' down."

"You know any posse people?"

"Just told you."

"I don't want to see you get caught up in nothing you can't handle."

"If I did know, could I tell you?"

Hawk hesitated.

"No. I don't think you could."

"That's what I'm sayin'.

You think it's a crime for us to kill them, but it's okay if they kill us. What about them Keepers? They got a straight murder license."

"They enforce the law."

"Oh hell no. Slavery was law too. Fuck that shit.

Law and justice two different things."

The banging of the garbage truck woke him. He didn't know when Dennis left but the empty six packs attested to a lengthy pow wow.

He'd made a lot of promises last night. He was going to have to keep them. Closing the windows and grabbing the keys he bounded down the back stairs. He was in a hurry to get to work but he was going to be late. The garage door was open and the Cobra was gone.

15

DE LA CRUZ

W ho are you?" Hawk asked the unfamiliar female sitting at his assistant's desk.

The woman stood up. Extending a slender copper hand she answered,

"Adelina Flora Bella de la Cruz. Pleasure to meet you."

Hawk was startled. This was the last place he'd expected to see a woman as stunning as this. He hoped his appreciation didn't show. When she'd said her name it was almost like she was singing.

Her voice sounded like warm honey poured over sweet peppers. She had invasive amber eyes that blasted through a man's defenses like a blow torch through cotton candy.

"The pleasure's mine Ms de la Cruz."

He hoped his tone was measured.

"Please" she said.

Call me Adelina."

"Where's Mr. Louis, Ms de la Cruz?"

Her dark grey dress was modest enough in design, but its soft woven fabric clung to her contours like melted cheese on a chili dog. Hawk struggled to maintain strict eye contact.

Even though her outward manner was strictly professional, there was nothing she could do about her underlaying sensuality. She wasn't trying to be sexy. It was effortless.

"Mr. Louis took emergency leave sir. Personal matter. I was told you'd been notified" she said.

Hawk wondered if anybody had called last night that he'd forgotten?

"Don't remember that" he said.

Who hired you?"

"Human resources assigned me sir, but Mister Nick Carlsen was my reference."

Hawk's defenses sparked. Was Carlsen trying to sic this woman on him?

"Get me Regional Director Walters at Lompoc" he said before abruptly walking away.

Almost as an after thought he offered a lukewarm,

"Welcome aboard."

The modular bungalow was situated on site for efficiency purposes. The staff were holdovers from the previous administration and he hoped this new addition didn't upset the work dynamic.

He'd moved himself on site ostensively to show he'd go to extremes to complete his orders, but the deeper truth was, he simply wasn't comfortable in D.C.

Whenever he'd entered the Bureau's 1st Street headquarters he'd felt like a display mannequin.

Worse, he sensed mockery behind his back. It wasn't that he couldn't handle pressure, he'd led combat fighter squadrons after all. But this duty was different.

Rather than feel like a fish in a bowl, he'd chosen to be on site where he could be publicly invisible and still keep busy. He knew staffers at the DOC, as well as the BOP, thought he was weird. What kind of department head deliberately made themself an outcast? But whatever they thought didn't matter. His goal was to get the job done and get out of here.

Hawk ordered Regional Director Walters to search all Immigration detention facilities for Dennis' family.

When he'd finished the call he dug through his pockets and fished out the paper Dennis had written on.

He ordered de la Cruz to contact the Assistant Director of Correctional Programs.

"Tell him to search all privately owned California immigration detention centers."

He handed her the paper.

"Get that to legal. Have them draft writs of habeas corpus for those names."

As de la Cruz hurried away he called after her,

"And have Enterprise come pick up their car."

While he waited for a response from the AD of prison programs, Hawk distracted himself with product management reports.

MTC staff had handled all the details in the stack of files on his desk. He was looking at the pile when a farm equipment order, inside a mound of recent Carlsen approved purchase orders, caught his eye.

'There's enough hardware here to cultivate an entire state' he thought.

On a hunch he began searching the camp survey map. Before he knew it it was 5 o' clock.

Still no word from Lompoc, but Dennis had called three times. Hawk had de la Cruz call Walter's back.

A few minutes passed before she ducked her head in.

"Director Walters is gone for the day sir. His office says they're still waiting to hear from a couple of facilities but so far no trace of your people."

She waved a sheet of paper overhead.

"They sent over a list of respondents."

'What about what's-his-name over at Correctional Programs?" Hawk grumbled.

"Hector Hernandez sir" she answered.

Her voice betrayed a hint of irritation at his not recalling the Hispanic director's name.

"His office says that none of their facilities have them either."

"Well somebodies got them. Check everything in the county that has bars. I'm talking city jails and Juvenile housings too. Find them."

"If you don't mind my asking sir, Do you know them? Who are these people?"

"I do mind" Hawk replied more harshly than he'd intended.

She couldn't know this was personal.

"Just some people who have been mistakenly detained.

I'm trying to keep a lid on Hispanic deportation mismanagement" he said calmly.

"Are they good candidates to represent a test civil case?" she asked.

The question made him suspicious. People in jobs like hers generally didn't care about immigrants, even if they were immigrants themselves.

When Hawk asked why she cared, the temperature dropped in her eyes.

"I think we all care about justice sir."

'I agree' he thought, but said instead,

"I should think we would too Ms del la Cruz.

But hence forth I will appreciate your not involving yourself with matters into which you've not been invited."

It stung but she didn't show it.

"Yes sir" she answered, turning on her heel and dismissing herself.

His eyes followed her out of the room.

'You fine' he thought, 'but you ain't that fine.' But really, he knew she was.

Eventually he stopped taking Dennis' calls and let them go straight to voice mail. Days turned to weeks and Dennis stopped calling.

Then, without any national or international outcry, cities like Pine Bluff Arkansas, Monroe Louisiana, Fort Pierce Florida, became virtual internment camps.

Everhart had wanted to go so far as to propose a constitutional amendment excluding Blacks and Hispanics from the bill of rights, but Guillory managed to keep him from it.

The restraining of the President not withstanding, the administration's labor aspirations remained intact. Hawk's suspicions about the farm equipment were confirmed when tons of Carlsen ordered seed showed up in the camp's far flung fields.

"Those were my orders" Carlsen replied when Hawk asked about it.

"You got issues, take em' up with Everhart."

Across the country detention camps were filling up faster than the bureau's ability to expand. It wasn't long before immigration detention centers, private camps, and all federal camp installations in the California system were linked by rail.

Carlsen had planned to position foundries and factories at the center of the development, while reserving the vast outlaying acreage for agriculture.

From the looks of things there'd be plenty of hands available for the anticipated work ahead. With the administration's encouragement, party controlled city councils issued ordinances, mandating barricades, if three or more residents were charged with sedition.

Kellogg had coerced city councils into requesting the interventions. That way, Everhart could claim the government wasn't initiating isolations, but rather, was responding to petitions for assistance from the cities themselves.

The result was that millions of people continued to flee West where they hoped for more lenient state governments. From New Mexico to Washington, states took on completely new complexions. Yet predictably, arrests in those places went up in direct proportion to the increase in migration.

Economic pressures brought on by the increase in population influxes quickly pushed affected state budgets past their breaking points. Frustrated by the federal government's withholding of social program funding and entitlement payments, several states threatened secession.

In the wake of strained resources, the barter system took hold in many of the shanty communities that popped up like mushrooms across a new frontier. People began organically helping each other survive. 'Freetowns', as they came to be called, took on the feel of 1960's hippie communes.

Hawk was considering handing in his resignation when he received a strange dictum from the administration.

Everhart directed him to issue an edict to all Federal correctional facilities. To wit.

'Any prisoner who dies in the custody of, or while otherwise incarcerated by, a federal correctional officer or institution, will be buried at the place of death, or some other, federally approved facility.

Relatives will have no claim to the body'.

He wasn't sure why, but he took it as a sign to stay put.

———

De la Cruz cradled a manila folder under her arm as she leaned against the doorjamb. Without looking up Hawk asked what she needed.

He knew she was there by the scent of her perfume. It had the fragrance of lilac that for some reason put him in the mind of Jacaranda trees.

"Your signature" she replied, concealing her annoyance that he hadn't bothered to make eye contact.

"Drop them on the desk please" he said still studying the computer screen.

She inwardly mocked his ignoring her. She knew as soon as she walked away he'd be staring at her ass.

In the months they'd worked together, never an unprofessional word had passed between them, but every now and then, they did catch the other one looking.

On the opposite end of the emotional spectrum, Hawk had had his fill of analyzing gradation, water flow, and similar charts.

"Budgets, blueprints and progress reports just ain't who I am" he muttered aloud while closing out the current spreadsheet.

He was questioning his sanity when the news broke. Everhart had ordered Governor Booker to put California's National Guard on alert.

Hawk immediately put through a call to Sacramento.

The first words out of Bookers mouth surprised him.

"I'm not doing it" he said without prelude.

"Thank God" Hawk exhaled.

Everhart can't wait to get into Los Angeles. It's starting to look like a concentration camp out"

The line suddenly disconnected and as he set the receiver down he noticed de la Cruz still looming in the doorway.

Her ability to materialize out of nowhere was disconcerting.

"How long have you been standing there?"

"I never left."

He didn't know what to make of her having overheard him nay say the President. 'Too late now' he thought.

"Go ahead" he challenged her.

Tell your friend Carlsen what I said so Everhart can fire me."

A pinch of vexation twisted her lips.

"If that's what you think" she replied,

then why not just fire me instead?"

Resting a hand defiantly on her hip she waited for his response. Hawk was stymied by the gauntlet toss. He hadn't expected such a direct reaction. He didn't want to fire her and he didn't want to address the reasons why. Retreating to his computer he said the only thing he could think of.

"That will be all Ms de la Cruz."

16

WE DON'T HAVE NUTS

Luis Reyes lay on the top bunk in the 10 x 15 cell staring at the ceiling. His closely cropped salt and pepper hair exactly matched the thin mustache resting over his equally thin lips. At 5' 8" the thickly built man in his mid forties fit comfortably on the jail issue mattress.

Reyes couldn't have been more relaxed if he'd been kicked back on a beach in Mazatlan.

His mood didn't stem from his familiarity with prison life. He was chill because he knew he wouldn't be here long.

Luis Martinez Reyes was the head of the Mexican Mafia.

A race riot/gang war at San Quentin, had forced authorities there to transfer him, but something got screwed up. Reyes should've been at Pelican Bay, Northern California's supermax. No way Reyes belonged in a low security facility like Camp Brown. He was here because of a digital mix up. He knew the mistake would be rectified sooner than later, but he didn't care. He was doing life. This escapade was merely a distraction from the mundane ordinary.

Danny Ortiz, who now went by the name Angel Salido, had no

idea who the guy sharing the cell was. He was just glad that he'd made it here himself.

The three weeks he'd spent in the Ann Arbor County Jail had been one long sphincter squeeze. There hadn't been a minute he didn't wonder when the Keepers would show up and drag him out of the cell. He worried even though they couldn't possibly know who he was.

Because the agents who'd arrested him thought he was an illegal, they figured the reason they didn't get a hit on his prints was because he'd never been printed in the states before. That wasn't it.

The morning he'd heard his alias announced on the intercom he hadn't known what to expect. Was this the day they found him out? He was relieved when he saw the transport bus. He didn't know where he was going but at least he wasn't going to die. Not today. Not here anyway.

Nurturing something that felt mildly like hope, he shuffled obligingly onto the bus. Slinking into a window seat he stared blankly out the grimy reinforced glass into the uncertain future.

All during the numbing ride, he'd thought he'd been headed to the border. He was surprised and depressed when four days after leaving Michigan, he'd rolled up to the gates of Camp Brown.

Looking around at the camp's newly constructed pods, Danny knew things were getting worse. But no matter what, he still needed to get back into the U.S. from wherever he might land in Mexico. 'What if they lock me up there too?'

He forced the thought from his mind.

Reyes sat on the upper bunk with his feet crossed underneath and his back propped against the wall. He ostensively read a bible, all the while surreptitiously giving Danny the spy eye. Slowly thumbing through the New Testament, his eyes flitted between the tissue thin pages of the King James and Danny's movements. Reyes hadn't been in a general population situation in years and experience had made him unnaturally suspicious.

Reyes had spent decades observing people and their motives.

Watching Danny's forlorn expression as he pressed his face against the glass, told him Danny wasn't a threat. Just another guy down on his luck.

Ordinarily Reyes would have kept to himself but for reasons only he knew, he spoke to Danny.

"Where you from?" he asked matter-of-factly.

The question made Danny leery.

"I don't bang" he answered cautiously.

"That's not what I meant" Reyes assured him, allowing a smile to validate his sincerity. Danny wasn't in the mood to talk but figured no sense being an ass-hole.

"Austin, by way of Long Beach" he answered.

You?"

Reyes' smile broadened.

"We're neighbors" he laughed.

Jerking both thumbs toward his chest he said,

"Hawaiian Gardens."

As Reyes laid the bible aside, and swung his feet over the side of the bunk, Danny caught a glimpse of a black hand among the many tattoos under Reyes' shirt.

"Where they pick you up at?" the crime boss asked.

"It's a long story."

"Look around" Reyes chided, glancing at the grey walls and glass,

I think we got time."

After he'd told Reyes about the attempt to rescue Blacks in Michigan and the shoot out that followed, Reyes revealed his identity.

"Why you wanna help Blacks?" was the only thing Reyes wanted to know.

"At the time it wasn't about being Black" Danny said.

It was about people in trouble."

"Who has more trouble than Mexicans?" Reyes asked.

"That's the thing" Danny said.

You know the saying. The enemy of my enemy is my friend."

Reyes knew little of world politics and Danny knew even less about jail house protocol. But intake orientation at Camp Brown was a three week process and both men were quick studies.

On the very last day of orientation, guards arrived at the cell before sun up. While being cuffed up Reyes let Danny know that he'd get the word out concerning their conversations.

Danny figured Reyes would go directly into segregation when he got wherever he was going. He didn't figure to hear from him for a while, if ever. But barely a week had gone by before Hawk noticed the Hispanics had completely shut down their normal activities.

There were no card or domino games on the yard. Nobody was balling. Instead, organized calisthenics, close order drills and self-administrated martial arts exercises were taking place.

None of this was happening among Black inmates. Some of the guys were suspiciously watching the Hispanics, but mostly they were balling, joking, slapping dominos and going about their regular routines.

Hawk asked a young correction officer about the change in dynamics. Spencer Wilton, a wiry 28 year old with a coarse complexion and a pronounced overbite, shrugged his bony shoulders and seemed as perplexed as Hawk.

"Beats me sir" he said.

Never seen nothing like this before. Marching Mexicans. That's different."

"Get with the deputy warden" Hawk said as he walked away.

I want answers by morning."

———

The next morning Wilton stood by with a prisoner in tow. Hawk leaned back in his chair and examined Danny.

"This our guy?" he asked.

"I don't know sir" Wilton replied.

Says his name is Angel Salido. Other than this arrest, he's not in the system.

Wilton handed Hawk a report and added,

He doesn't speak English."

Hawk's nod indicated Wilton's dismissal and he turned to the prisoner.

"Sit down" he said.

When Danny continued to stand, Hawk pointed to a chair.

"Ms de la Cruz" he called,

I need you to translate."

Studying the subdued figure in front of him Hawk mulled the possibilities.

Somebody had convinced the hardest Mexican gangsters in the system to submit to unprecedented discipline. Was this that guy? He directed de la Cruz in a series of questions.

"Ask where he's from.

How long he's been in the country.

Where he's worked.

How long.

What he knows about the drills.

Why his name comes up in this investigation?

If he's related to anybody in the institution?"

Danny gave generic answers in Spanish. Nothing he said or was evident in his demeanor suggested he had any connection with gang maneuvers.

Slapping the pages of the report Hawk turned to de la Cruz.

"All Hispanics, no matter the country of origin, must adhere to regimental orders" he explained.

Says a new intake named Angel is the source of that edict. Ask him the meaning of regimental orders."

Danny stared absently at the floor and merely shrugged at de la Cruz's translation.

"Have him take off his shirt."

Danny methodically removed his shirt revealing unmarked skin.

There was nothing to identify him as any kind of gang member, much less a shot caller.

Hawk got up, came around the front of the desk and sat on its corner. The Marines had trained him how to conduct himself when he personally was under interrogation, but he wasn't skilled in extracting information.

"Ask him again about his connection to Reyes?"

Danny continued to downplay the relationship in Spanish.

"Nothing, I don't really know him. He was my cell mate before he was transferred. That's it. He didn't talk much."

Regardless of the absence of physical evidence something about Danny's demeanor didn't reflect the man he was presenting. He kept his head down but although he appeared docile enough, Hawk sensed an intangible fortitude in his nature.

As Hawk reassessed his charge he let his gaze drift from the top of Danny's head to the tips of his toes. After a moment Hawk stood up.

"I think we're done here" he announced.

You can go Ms de la Cruz."

Startled by her sudden dismissal de la Cruz hesitated. Hawk looked toward the door indicating she should leave.

As she walked by he shook the report in the air and declared,

"The incompetence of this bullshit is staggering." He called after de la Cruz.

Get Wilton to take this guy back to his cell. Whoever our guy is, this ain't him."

Flopping back in his seat he spun the chair around turning his back to Danny. After a moment he violently back-handed the report scattering sheets of paper across the floor.

"Ridiculous" he scoffed.

I'm looking for a Mexican named Angel, in the California prison system. How many can there be?"

Spinning back around he yelled out the door,

de la Cruz, check on the author of this report. I wanna know everything about whoever wrote this shit. Find out their credentials and who assigned them to this department. But first, get me something to eat, I'm starving. Coffee too."

He turned to Danny,

"You want a burger?"

"Yeah" was in the air before Danny realized he'd spoken.

It was the first time he'd used English in weeks.

Hawk yelled to de la Cruz,

"Hold the Wilton call."

Turning to Danny he asked.

"You wanna tell me what's going on?"

Instead of answering, Danny asked what gave him away.

Hawk pointed to Danny's hands. Danny looked down at his smooth unblemished hands and understood.

"What's your name?"

Again Danny answered with a question.

"Why do you help them?"

"What?"

"White people."

"Just tell me who you are and what you're up to."

"My name is Danny Ortiz."

"What's going on Danny?"

"Really?"

"Really."

"Okay, since you need to know anyway."

Danny threw up deadpan jazz hands.

Surprise, we're fighting back. We're not like you. We're not going passively to the fields or the ovens either."

'What like me?'

Hawk leaned forward.

"I don't know what you're trying to accomplish inmate" he said.

But you don't get to tell me what you will or will not do. And understand something. The only one deciding what happens around here is me."

Danny's deferential demeanor dissolved into frank speak.

"With all due respect sir, you don't decide anything.

You *can't* decide because you're not the head.

You're merely the finger, that pulls the trigger."

"Careful" Hawk warned.

Danny ignored the warning.

"I was like you once" he said.

I used to believe in liberty and justice for all too.

He shook his head.

It just ain't true."

The ease of Danny's transformation puzzled Hawk.

Was this inmate being purposely insubordinate or just inappropriately sincere? D"isn't matter. When it comes to what happens to you personally" he said,

And I mean every breath you take; I'm head nigga in charge. You'd best not to forget that."

"No sir, I won't sir" Danny replied.

He reassumed a softer posture.

Looking around the office he focused on Hawk's portrait hanging on the wall.

Clothed in dress blues, Hawk bore a confident smile, proudly displaying his chest candy.

Shifting his focus to a gold fringed American flag tucked in the corner, Danny said,

"I meant no disrespect, but can I ask you something?"

Hawk allowed his silence to be taken as consent.

First you were a soldier. Now you're the country's top prison boss.

Basically you spent your whole professional life, up to your neck, helping to perpetuate a system that stands firmly on that self same neck.

I look around this room and I ask myself, who's really the prisoner here? My question is; What's the thing, the one thing, about all this shit that fucks you up the most? Sir."

Hawk's face tingled, but he kept it poker and let Danny talk.

"The thing that bothers me most" Danny said,

Is the look in our women's eyes.

The look that says she knows we can't protect her.

That at the end of the day, the system, and by system I mean White men, can do anything they want to her, and there's nothing, not a goddamn thing, we can do about it."

Dennis flashed across Hawk's mind.

And even though she knows the consequences for men of color who stand up to the system, whether she admits it or not, the fact that we haven't chosen to die in deference to our manhood, impedes her ability to fully respect us."

Deep down Hawk agreed with Danny but wasn't in a position to say so. He was uncomfortable and about to change the subject when Danny asked.

"You ever hear of something called phantom sensation?" It's like when amputees claim they can still feel their missing limbs."

Danny leaned forward leisurely placing his forearms on his knees.

Well, that's what's up with us whenever we think we feel our nuts."

He leaned back in the chair.

And if you think that by merely kissing their ass, they're ever going to accept you as their legal equal, you're just flat out delusional. You need your own country for that."

Later, after he'd had Danny taken to the hole,

Hawk sat at his desk drinking Jack Daniels from the bottle until he passed out.

17
HOLLOW MAN

His tongue was dank like a bathroom sponge.

She handed him a cup of coffee.

"What?" he muttered to the blurry vagueness that was de la Cruz.

"Hispanic prisoners" she repeated.

"What about them?"

"You put Ortiz in segregation and Hispanics went on hunger strike."

Hawk thought he heard a hint of pride in her voice.

Then it dawned on him what she was saying. Wide awake now, his head thumped hard.

"All of them?"

"All of them."

At his core Hawk was reactionary. He wasn't one to start things and would rather row the boat than rock it. But when things went off the rails he went on autopilot. Identifying problems and solutions on instinct was his forte even though he didn't rely on it.

"Contact Lompoc H&R" he snapped.

Have them transfer one Wesley Painter here right away."

"Who's that?

"Gate guard."

De la Cruz's eyelid spasmed.

"Okay?" she said.

Hawk needed an ally who'd be loyal solely to him. In an attempt to pump himself up, he slapped his hands together making a loud pop.

"It's bout to get a whole nuther level of stupid up in Brown town" he said.

Needs me a trusted somebody up in here right about now."

While de la Cruz was intrigued by the unexpected appearance of 'hood' Hawk, she chaffed at the notion of not being considered trustworthy.

The phone rang.

de la Cruz picked up and her mood abruptly changed.

She half whispered though she didn't know why.

"Governor Booker for you sir. Sounds urgent."

Assuming her customary place against the doorjamb she waited for Hawk to answer.

"You just going to stand there?" he asked.

She shrugged as he lifted the phone to his ear.

"Yes Governor."

"Director Hawkins, we have a situation."

"Yes sir?"

"Here're the cliff notes.

A woman in the West Adams district identified 12 air toxic chemicals in the water, blah blah blah. You want the particulars?"

"No need sir."

"To make a long story short, people wouldn't pay their bills and DWP shut the water off. Right now there're hundreds of people in the streets."

Hawk picked up the remote, clicked on the TV and there it was. Streets clogged with angry protesters. The kyron scrolling under the live image read,

'Riot In Los Angeles'.

Cars, trucks, busses and people choked the thoroughfares. Nothing budged in any direction. Hawk immediately recognized the public safety risks.

"How can I help Sir?"

"Don't call me sir."

"Force of habit."

"Everhart has requested the Guard be deployed to the Crenshaw district.

Says if I don't move he'll call in troops himself."

Hawk had visions of tanks rolling down Adams Boulevard and asked,

"Can you stall?"

"For a time."

"Then what?"

"Is there a gentlemen by the name of Caleb there?"

At that moment there was a rap at the door.

When de la Cruz turned around, a pale, hollow looking man in a light grey suit, brushed in past her.

"Caleb?" Hawk ventured.

The hollow man nodded.

Hawk motioned de la Cruz out of the room. As she closed the door Hawk faintly heard Booker saying goodbye. Hollow man handed him an envelope with no indication of its contents.

After reading the note Hawk asked,

"Is this what I think it is?"

"It's what it says it is" Caleb answered.

"The Governor wants you to command the California Reserve."

'That's crazy' Hawk thought but said instead,

"What about the regular Guard?"

"The Governor's going to volunteer them to Greens Point."

Greens Point is a predominately Black enclave in the greater Houston Texas area. It's accurately known to locals as Guns Point and was a logical next target for the administration.

Suddenly a bigger picture sprung into focus.

Hawk realized that with the regular Guard out of state, as Commander of the Reserve, he'd actually be the de facto Commander of the California Guard.

Hollow man recognized Hawk's conclusion and nodded concurrence.

"Booker trusts you" he said.

"Let's say I accept that.

It still doesn't explain why Everhart would trust Booker to back him up in Greens Point?"

Something akin to a smile attached to Hollow man's lips.

"Governor Booker told the President that he'd seen the light. Turns out it's pretty easy to convince a man that you believe he's right."

Hawk shook the letter in the air.

"Booker's considering seceding?

Why's he trust me like this?"

Hollow man's smile dissolved.

"Only he can answer that sir."

Hawk wasn't comfortable. These were uncharted waters. Was this a trick? A test? He challenged Caleb.

"If we try to secede Everhart is sending in troops."

Hollow man shook his head.

"Not right away" he said.

Too many minorities in the ranks.

He can't be sure that they'll go along with firing on other Blacks."

Attempting to quell Hawk's obvious skepticism Caleb continued.

Seceding's not a done deal, he said.

It's just an option."

"Helluva option" Hawk replied.

"If we secede, we'll be sovereign" Caleb said.

Any aggression against us becomes an act of war."

"A war we can't win" Hawk countered.

"He won't chance it" Caleb insisted.

We have allies who've assured us of their support for U.N. sanctions."

Hawk still wasn't convinced.

"You'll excuse me but that sounds shaky as hell.

What makes you think Black troops won't go along? They've gone along so far."

Caleb shook his head again.

"Not true.

Black and Hispanic troops, including officers, were removed from detail in every barricade case."

"You sayin' only White troops engaged in ghetto operations?"

Caleb remained stoic.

'So that's how it is' Hawk thought.

It was the first time he'd ever thought of Whites as the enemy. He immediately checked himself. All white people weren't problematic. Hell, Booker was white.

"If I agree to this, Booker has to delay the announcement.

It can't be known right now. Some things I need to do first."

Hollow man accepted the response but added,

"He's going to want an answer soon. This thing has a short fuse. Everhart's latest fiasco is demanding that all Governors add the designation 'Church' to their state names."

Hawk almost farted.

"You mean like, The California Church, The Ohio Church?"

"Exactly.

But it gets worse. He's moving the Capitol to Corpus Christi Texas, and there's rumors of an executive order changing the name of the country to the United Congregations of Christland."

"That's ridiculous" Hawk blurted.

The courts won't allow it."

"He owns the courts" Caleb parried.

Besides, a court battle will take years and by then he'll have solidified power to the point where no ruling will go against him."

"Jesus"Hawk sighed.

"Jesus indeed" Caleb echoed.

"If I agree to Booker's request I'd need to resign my position."

"I don't know" Caleb replied.

Everhart might think it's a good idea to have his Boy in charge of the California Guard. So long as he believes you're that guy.

It's never been done before but hey, one job's federal and the other's state. I don't know of any law against it."

The door burst open and de la Cruz crashed wide eyed into the room. She couldn't immediately find words.

"The Blacks" she finally managed.

Hawk instantly understood.

He hustled Caleb to the door.

"Tell Booker I'll do it.

Let me know when the Greens point deployment gets under way, I'll be ready."

Caleb turned around.

"We're not in this alone" he said.

There was a surety in his voice that Hawk didn't share.

As soon as the door closed he turned to de la Cruz.

"What happened?"

"I don't know.

Wilton said nobody's talking about it. It's weird. He said everybody just stopped eating all of a sudden."

"Call Pelican Bay" Hawk snapped.

"Have them get Odell Giles down here immediately."

He answered the question before she could ask.

"Black Guerrilla Family" he said.

Suddenly, a camp that had until recently been merely a plan in some autocrat's head, was now the epicenter of a swiftly changing dynamic in the California military and prison system.

Hawk knew what would happen if it got out that both Blacks and Hispanics at the camp had revolted.

There wouldn't be any negotiations. Keepers wouldn't just storm the camp; they'd level it. He believed in law and order but that's not what would happen here. He turned to de la Cruz.

"After you call the Bay get Ortiz in here."

He didn't know why the prison gangs were striking and even though there was nothing he could do about it, he wondered how to stop L.A. City cops from overreacting in his West Adams neighborhood.

Governor Booker had ordered the mayor to hold the LAPD back until he gave the word. Hawk could only hope the order held because that was as good as it was going to get for now.

He had a bad feeling. He comforted himself with the knowledge that should things get crazy, at least he'd be in command of the National Guard. He didn't want the Guard in his neighborhood but he wanted the Keepers there even less. His thoughts were interrupted by the arrival of Wilton and Danny.

Under the circumstances Danny's demeanor was far too casual; like he knew something Hawk didn't.

Dismissing Wilton and removing Danny's cuffs Hawk got to it.

"Okay, what will it take?" He asked.

Danny casually rubbed his wrists before sitting down.

"Just like that?" he said.

"Just like that" Hawk answered flatly.

"Okay then" Danny nodded.

I want to be be free."

"I don't have time for bullshit " Hawk said.

What's it gonna take to call off the strike?"

"Like I was saying" Danny answered,

I want to be free to control my own program without interference."

"Your program? That's insane. Why would I agree to that?"

"Because it makes sense."

"Not to me."

"Let me explain it like this."

Danny leaned forward in his chair.

The longer you wait, the slimmer your chances get."

Hawk stiffened.

"My chances?"

Hawk was irritated.

I don't think you understand the situation" he said.

"That's funny" Danny smiled.

I was about to say the same thing to you."

Hawk was constraining the impulse to go authoritarian when Danny asked,

"You think you're just gonna walk away?

That they're not going to do to you what they're doing to every other Black person?

What rational would justify that line of reasoning?"

Knowing Hawk received the question as rhetorical, Danny continued.

You better face the fact that you ain't getting off 'Scott' free. Cause at the end of the day, you ain't Scottish.

Sooner rather than later, they're coming for you too.

Time you understood that the men in these prisons are the closest thing you have to friends."

Hawk leaned across the desk and stared intently at his charge. It didn't take a genius to understand this wasn't your everyday jailhouse hustle.

"Who are you?" He asked.

Danny ignored the question.

"You better start getting your people organized" he advised.

"What people?"

Danny continued ignoring him.

"And you better do it while you can. I hear Kellogg's moving on Homestead Florida next."

The words hit hard.

"Who are you?" Hawk repeated.

"Danny Ortiz, Austin Texas. I told you that."

"What do you know about Homestead?"

Rather than answer, Danny asked instead,

"You didn't know about it did you?

They didn't tell you did they?"

It was true. He hadn't been told.

"I wanna know how you know" Hawk insisted.

Turning to the door he called for de la Cruz.

When she came in he wrote something on a tablet, tore off the page and handed it to her.

"Run that name along with this guys prints and get back to me."

De la Cruz hustled out as Danny asked sarcastically,

"You didn't do that already?

Doesn't matter. Nothing's coming back".

"We'll see" Hawk answered.

"Look at me" Danny said.

What do you see?"

He didn't wait for an answer.

When people look at me, they don't see a nice guy, or a productive citizen contributing to society. They see a scary Mexican. All cover, no book. They have no idea who I am."

"Choir here" Hawk said.

Danny slouched back in the chair and clasped his hands behind his head. There was no whimsy in his voice when he reminisced,

"There was a time I'd-a done anything to be accepted by White people.

I tried to look like them and talk like them. I tried to erase everything Mexican about me. I hated my accent. To me it was like having a giant scarlet letter leap out of my mouth every time I opened it.

So I practiced sounding American by imitating people on TV. And God the TV. Whenever they showed Mexicans, we were dirty, poor, dopers, prostitutes and shit."

"Choir" Hawk repeated.

"I hated that" Danny said,

That wasn't me. I had to escape that image no matter what. But that took money. I didn't have any, so I studied. Hard. You know what I'm talking about."

Hawk involuntary nodded.

Got good grades, stayed out of trouble. I was actually quiet back then. And yeah, it worked. I graduated college, got a good job with a great company, the whole bit."

Hawk knew a con job when he heard one and suddenly interjected.

"Then you met a girl and fell in love, but then she got deported. She wasn't pregnant was she?"

"No" Danny answered, intentionally ignoring the intended slight.

Nothing like that.

But one day I realized, that by simply doing my job, I was sharpening the knife that slit my own throat."

"Job?"

Danny stuck a finger in the air.

"Hold that thought" he said then slowly looked around the room.

"I was educated but I was ignorant. I never knew North America's history with South and Central America. I was so busy trying to become American that I didn't realize I was already American.

I'd been American since before Europeans ever set foot on the continent. But at the time I just wanted to fit in. I never studied U.S. Latin American policies. I just didn't know any better."

And no, he said evenly,

She wasn't deported. She was murdered."

Danny's bluntness had the ring of truth.

Maybe this wasn't a con.

"I'm sorry" Hawk stammered. I didn't mean"

Danny waved him off.

"Forget it.

All I'm saying is, we ain't brainwashed; We're whitewashed.

Believing in assimilation as a means to equality is a mistake.

Truth is, most minorities suffer from mass Stockholm syndrome. You know who gets the syndrome right?"

Hawk remained silent.

"Yeah you do" Danny cajoled.

"Hostages."

Hawk avoided the perspective by asking how the girl died?

Danny wasn't sure he wanted to share the details, but decided to subordinate his privacy to further later designs.

"Ever hear of an outfit called Stratfor?" He asked.

"Doesn't ring a bell."

"It's a private intel company that government agencies use to handle their overflow.

One of our contracts was with NSA; Collecting data on Central and South American gangs."

"You were a spy?"

"No, I was a cyber security specialist. Encryption, hacking and data analysis. She was the spy."

"You worked together?"

"No. We worked in the same field, but not together.

Vanessa was a double agent. She worked for us and them."

"Who is them?"

"Guatemalan government."

"Who killed her?"

"I don't know.

She was in the slums of Guatemala City, meeting with the Zetas when she disappeared. Guatemala military police found her body stuffed in a refrigerator on the back of a flat bed. She'd been there for days."

"Geez. I'm sorry" Hawk offered again.

Danny shrugged. Hawk gingerly pressed him.

"Why's she meeting with gangsters?"

"She was briefing them on U.S. plans to back a Guatemalan government offensive against the remaining Mayan people."

Hawk wanted to be sure he was understanding correctly.

"She was giving the gangsters information?"

"Yes."

"Why?"

"The government planned to redistribute the land; Herd the Mayans onto reservations.

Zetas aren't gangsters to everybody. They're Robin Hoods to some people. They use crime to raise money but some of it goes to supplement the Mayans."

"So she's playing both the Guatemalan and U.S. governments?

"Yeah, try to keep up."

"Okay, again, why?"

"Who knows. Maybe she just decided she didn't want to be part of the problem anymore."

Hawk shook his head.

"Why-ever she did it, she was kick-ass. Triple agent is definitely kick-ass."

Danny looked at the floor. His lips crimped.

"Not kick-ass enough" he said.

Hawk never discussed politics with other officers when he was in the Corps. His was just to do or die, and that was the way he'd liked it. He'd always accepted who the enemy was. It was whoever his superiors said it was. Now he wasn't so sure.

"Why didn't ICE flag you when they ran your prints?"

A look of satisfaction came over Danny as he folded his arms across his chest.

"I scrubbed my identity before I left Stratfor. I don't exist."

Suspicious of the ease with which Danny offered the confession, Hawk asked him why he was so forthcoming.

Danny answered simply,

"I'm trying to help you."

'Who did this guy think he was?'

"Did Reyes authorize you to direct these operations?"

"I don't have any power."

"I'm not asking if you personally have any power.

What are regimental orders and who gives them?"

"The orders are simple. Take whatever action necessary to preserve life and dignity."

"Who gave this order?"

"Not me."

"But you're key.

"No Director Hawkins, truth be known, you're key."

"Explain that" Hawk demanded.

"You have resources at your disposal. But you won't have them for long. You should use them while you can."

Hawk took the remark as a threat.

"Do you know what will happen if I call in assistance?" he said.

"That's not something you want to do" Danny answered. You don't have much time. This isn't something we chose. It's just the way things turned out this time."

Hawk suddenly wondered if the gang strikes were mutually agreed to.

"Why are the Blacks striking?" He asked.

"Are they?" Danny said.

I don't know anything about that. You'd have to ask them."

When it looked like Danny was through talking Hawk warned him.

"You're setting yourself up for some shit you ain't ready for."

Rather than react defensively, Danny curtly jabbed at what he considered to be Hawk's soft underbelly.

He stroked his chin absently replying,

"At least I have a country I can call my own.

You? You can't even speak your own native tongue.

You don't even know what it is.

Most of your people have never even seen Africa, let alone want to live there.

You're so whitewashed that you choose to remain an unwanted guest, in a house you were forced to build, rather than identify as African.

And you absolutely refuse to accept the undeniable fact, that this, is not, your country."

Danny appeared more disappointed than angry. Like he couldn't believe Black people hadn't rebelled years ago.

"Talking about, I pledge allegiance" he said.

Ain't that a bitch? Allegiance to What? 400 more years of the same shit?

What you need to be saying is kiss my ass. Face it. As far as you're concerned the bill of rights is a bill of goods."

Until now Danny's demeanor had been dismissive. Now his manner became more controlled.

"You personally, have the wherewith all to change things. If it's not already too late" he said.

The accusation of being ashamed of his blackness was too crucial a charge for Hawk to leave on the table. Partly because there was truth in it. But rather than exhort the virtues of his Blackness, Hawk characteristically defended his patriotism.

"This is very much my country" he declared.

And I'm the last one to be a traitor."

He meant it. But it seemed to Danny that he'd gone too far when he said,

I serve and I protect. I <u>am</u> the law!"

Danny rocked backward.

"Oh My God. We had this conversation already. You can't be the law. You need your own country for that!

Let me tell you who you are.

This is you.

To serve and protect rich people from poor people in general, and black and brown people in particular.

You're an occupying terrorist organization, that murders people of color, under color of authority, at the behest of your monied masters in order to maintain the status quo."

Danny was accusing Hawk of being a house nigga. The Judas goat of Black people. The supreme insult.

This kind of attack usually came from progressive Black activists. He wouldn't take it from them and he wasn't going to take it from Danny.

"I'm the nuts and bolts that hold this whole thing together" he asserted.

It was this foundational belief that sustained him, and he was non-deferential in his contention that,

"Without me, the strong would eat the weak."

"My point exactly" Danny fired back.

The weak *are* being eaten. But there're too many of us to digest now.

To Whites we're a virus that's spiraled out of control.

A human epidemic that can't be contained and threatens to over-whelm the host."

There were aspects of the argument again that Hawk agreed with and rather than debate inauthentically he said instead,

"This matter is closed."

"Have it your way" Danny said before adding,

Just remember, you're a liability now."

"What's that supposed to mean?"

"Look at it from their point of view" Danny said.

Black soldiers who come back alive, have outlived their usefulness."

He wanted to tell Danny to kiss his ass but he needed him so he said instead,

"If you wanna survive you'll end this strike."

18

I HAD A DREAM

Hawk made a point of avoiding people from his old hood. Their accusatory glares weren't easily warded off just because he wasn't ashamed of his job. But this morning, while watching prisoners being led off of arriving busses, he saw Dennis Cox.

His stomach pinwheeled as he watched the feeble figure, head bowed, shuffle beleagueredly into the intake building.

When Hawk saw the skeletal frame disappear behind the mechanical doors, visions of Dante's Devine Comedy popped in his head.

He raced to the building.

Once inside the cavernous field-house he sifted through the sea of despondency looking for his friend. He couldn't single him out. Everybody looked the same. Ghosts.

Finally he spotted him. Sitting on a bench slouched over, frail and withdrawn, Dennis seemed more child than man.

When Hawk tapped Dennis' shoulder he felt bone beneath the threadbare stained shirt. Almost catatonic, Dennis didn't notice Hawk at all.

Careful not to startle his friend, Hawk quietly asked how he was doing.

Dennis slowly looked up. His eyes were vacant.

After a moment a flicker of recognition registered.

"Hawk?" His voice more air than tone he asked,

What they get you for?"

"They didn't get me Den, I'm here to help you."

Dennis stared past Hawk for a moment before turning absently away.

A familiar voice suddenly caught Hawk's attention.

He turned to see a perturbed de la Cruz hastily making her way toward him.

"I've been searching everywhere for you" she sputtered.

The instant Dennis saw de la Cruz he stood up.

Struggling to gather enough air to gain his voice he gasped,

"Sylvie, I knew you'd come back" he said.

Looking as if he'd just seen the risen Christ he implored the bewildered aide,

"Let's go home now baby, let's go home."

De la Cruz turned to Hawk.

"He thinks you're his wife" Hawk explained.

She's Mexican."

"You know this guy?"

"No. Not this guy."

Dennis stretched toward de la Cruz.

"I thought you didn't want me no more baby" he gurgled.

Hawk stepped between them.

"No Den, this isn't Sylvia" he said.

This is Adelina, she works for me."

De la Cruz took a step back. It was the first time she'd heard Jesse speak her given name. The sound of it, formed with his own breath, was unlike she'd ever heard it. Her face burned.

Dennis didn't hear any of it. Reaching again for Adelina he repeated,

"I knew you'd come back."

Hawk held him back. The body he restrained felt more like broken pretzels in Saran Wrap than flesh and bone.

Suddenly the fact that he'd helped enforce policies that had cost his friend his family, his freedom, and maybe his mind, hit home.

Alarmed by Dennis' condition and compelled as much by guilt as compassion, Hawk called for assistance.

Orderlies appeared and led Dennis away, leaving Adelina to gently offer her sympathies.

Unaccepting of condolences, Hawk walked away. Before disappearing he called over his shoulder,

"Get me the prognosis ASAP."

de la Cruz suddenly remembered why she'd come and yelled after him.

"Your special assistant is waiting for you in the office."

He'd barely walked through the door when he heard the buoyant greeting.

"Wesley Painter reporting for duty sir."

He took Painter's eager hand and gave it a firm shake whereupon Painter fairly gushed.

"I can't believe you remembered me sir. I'll never be able to properly thank you."

Hawk pushed Dennis from his mind and summoned his commander persona.

"Glad to have you aboard Painter."

Considering what was at stake, Hawk hoped he'd picked the right man for the job.

"Any trouble finding me?" he asked.

A sheepish grin crept over Painter's face.

"Not at all sir" he snickered.

"Around here, seems like everybody knows everything about you."

Expelling a self deprecating chuckle, Hawk admitted to being a kind of a freak show.

Looking the new guy over he quickly accessed Wesley's sense of style. His navy blue suit and well worn black shoes were presentable enough but not quite up to Hawk's standards.

Pointing to the hardwood chair crammed by his desk he cordially directed Painter to sit. Painter's commitment showed in his posture as he sat ramrod straight on the chair's edge. This was the attitude Hawk hoped for.

"You excited?"

"Yes sir" Painter beamed. "I sure am sir."

"Ever been to Homestead Florida?"

While Hawk briefed Painter on what to expect and what was expected of him, de la Cruz returned.

Before Hawk could ask about Dennis she announced,

"He doesn't know where he is sir. He's in and out of lucidity. Doctor needs to run more tests. Says she'll know more in a day or two."

Hawk thanked her before introducing Painter.

Still chaffing over being considered less trustworthy than the stranger, de la Cruz offered only a curtesy smile.

"We've met" she said curtly.

If Painter took it as a slight he didn't show it.

Hawk, on the other hand, sensed her displeasure, but since he didn't know the reason for her vexation, he proceeded affably.

"Ms de la Cruz, Please see to it that Mr Painter patronizes a proper haberdashery. Expense it."

He turned to Painter.

"We have appearances to maintain. No offense."

Painter assured him none was taken.

De la Cruz had enough of the best foot forward play. Painter annoyed her. She knew she was being irrational and that annoyed her more. If her boss didn't trust her so what, what did she care? But she did.

"I know just the place" she said coolly even though she had no idea where to shop.

"When would you like me to take him?"

"Today is good" Hawk nodded.

"This afternoon then" she replied and slipped through the door before anyone could respond.

————

Hawk was having trouble figuring out his current situation's end game.

All of the scenarios looked bad.

He was out of the top administration loop, troops were on the verge of invading his old neighborhood, he had institutional compliance problems, and to top it off, war with Islam could break out at any second.

What the fuck, seemed the only appropriate response.

"You get Painter squared away?" he asked when de La Cruz returned.

Instead of answering she assumed her customary lean against the door jamb. A wistful melancholy shrouded her face.

"He called me Sylvie" she said.

Wasn't that the name on the list you gave me? Sylvia Cox?"

"Yeah." Jesse was surprised she remembered Sylvia's last name.

I told you, he thought you were his wife."

"Kids still missing?" she asked.

Jesse didn't look up, only nodding in reply.

She could see the question rubbed hard.

"You're not blaming yourself?" she back-handedly encouraged him.

He spun the chair away from her and stared out the window.

"Of course not" he lied.

She sensed his penance but decided to intrude anyway.

"It's not your fault. You did everything you could."

"Did I?"

Although his back was to her he could feel her eyes on him and he straighten his shoulders.

"You're a good man Jesse.

Nobody could ask for a better friend."

She was trying to help him off the hook but he wouldn't let her.

"You don't know me" he insisted.

Rather than be put off by the rebuff, she responded with absolution.

"I think I do" she said.

It was an unadorned statement.

A simple opinion. Yet the ease of its conviction served as a much needed balm to his wounded spirit.

Ever since he'd known her he'd thought Adelina was one of the most beautiful women he'd ever seen. But in this moment it was like he was seeing her for the very first time.

More than outward good looks, she epitomized what it meant to be beautiful on the inside. She was simply the personification of what it was that Willis was talking about.

His throat closed around a tongue that suddenly felt like lead. He knew his mouth was open and hurried it shut. Though slightly embarrassed, Adelina otherwise enjoyed the moment. Stifling a giggle she tentatively placed a hand on his shoulder.

"You okay?" she asked.

"Yeah" he gagged.

Just worried about my boy."

She mercifully played along.

"Doctor says you can see him tomorrow."

While no words relevant to the situation had been spoken, in that moment everything between them changed. Nobody knows how these things happen. Sages ascribed such moments to mystery.

Their personal paradigm having unalterably shifted, left nothing more to be said. Accordingly, intuition nudged Adelina from the room.

———

The next day, after dispatching a dapper Painter to Homestead, Hawk went to the infirmary.

He arrived to find Dennis struggling to prop himself up in bed.

The movie 'Malcolm X' was playing on a TV suspended on a stand in the corner.

"You been hoodwinked, bamboozled, led astray"

Dennis was quoting in tandem with the film's dialogue when Hawk came in.

Dennis turned to him.

"I never understood the Run Amok line" he said.

He clicked off the TV.

You been hoodwinked, I get. Bamboozled, I get. Led astray. But ain't nobody run amok."

Hawk hadn't expected to find Dennis awake, let alone lucid.

"Damn, look at you" he said.

Livin the life, taking in the flicks. How you feeling?"

"Don't mind me" Dennis answered.

I'm just another nigga sayin' what er'body already know."

Although Hawk was encouraged by the strength in his friend's voice, he wasn't sure he liked what he was hearing.

"What's that Den?"

"We just like the Jews" Dennis said.

Old testament and 1930's both. Been 400 years and Pharaoh still won't let my people go. You betta listen to me. You listenin'?"

"What're you sayin bruh?"

Dennis fluffed his pillow.

"Remember that time we went out to Bakersfield to yo momma sista place?"

"Yeah."

"And she had them animals?"

"Yeah?"

"You put the baby goats in the pigpen cause you wanna see em' play with the pigs?"

"Yeah?"

"But they kept fighting til you finally had to separate em'?"

"Why are you bringing this up?"

"Pigs ain't want them goats in they pen."

"Yeah I remember. So?"

"So you a goat in a pig pen. You been hoodwinked, bamboozled, and it ain't long fo' the trains come."

'Maybe it's the meds talking' Hawk thought as he leaned on the railing at the foot of the bed and tried to access his friend's condition.

"Trains?"

"Oh, trains comin'" Dennis repeated.

Listen to me. You listening?"

"Yeah, I am."

Dennis leaned forward. His eyes morphed into reptilian slits.

"I ain't never told you this before" he half whispered.

I ain't never told nobody this before, and I ain't lookin' fo no feedback neither."

Hawk got the odd feeling Dennis might say something important.

Dennis paused and considered whether or not to continue. After a moment, he did.

"Last week I had a dream. I don't have these kind-a dreams often, but when I do."

He stopped again. Hawk waited.

"When I do; They happen."

Dennis studied Hawk's expression.

Satisfied he was being taken seriously, Dennis continued.

"I seen trains in the dream. When the trains come, that mean it's about to jump off."

As crazy as it sounded, Hawk wondered if he was listening to more than med induced ramblings. Black people have a penchant for giving credence to dreams and divinations. Still, that didn't mean he wasn't skeptical.

"What does that even mean?" he asked.

"I don't know what it means" Dennis admitted.

But in the dream the trains left full, but came back empty."

"Left where?"

"Here, muhthafukka" Dennis blurted.

Then he asked a strange question.

"Why you was never captain of yo team?"

"What?"

"At S.C. Why you was never team captain?"

"Why you asking me that?"

"Just answer the question. Why you was never team captain?"

"I don't know" Hawk hesitated.

They tried to make me captain a few times but I didn't want it."

"Why?"

Hawk paused again and Dennis jumped in.

"I'll tell you why.

Cause you ain't want the responsibility that's why.

You ain't want to carry the weight of always havin' to win, always gotta be betta."

Dennis was sitting straight up now. His eyes and voice were crystal clear.

You knew, whether the team win or lose, you personally be alright.

You be a star, no matter what happened. But you don't want nobody lookin' at you like the leader. You ain't wanna carry er'body else weight."

Hawk wondered where Dennis was coming from, and better yet, where was he going.

"You took them Marine promotions cause they come with the territory. You couldn't turn em' down but you ain't really want em. They come with expectations. You just wanna do yo thing, get out with a pension. Now you on easy street. You a coward Jesse."

Hawk felt himself get hot. Nobody'd ever called him a coward before.

You scared to be a leader."

"Bullshit" Hawk finally protested.

"I led fighter squadrons."

"In a fight that wasn't yours" Dennis said.

It's bullshit alright. You think you mighta been doin' all that sky divin' an shit to prove something to yourself?"

'Hood' Hawk suddenly showed up.

"Nigga I ain't got nothing to prove" he declared.

Realizing he'd raised his voice Hawk looked around to see if he'd been overheard.

What do you want from me?" he demanded.

"What you want from yo-self?"

Unwilling to be forced down this path, Hawk changed the subject.

"You didn't ask me about your people."

Dennis instantly shut down.

"I know about my people" he said.

"You found them?"

"I ain't say that."

"Then what?"

"They been sold."

"Fuck you talkin' about?"

"You ain't find em' did you?"

"But that don't mean"

Dennis cut him off.

"Three months ago, she called in the middle of the night.

I could hear 'em beatin' her.

Girls screamin' in the background."

"Who?"

"They wanted money to let em' go?"

"Who was beating her?"

Dennis' eyes glazed over.

"Keepers sold em' to smugglers."

"What smugglers?"

"Smugglers nigga, I don't know."

"How you know they were smugglers?"

"She told me."

"Where is she?"

"She say Azerbaijan."

"What?"

"They work the mining camps in Kazakhstan."

"She's in the mines?"

Dennis' eyes went black.

"She in the *camps* he emphasized.

Hawk suddenly realized Dennis' family had been sold into sex slavery.

"They wanted me to hear her get beat" Dennis said.

I sold my house."

"You gave them the money?"

"Yeah."

"How much?"

"All of it."

"How'd you get it to them?"

"I put it in the bank. Sylvie gave them the account number. Ain't heard nothin' since."

"Why didn't you call me?"

"I did. Voice mail."

Hawk felt his nuts contract and instantly recalled Danny's admonition.

Dennis sensed Hawk's impotence.

"Ain't nuthin you can say" he offered. It's past all that."

Hawk still struggled for words.

"I'll get Kellogg" he fumbled.

"Nah fuck that" Dennis interrupted.

They dead by now.

If the Russians ain't kill em, Sylvie did.

She ain't let no shit like that go down."

Hawk felt numb but Dennis wasn't through.

"I asked you why you ain't wanna be Captain a that team. You still ain't said nuthin'."

"Okay, you wanna know, I'll tell you."

This seemingly small gesture was a big deal for Jesse.

He'd never shared the reasons for a lot of the decisions he'd made. He wasn't particularly proud of some of them but he'd been guided by principles that had been part of him since he could remember.

"During the Korean war" he began.

"The what!?" Dennis snarked.

"Nigga you want to hear the story or not?"

"I don't know. Do I"?

Hawk pulled a chair next to the bed and sat down.

"My Granddaddy was a paratrooper assigned to the 2nd Ranger Infantry Company Airborne. A segregated unit. Everybody, including officers, was Black.

So in December 1950, he deployed to South Korea.

That's when the company adopted the nom de guerre', Buffalo Rangers."

"Com'on man."

"Their war name" Jesse explained.

They served as a scouting unit for the 7th Infantry Division and you know what that meant. They were dropped at the front and were always first to run up on the Red Chinese."

Hawk checked Dennis' appreciation of the situation.

This was some close proximity shit" he emphasized.

There was no pride in his temper when he added,

Granddaddy was a hero. At least that's what the army said back in 51'. Black newspapers told it like this."

Hawk leaned forward and recited the old printed account from memory.

.　.　.

In early February 1951, 1st Sargent Stanley James Hawkins' platoon was attacking a hill just northeast of Seoul. During the fire fight they got pinned down and the unit's leader got killed.

Grandaddy took command. He rallied the men and despite the odds, convinced them to carry the charge up the hill.

With a machine gun and grenades, Grandaddy destroyed three hostile positions and killed seven enemy soldiers before the unit got pinned down again.

Grandaddy did what he could to push the men forward, but this time it was no go. Eventually heavy grenade fire drove them back.

He was struggling to hold his position when an enemy grenade exploded right in front of him. Shrapnel ripped into his chest, but he brushed off the medic and led another charge up the hill. This time they reached the top.

When he saw the bunker that was firing the mortars, Grandaddy went straight at it. He ran ahead of the platoon shredding the bunker with machine gun fire. The defenders ran off and somehow Grandaddy took out another machine gun. That's when the next grenade hit.

1st Sargent Stanley James Hawkins might-a been a hero to the army,

but Grandaddy wasn't no hero to my Granmomma.

When she got the news he was dead all she said was, 'He'd be alive today if he just hadda kept his head down and followed orders.'

Hawk got quiet and looked at Dennis as if to say, 'You understand now?'

Dennis flopped back on the bed and rolled his eyes to the ceiling.

"That's a good story nigga but what that got to do with you?"

"Everything" Hawk protested.

Momma had a hard life because of that. She needed a father; Her momma needed a husband."

"Ain't that a bitch" Dennis said.

How many niggas you know ain't had a hard life?

Far as that go nigga, you ain't had no daddy and you turnt out aw-ite."

The mention of his father triggered uneasy feelings. Neither Dennis or Hawk knew their fathers. It was a subject they hadn't talked about since they were kids.

As boys they'd ignored their mother's bad daddy rants and made a game of telling stories about the day 'Daddy Come Home.'

The tales were more like exaggerated Christmas wishes than fables.

They'd spin yarns about whose daddy would have the finest car, most expensive house, best clothes and so on. 'My daddy gone have this' one would say. 'Well my daddy gone be that' the other would reply, each always trying to top the other.

But by the time they got to middle school the stories had stopped and this was the first time the subject had come up in years.

If Dennis was willing to go there Hawk knew two things.

One, Dennis' mind was razor sharp, and two, he was serious as fuck.

"What's your point" Hawk asked?

Dennis sat up.

"Last night I had another dream."

"Okay Doctor King, what did you see?"

"You might got jokes, but this ain't funny."

"Okay, I'm listening. What did you see?"

"I saw you."

Now it was Hawk's turn to straightened up.

"In the dream there was a whole bunch-a people standing down in a big ol' valley. It was dark all around and you was standing on the top of this mountain. You was holdin' up some kind-a torch that made a light so bright it lit up everything around you.

But down below where the people was, it was dark as hell. They was all lookin' up to the light and reachin' out they hands."

"To who?"

"You nigga, ain't you listenin'?"

The hair stood up on Hawk's arms.

"Hey Dennis man, you gonna have to forgive me but."

"But nuthin', Thats when the trains come and went. All day. All night. You can't run from this."

"What run?"

"Nigga you Black Moses."

A nervous chuckle preceded Hawk's denial.

"I ain't no got-damn Black Moses got-dammit."

The response had no effect on Dennis who remained sanguine.

"You ain't got me to convince. I'm just tellin' you what the dream say."

"I don't care what the dream said. I ain't nobody's Black Moses."

"Who are you then? Dennis demanded.

Cause the way I see it, you either Moses or Judas."

A suddenly animated Dennis pointed a gnarled finger in Hawk's face.

Listen to me. You listenin'?"

"No."

"You betta, cause Keepers out here straight cuttin' muhfukkas tongue out. Squeeze a muhfukka throat, stick a blade in they mouth, twist and pull out a tongue. I seen that shit with my own eyes. What a nigga spose to do with shit like that?"

Hawk instantly heard himself repeating words he'd heard his mother say a million times. Even as he spoke he considered the irony of a man in his position, relating the wisdom of his mother. But she'd had a fine tuned instinct for survival. Her wisdom was the reason he was where he was today. And the words he repeated now had always proved true.

"We're gonna get through this" he said.

I don't know how right now, but we will."

Dennis managed a smile.

"I might-a questioned your judgement sometimes" he said. But never your word."

Hawk stood up.

"You're wrong about the Jew comparison" he said.

We're not the Jews. We've never been the Jews.

We are Pharaoh. We have always been Pharaoh."

————

Nick Carlsen was pissed. He'd come to the bungalow red faced and huffing over the absence of workers.

"How they gonna work if they don't eat?"

He acted like he didn't know that was the whole point. They weren't going to work, eat or anything else until they got what they wanted.

"What the fuck do they want?" Carlsen asked, to which Hawk still had no answer.

He suspected a major power play was underway but he hadn't figured out what the upshot was. Understanding what who wanted, and why, was the challenge.

Because of the strikes and heightened security, there'd been a delay in Odell Giles' transfer from Pelican Bay.

Whatever was going on with the Black inmates was coming from the top, same as with the Hispanics. Hawk couldn't get to the bottom of things until he spoke with the top.

When Wesley Painter called from Homestead he'd said exactly what Hawk expected. The conditions there were the same as anywhere else. But Hawk didn't need intelligence reports anymore. Nothing was secret. He ordered Painter back.

There was no way around it. To protect his old neighborhood he'd have to put the guard on the street. Staring at the stars and stripes hanging flaccidly in a corner, he realized their relationship was changed forever. Where once it had stood for justice and pride, the flag now represented betrayal and mirage.

As he thought about the many times he'd saluted it, having suborned his individualism to the principles it espoused, he felt shame and embarrassment. At the same time it also felt like he'd lost an old friend.

———

He was relieved when the news came.

T. Edmond Longstreet and members of the Moorish Scientific Temple, had convinced the West Adams crowds to disperse.

Word that Longstreet had been personally involved with convincing people to return to their homes gave Hawk pause. It had happened quickly and without violence. Utilities had even been restored. While Hawk was glad the guard wouldn't be called in, he wondered how Longstreet had pulled it off.

He immediately rerouted Painter to the California Military Academy at Camp San Luis Obispo, to await further instructions. It would just be a matter of time before the administration found some other pretext for sending the guard into South Central. Hawk needed to be ready. Wesley's job was to recon conditions at the Academy.

Prior to leaving for Homestead, Painter had wanted to know why Jesse had picked him as his right hand man.

"You're trusting me with some heavy responsibility sir" he'd said by way of asking why.

"You afraid you can't handle it" Hawk asked?

"No sir, I know I can but"

"Then why question my judgement?"

"It's just that you don't know me. You don't know anything about me."

"I know you enlisted in the Navy right out of Pacifica high where you graduated with a B average.

You served four years as a seaman and got an honorable discharge.

You started working at Lompoc a year before we met.

You married, Juanita Fields, your high school sweetheart. You have two brothers, one older one younger.

Your older brother Cecil, is a preacher, Baptist, Kansas City. Your baby brother Bruce, is doing six years, Pollock, Louisiana. Drugs.

Your mother Mamie, diabetic, lives with you and your wife.

No kids.

But to answer your question, I picked you precisely because we have no history. I never get close to my wingmen.

I trust them but I don't form personal relationships with them. Things happen. I'm not trying to be your friend."

Painter was impressed by the background check but disappointed by the revelation he wasn't considered a friend. He didn't show it.

"Yes sir" he said feigning agreement before quickly adding,

"I'm not going to die sir?"

The San Luis Obispo facility was headquarters for western based National Guard training programs. Hawk planned to order all Guard brass there for a newly created protocol orientation. But first he had another move to make.

19
UPPER ROOM

Things had moved faster than Hollow man had originally indicated. The Capitol had indeed already been moved.

The construction had been secretly completed and the administration had already installed operations there.

The new Whitehouse was located on a small peninsula situated at the confluence of the Corpus Christi and Oso Bays.

Ward Island, once occupied by Texas A&M University-Corpus Christi, was now the center of Federal power.

What once had been the Miramar Apartments, a complex that housed university students, was now an enclave of modern office buildings, known collectively as

"The New Jerusalem."

The relocation of the capitol was intended not only as a major physical change, but also to symbolize significant legislative and policy transformation as well.

Taking advantage of super majorities in both houses, Everhart called an emergency session of congress. With the sweep of the pen he signed into law the most extraordinary tax bill in the history of government. He called it the Jubilee Income Tax bill.

The law was based on the principles set forth in the Old Testament book of Leviticus.

According to tradition, the year of Jubilee was a time of new beginnings, and in keeping with that spirit, all debts were forgiven. And so it happened that every taxpaying citizen instantly became a debt free American.

Yet while the bill abolished the income tax, it replaced the government funding tool with a compulsory national tithing system.

In the new system, instead of paying taxes into the U.S. Treasury via the internal revenue service, Christlanders (as citizen were now called) as well as businesses, were compelled to annually contribute ten percent of the value of all their earthly goods, to the Treasury of the United Congregations of Christland.

A charter was created to establish The Bank of Christland, as the successor to the Federal Reserve, which was also abolished. Through Guillory's Jesuit relationships, the Vatican Bank was persuaded to increase the contribution of its vast gold reserves from 20 billion, under the Fed controlled economy, to 3 trillion, under Everhart's Bank of Christland.

Guillory also called on the Rothschilds to influence European central banks to underwrite further reserve support to shore up confidence in the new economy.

Contrarily, Angus Kellogg wasn't worried about the strength of the economy so long as the strength of the military remained intact.

Guillory was more circumspect.

To further hedge his bets, Guillory had made large buys of cryptocurrencies. Since transactions in digital money had no need of banks, and were therefore difficult to trace, he'd conveniently forgotten to mention these transactions to Everhart.

Under new regulations it was now illegal to knowingly sell Treasury bonds, now called 'Trinity' bonds, to Muslims.

Trade with Muslim countries was likewise discontinued. Such was the state of the Union when Everhart met with his inner circle in the new West wing, dubbed 'The Upper Room'.

Although most of the bureaucratic buildings in The New Jerusalem were reasonably accessible, the 'Upper Room' was far less so.

The sanctum was housed in a fifty foot high, steel and glass pyramid that sat atop a forty story executive building at the center of the complex.

It was protected by camouflaged anti-personal weaponry and surface to air missiles while its exterior was layered over with a hyper reflective cloaking material that made it virtually invisible.

The massive suite provided a 360 degree view of the island, encompassing both Corpus Christi and Oso bays.

To penetrate the Upper Room was essentially a black ops mission.

Entering through the main administration building, Hawk was led by Keepers, through a maze of doorways, past sensors that measured his breathing, body temperature and heartbeat while lasers scanned every pore of his body.

The passageway that led to a concealed elevator was made of continuous sheets of a mirrored material that had no apparent seams or openings. He couldn't tell where one something ended and another began.

As they exited the elevator he was surprised to see a contingent of heavily armed Keepers guarding the landing. The landing existed for the sole purpose of dissuading any intruder from gaining further access to the building.

After disembarking the main elevator they entered an access lift. There was no direct route to the Upper Room.

You had to go through hell to get there.

Hawk wasn't sure why he'd been summoned here.

In the wee hours Keepers had shown up at the trailer and told him to get dressed. He'd been air-lifted to a municipal airfield where he'd boarded a private plane to Corpus Christi.

The access lift came up through the floor of the Upper Room and Hawk stepped off into splendor and anxiety. Without a word the

Keepers saluted the men in the room and disappeared as the floor closed over the opening.

Hawk didn't know if he should be worried but he was.

Did Everhart know about his conversations with Booker? He was about to find out.

"Good to see you Hawk, been a while."

Everhart's greeting came with a smile.

If the smile was intended to put Hawk at ease it wasn't working.

"Pleasure's mine sir."

The view was impressive. From this height the expansive land and seascapes gave him a feeling almost like flying.

But it didn't put him at ease.

Everhart noticed the discomfort.

"No worries Lt. Colonel" he said.

We just want to hear your thoughts on the efficacy of your programs. How do you see things going?"

Hawk knew it was more than that. That conversation could have been had over the phone. He tried to sound confident without over-selling it.

"Program's coming along great sir."

He looked to Kellogg for validation. It wasn't forthcoming. He kept talking.

Construction's having some challenges as regards bedrock depth in the far north acreage, but we're still on schedule and under budget."

Everhart offered Hawk a drink which he readily accepted.

"Not what I'm asking" he said.

How's our prison industries enterprise program doing?"

Hawk took a sip of the cognac and steadied his tone.

"You're aware of the strikes."

"Why are they striking?"

Hawk still didn't know but he wasn't going to say so.

"They're afraid" he ad-libbed.

"Of what?"

"Of you. I mean the ghettos sir."

Everhart wanted to know what they expected to gain?

When he heard himself say

"I don't know sir"

the phrase 'bad answer' instantly rang in his head.

Angus Kellogg picked up on it like a psychic.

"Wrong" he rumbled.

If you don't know, you damn well better find out.

Who's in charge of that program?"

"I am."

"Not for long if you keep not knowing shit."

Angus stood up and walked over to Hawk.

His face clouded over like Tuesday in Seattle.

Make no mistake. This is what's going to happen" he said.

You're going to go back to that camp, and you're going to root out every shit stinkin' shred of insubordination everywhere you find it. You're going to wring it out, beat it out, stomp it out. And when that's done, you're going to see to it that the same thing happens at every other federal institution in the system."

Angus stepped close enough for Hawk to feel his breath.

You're going to crush some skulls.

I want a body count on this.

No way the monkeys run the zoo.

Next report I get about inmates not working, I'm coming there myself. And you don't want that."

At that moment Edric Everhart and Guillory also stood up.

All three men towered over Hawk who remained seated.

Everhart posed the pertinent question.

"You have any problems with this?"

Hawk did have a problem. If he was ever going to quit, now would be the time. He wanted to get up and walk out but his gut said not to.

"No sir" Hawk lied.

He wondered if his smile appeared too forced.

Everhart's eyes conveyed consequence.

"I want to know everybody involved in this strike. Everybody. I want names and I want them two weeks ago."

"Yes sir. I'll get to the bottom of it. Segregation units are already past capacity sir."

A trace of apprehension colored Kellogg's tone as he turned to Everhart.

"I've ordered transports to the agriculture districts but"

Kellogg suddenly went uncharacteristically silent. Everhart raised an eyebrow.

"But?"

It was the first time Hawk had seen a chink in Kellogg's confidence. Kellogg tossed back the remainder of his drink.

"There's talk that if the prisoners are forced into labor, they'll revolt."

Everhart smirked at the warning.

"I should think that'd be right up your alley Angus."

"That's the thing" Kellogg explained,

Other than the Keepers, no telling who can be trusted. At this point there's a high probability of noncompliance. There're sympathizers throughout the ranks."

All eyes instantly trained on Hawk who blurted,

"Then we send in the Keepers."

He'd said it on instinct.

He didn't know what else to say. Anything less would've been construed as disloyalty. Guillory's reaction surprised him.

"We can never jeopardize California" he declared.

It's literally a gold mine. The annual tithes alone are worth billions and the natural resources are" he paused.

I don't know, what's the phrase for, you can't spend it all? It's called the golden state for a reason."

Hawk was starting to feel better when Kellogg added,

"I don't like you Hawkins.

Far as I'm concerned you're not team material."

Keeping his seat so as not to exacerbate the situation Hawk asked,

"What's that mean?"

"That means your ass is hanging in the wind" Kellogg growled.

And if you know what's good for you, you'll find a way to pull your pants up.

We don't carry dead weight around here son.

Not the convicts and not yours. This is not a drill."

Kellogg's intended intimidation merely reminded Hawk of every coach or drill sergeant he'd ever known.

He reacted as he always had. Inwardly he brushed the words off, while outwardly appearing to accept whatever was being said.

"If you can't get the job done" Kellogg declared,

Then it falls to me. And when it gets to me, I got the shit that'll get butter from a duck. And you're looking more like a duck than a Hawk to me."

Guillory, as was his custom, interceded on behalf of civility. Laying a hand on Kellogg's shoulder he soothed,

"Now now Angus, I'm sure Lt Colonel Hawkins understands the situation."

Father William Guillory's soft tones were again in contrast to his words.

He knows if he fails his given task, it's not you he has to worry about. It's the Keepers who should have his attention."

Hawk couldn't believe it. These motherfuckers were actually threatening him. This thing had turned into blood in blood out. He couldn't quit if he wanted to. If he didn't do what they wanted, they'd kill him.

It was a fact he'd never considered.

Everhart slowly swirled his cognac before draining the glass.

"I'm the only one any need fear" he said.

He wasn't the same man who'd been recruited by the C street group. Power had affected him in uncharitable ways. His instructions left no doubt about his mounting psychosis.

"You go back there" he demanded,
And you tell those mongrel bastards it's time they all understood
who their real fucking Jesus is.
It's me Goddamn it.
I'm their Jesus.
I'm the only one who can save them."

20

TRAINS

A detail of Keepers escorted Hawk back to the airport.

This time there was no private jet.

The ticket agent eyed him suspiciously.

He knew it was because he didn't have any luggage.

He didn't feel like talking and hoped he wouldn't need to explain anything to anybody. Stuffing the boarding pass in his pocket he flopped down in a window seat and reclined.

His eyes closed but he didn't relax.

It was clear there wouldn't be any more executive level discussions. He needed time to sort things out but he didn't have much. To keep bad things from getting worse, he needed to gain the gangster's confidence without losing faith with the government. He wondered if he was doing the right thing.

From Corpus Christi to Los Angeles is a fairly short flight and it wasn't long before the pilot was alerting passengers to prepare for landing. Gazing out the window watching the wing flaps lower, Hawk reflected on being threatened.

Who the did they think he was?

Did they actually believe he would deliver the body count

Kellogg demanded? He'd killed on orders before but this was differ-ent. Wasn't it?

The sharp squelch of rubber hitting the tarmac at 200 miles per hour jolted him back to the moment. As the jet liner rumbled down the runway he automatically progressed through the landing proce-dure in his mind.

That's when it hit him.

He couldn't hide behind the Nuremberg defense anymore.

I was following orders was merely a confession of cowardice.

Amid the high pitched whine of reversing jet engines he made a decision. He wouldn't sharpen the knife any longer.

Coincidently, at that moment, unbeknownst to Hawk, a coalition of Hispanic gangs were also changing course.

From as far south as Guatemala, to as far north as New York City, erstwhile separate gangs were coalescing and adhering to a central-ized code of conduct. Because the major drug cartels believed they could use any new found leverage to their advantage, they not only didn't interfere but provided arms to the endeavor.

Most notably, Big Homies demanded any weak links be summarily dealt with.

The edict was,

'If there is a known problem, be your own green light.'

But Hawk didn't know about that yet. At the moment he was wrestling with other issues.

It was the middle of the night when he leapt out of bed.

Jamming his hand in his boxers, he cupped his genitals.

For a second he stood in the dark, sucking air and clutching his package. After a few moments the tension drained from his body and he slouched down on the side of the bed.

He'd never shown a false face to his superiors before.

His subconscious fears of the possible consequences had given him nightmares. In the dream Keepers had broken down the door, tied him up and castrated him. It felt real.

Even now he wondered if instead of a dream, he'd had a vision.

What if it was like Dennis' dreams?

He'd barely closed his eyes again when a loud clamoring jarred him back awake. Alarms shrieked over a chorus of screams. Yanking back the tiny trailer curtain, he scanned the darkness for the source of the commotion.

Across the way, out on the yard, search lights slashed eerie criss-cross patterns through the blackness.

The tempestuous squalling of the Klaxons heightened the anxiety and confusion.

Jail break!

As his eyes adjusted to the darkness, the silhouette of a freight train loomed into focus.

Dennis' train.

Leaping into his pants and grabbing the Glock from the armoire, Hawk raced to the yard.

He got there just as a crush of detainees stormed the locomotive. Charging the diesel's cab, the mob smashed its way into the control console. The engineer didn't put up a fight but they beat him down anyway.

As hundreds of men stampeded the yard, Hawk saw all the pod doors were open. It couldn't be accidental.

None of the guards on the yard were armed.

Their nightsticks and mace were useless against the desperation plowing through them. Amid the cacophony of hysteria certain protests stood out.

"Them days is over." "We ain't slaves."

This was the rebellion that Kellogg had warned against. The men were being transported to work the fields but something had gone terribly wrong.

Gun fire erupted from the towers.

A deluge of ordnance rained down drenching the yard in shrapnel and blood. Everybody hit the dirt. As the men clutched the ground scratching for cover, the train suddenly lurched forward.

The steel wheels squeaked, the box cars creaked, and the train started rolling. Hundreds of men abruptly scrambled to their feet. It was either stay here and be slaughtered or escape on the train.

Laying on his stomach, Hawk watched detainees chase after the box cars. He instinctively drew a bead on a fleeing inmate before he realized he couldn't squeeze the trigger. He tossed the gun aside.

Worming his way on his belly, trying to shield himself from shrapnel ricocheting off the tracks, he searched for cover. The towers had the yard in a crossfire. There was no where to hide.

Pinned down by overwhelming firepower, facing imminent death, Hawk was struck by the irony.

He'd been in this situation plenty of times, but he'd always been the one in the tower. Now he just hoped he wouldn't be the recipient of the authority currently being dispensed over the yard.

When the shooting finally stopped, the pregnant silence brought hope of deliverance. Hawk was clinging to blades of grass when a series of thuds pounded in his ears. He quickly realized it was his heart. A moment later a voice came over the P.A.

"Attention Camp Brown Staff;

Stand up. Raise your hands over your head and walk to the center of the yard. All others stay down."

Hawk joined a group of twenty or so who slowly raised their hands and did as they were told.

A female officer was stepping over a body when a detainee stood up alongside her.

When the detainee raised his hands and tried to blend in, the officer screamed to the tower while pointing,

"He's not staff! Shoot! Shoot him!"

A search beam played over the couple before a short burst of machine gun fire killed them both.

Afraid he'd be next, Hawk called out,

"This is Director Hawkins. Don't shoot."

With his hands still raised, he stepped away from his group. Covering his eyes against the blinding searchlight streaming from the tower, he called again.

"I'm in command, Drop a weapon."

The tower ordered him to halt and prove his identity. Hawk wanted to know how he was supposed to do that.

Staff members on the yard backed him up but the tower still balked. A Black guard ended the standoff by throwing a weapon down.

Hawk picked it up and walked to the middle of the yard.

Holding the barrel skyward he squeezed off several short bursts.

"Listen up" He barked to the detainees still on the ground.

First move, last move.

Tower, get more guns down here."

Later, as detainees were being hustled off to whichever pod was closest, Hawk ordered a detail to drag the dead to the middle of the yard.

In short order the stack had grown into a heap.

'Must be at least a hundred men here' he thought.

He'd have to account for them. He was ready. Staring into the distance, he wondered about the men who'd made it on the train.

As the locomotive barreled along unencumbered by skilled operation, a nervous escapee stood over the battered engineer.

"Bet not die on me" he threatened.

"That'd be my choice" the engineer mumbled.

He was badly beaten and struggled to keep his outstretched foot on the dead man's switch.

"Where we headed?" the escapee demanded.

"We were supposed to be going to Mesa Verde to pick up more workers."

"Mesa Verde. What's that?"

"Ice industries processing center."

"Most us Black, fuck we got to do wit ICE?"

"I'm just driving the bus mister."

"Well slow this muhfukka down."

21

ROOSTER GILES

Odell Roosevelt "Rooster" Giles, a sleight man in his mid fifties, had come to Los Angeles from Chicago.

His interstate migration hadn't been planned so much as resigned to.

The catapult that had hurtled him west had been the result of a routine drug sting gone bad.

Rooster, and two other members of the notorious Chicago street gang El-Rukn, had thought they were setting up a double cross, when in fact, it was the other way around.

Tootie and Carzell, were low level street soldiers who'd brought Rooster in on what they'd believed was a sure thing. The oldest sting in the game. They'd pose as buyers, then rob the dealer once the dope appeared. Everything went according to plan until Tootie inexplicably asked for a sample.

When the target cut into the package, the markings on the wrappings caught Rooster's attention.

A recent drug seizure at Mid-Way airport had made a splash in the local news. The markings on the packages in front of him were the same ones he'd seen on T.V.

Odell Roosevelt Giles didn't like killing, but at his core, he was a practical man.

When you kill a cop in Chicago you basically kick open the gates of hell. Say what you will about honor among thieves, Rooster knew if Tootie or Carzell got caught, he got caught. He'd briefly considered killing them too but left on a red eye to L.A. instead.

Rooster had survived Chicago's treacherous Westside by natural pragmatism. Recognizing he didn't have the greatest retirement plan, he wasn't averse to being ruthless when he had to be but his main attribute was shrewdness. He had a keen sense of human nature and a unique ability to discern and accommodate the needs of others.

He garnered his street name, not because it was short for Roosevelt, or because he was cocky, but because of his distinctive walk. He walked with a kind of soft strut that conveyed assuredness sans self aggrandizement.

He carried himself simply, like the cock of the walk.

Rooster was twenty years old in the spring of '92 when he'd landed at LAX. He'd made his first money in L.A. by taking advantage of the Rodney King riots that were in full effect on the night he got to town. What some had seen as catastrophic social disintegration, was to him, the greatest stroke of luck ever.

Joining in the smash and grab parties that were taking place all over town, he'd taken only things he could easily carry. Cash, jewelry, stamps, whatever he could sell quickest. He'd run toward the storefront fires like a stripper to a free clinic.

Black Los Angeles is a sprawling area, and on the second night of the riots, he'd stolen a car and found himself on Western Avenue.

Western is one of those streets that runs from one end of town to the other. Scanning the landscape on 31st and Western, a small pawn shop caught his attention.

He saw the fire that was burning two storefronts down, but he figured he had plenty of time before it reached the pawnshop. If it got there at all.

Leaving the car in the street, he'd pushed his way through a cluster of people who were looting a small hardware store.

He came out holding several empty sandbags and a 18 pound sledge hammer. He'd hurried around to the back of the pawnshop, but he'd found the rear entrance impregnable.

The sledge hammer merely bounced off the reenforced steel back door.

A tiny taco hut was all that separated the fire from the pawn shop now. Its back door proved to be a different story. One good swing with the 18 pounder and he was in.

Another few swings and he was through the common wall and into the pawnshop. Under the circumstances the alarm that went off was less than meaningless.

Smashing the glass display cases as fast as he could, he'd filled the empty sand bags with watches, rings, gold coins and whatever else he could fit. He was in the shop for only a few minutes but when he'd turned to leave, the fire was already licking through the hole he'd made in the wall. He couldn't go that way. The back door was still the back door and the front door was two inches of slotted steel bordered by windows too small to fit through.

He looked to the ceiling. Nothing. There was no way out.

If the fire got through the common wall he was afraid the roof would collapse.

Suddenly red lights swirled up out front. Fire trucks bumped up on the curb and barrages of water cascaded into the taco hut. With the flames still raging he dived through the hole in the wall. It felt like he'd jumped into a furnace.

Fire ants crawled through his lungs as he rolled to his feet. Everything smelled like burning tacos. He couldn't see through the smoke and if the shop flashed over he knew he'd die. He was reconsidering his life choices when a direct hit from a firehose sprawled him to the floor.

Choking and bleary eyed, he was sopping wet when he'd crawled out the back door. Stopping in the alley to catch his breath, he heard a gunshot.

He should have been scared but he wasn't. On the contrary, he was exhilarated. He'd just come through hell and survived. At that moment, soaking wet and clutching sacks of booty in both hands, he was an invincible Black pirate.

His water logged shoes sloshed with every soggy step back to the car. He'd driven at least 5 miles before he realized he'd been grinning the whole way.

Eventually the Governor sent in the Army National Guard. President Bush the 1st, deployed the 7th Infantry Division and the 1st Marine Division. But before order was restored, 63 people died (officially), 2,383 people were injured, and more than 12,000 were arrested.

Odell Roosevelt Giles wasn't included in any of those numbers. By the time the military showed up he'd made enough money to nail down a 1 bedroom apartment in Inglewood.

His instincts eventually led him to the local Bloods gang. He'd been hawking jewelry on the street when a black S class Mercedes slid up curbside. The oft spoken phrase 'Wanna buy a watch' seldom had more unexpected results.

Lemon Jimi, Big homie in the Inglewood Family Gangster Bloods, liked Rooster's merchandise. The problem was he didn't want to pay the ask. Instead, he made Rooster a counter offer. Two, 3 carat pave' pinky rings, and a Rolex Yacht-Master later, Rooster had his first kilo of L.A. cocaine.

But what got Lemon Jimi's attention was Rooster's quick return for the double up. The gang boss liked the fact that Rooster hadn't personally used a single gram.

It soon became apparent that the two gangsters were kindred spirits, and they became instant boys. Lemon Jimi showed his affinity by giving special dispensation to jump Rooster in the Bloods without initiation.

Rooster got another break when he learned that Tootie and

Carzell had been assassinated by Chicago police in an unrelated case. With them out of the way, the door to Chicago was wide open.

Combining his understanding of human nature with carefully selected key alliances, Rooster rose quickly through Blood ranks. Inside of two years he'd become the gang's top earner. Not only was the Chicago connection a distribution goldmine, but he'd made a veritable fortune on the L.A. crack market.

But before all that happened, he'd first made his reputation the old fashioned way.

He'd been living the mid-level street hustler's pseudo glam life, when an age old problem reared its head.

He discovered one of his crews was shorting the money. After he'd made sure they were definitely stealing, he'd gone to Lemon Jimi to get the go ahead to do what he needed to do.

On a grey evening in late June Rooster coasted a battered VW bug to a silent stop along the curb on Van Ness street. He walked the last two blocks to the tidy craftsman in the quiet neighborhood. He didn't want to be seen carrying a gallon of high octane gasoline and an A-K 47 down the street so he kept to the alley.

When he'd gotten to the house in question, he'd looked around the backyard for kid's toys. Not seeing any, he'd laid the A-K on the ground and deftly unscrewed the top of the gas can. He stuffed in a short rag and with a flick of a Bic, the rag was lit.

As soon as he'd gotten both hands on the handle, he'd half discus slung the container through a second story back bedroom window. A giant fireball exploded as he'd picked up the A-K, walked calmly around the side of the house and planted himself in the front yard.

The explosion immediately brought out the neighbors.

Rooster listened as shouts from inside the house were followed by the front door bursting open. He waited until everybody made it out before he squeezed the trigger.

The chipper clatter of the short bursts didn't so much as set off a car alarm but they did achieve their objective.

As the neighborhood watched, Rooster walked up on the porch, stood over the fallen bodies and emptied the clip into the corpses.

He'd pitched the Russian import into the house as he'd run off. Leaving the hoopty on the street, he'd caught the bus back. He'd learned some things about L.A. since the riots. He wasn't going to risk a random traffic stop.

Odell Rooster Giles was after all, a practical man.

The house eventually burned to the ground, collapsing over the gangster's bodies and burning them beyond recognition.

Because the incinerated corpses were riddled with bullet holes, the press quickly dubbed the crime, the "Swiss Cheese Barbecue Massacre".

It didn't take long for word to spread that Rooster was behind the killings. From that day on he always got the proper count.

In time, he'd bought a four bedroom home in Fox Hills, a middle class neighborhood close to his Inglewood stomping grounds. He wasn't retired but he left the bulk of the day to day to his lieutenants. Law enforcement was never able to catch him dead to rights and absolutely nobody would flip on him.

But there's no such thing as sanctuary in the dope game.

He'd made a lot of money and a lot of enemies.

Envy made him the target of skullduggery.

After surviving several assassination attempts, he'd moved to Palmdale, a sleepy, working class, white suburban development about 25 miles northwest of L.A.

For a time things settled down.

Then Lemon Jimi turned up dead.

Building maintenance workers found his body cut up in a duffel bag. Somebody had stuffed him under a stairway in a strip club he owned out by the airport. Police first thought he'd been the victim of a rival gang attack but it turned out Lemon Jimi was on the down low. A gay lover had murdered him in a jealous rage.

After Jimi's death, Rooster was sucked into the inevitable power vacuum that followed. You do what you have to when you're a practical man. Through negotiations, and less diplomatic means, Rooster successfully defended his first round position for leadership of the gang.

But just when it looked like he'd seize control of the Family, he'd been detained as a material witness in a grand jury investigation. The state was squeezing him and he'd found himself locked up in a no bail situation.

Business wise, little changed for Rooster.

He continued running his operations out of Pelican Bay. Being inside was an inconvenience to his liberty but not to his money making. The Swiss cheese Barbecue massacre, coupled with his attempted assassination survivals, had made him an urban legend. He pretty much owned any joint he was in. He'd become the head of the BGF after a consensus by shot callers.

Now he was staring at Hawk.

"You sayin' you can make this grand jury shit go away?"

"That's what I'm saying" Hawk answered.

"And all I gotta do is make these niggas eat?"

"Well that's not the goal anymore."

"What's the goal now?"

"What kind of man are you?"

"What kind of question is that?"

"The kind that needs an answer."

"Why you ask me that?"

"Cause I need to know if I can count on you?"

"For what?"

"What's the strike about?"

"Survival.

We saw the Mexicans changing shit up, so we changed shit up too. We got no idea what they up to. Mexicans some extreme muhfukkas. But it's deeper than that. They ain't stupid. If they makin' moves like the way they doin', it's a reason."

"You know the reason?"

"What I just say? All I know is, we see what's happening and we ain't havin' it. Ya'll ain't gettin' shit else outta us. We just gonna do our time and that's it."

"How does not eating help you?"

"Ain't got nothin' to do with ya'll. It's for us. A discipline thing. We ain't taking it to the death just yet. We just getting niggas minds right for when the time come."

"Yeah" Jesse said.

I wanna talk to you about that."

22

I GOT SHOVELS

Sectioned off by race, the detainees stood silently under the noon day sun and the heavily armed watch of the California National guard.

Flanked by Angus Kellogg and Governor Booker, Hawk presided over the gathering from an ad hoc stage.

At the base of the stage were the bodies of the last night's carnage. It was 'Hood' Hawk who took the mic.

"I got shit to do so I'll keep this short" he announced.

Now I don't know what you *thought* was gonna happen when you pulled this shit last night, but you bout to find out. First. Understand something."

He paused to roll up his sleeves.

"You muhfukkas gettin on them trains if I got to drag your stinkin' asses on board myself.

Understand something else. Contrary to what you might-a heard; This *my* house. I run this shit.

You wanna run it, you gotta take it from *me*."

Snatching the mic off the stand he walked to the edge of the stage.

Now I don't know about you, but I been all over the world. From South Central L.A. to the South China sea.

And ain't no place I went, did a muhfukka *ever* take one got-damn thing from me. Hear me?

I go wherever I wanna go, and when I get there, I do whatever I wanna do.

You know why?"

He paused, pointing at Kellogg and Booker.

Cause everywhere I go, I bring the awesome power and the dreadful might of the U.C.C. government with me.

And if I'm in a fight, they in a fight."

Hawk went back to the podium and placed the mic back in its stand. Kellogg whispered something in his ear as he turned back to the assembly and announced,

Now I'm gonna ask one simple question.

And when I do, I don't wanna hear no whole bunch-a I'm Spartacus shit.

I start hearin' that shit and I'ma just start shootin' muhfukkas."

He pointed to the bodies at the base of the stage.

Whoever had the balls to call this shit to order, need to find them again now. If you a leader, let me see you lead. I wanna know who green lit this shit and I ain't got all day."

Stepping back from the mic he folded his arms and waited. A few silent moments later he stepped back to the mic. Pointing to a random Black detainee he motioned the man up on the stage.

"Tell me your name son" he commanded.

"Crossley 32477" the detainee quietly answered.

"WHAT!"

"Sir, Crossley 32477 sir!"

"That's better. Okay Crossley, did you start this shit?"

"No"

"Are you stupid Inmate? Respect me."

"Sir, No sir! Yes sir"

Getting directly in Crossley's face Hawk demanded,

"Who started this shit Crossley 32477?"

Crossley shrank back.

"I don't know."

"Oh. So you just gone keep on disrespecting me."

"No sir, sir. No sir"

Hawk suddenly produced the Glock from the small of his back. Kellogg and Booker watched passively as he jammed the pistol in Crossley's face and ordered,

"On your knees."

With his hands in the air Crossley immediately dropped.

"Sir, Yes sir, yes sir"

Hawk stood over Crossley and placed the gun to the crown of his head.

"Too late now muthafukka.

I don't give a fuck if you started this shit or not, you gone respect me."

Hawk looked out over the yard.

All you muhfukkas gone respect me. Now we gone start with this bitch here and we gone keep fuckin' up the count until I find out what I want to know."

He turned back to Crossley and racked the slide on the Glock 23.

When the mechanical 'Kla chank' resounded through the PA system a commotion erupted in the assembly.

Hispanic detainees broke rank to let Danny Ortiz make his way down front. Rooster Giles quickly joined him.

Hawk looked at the men making their way forward and nodded.

"Congratulations" he said.

Today you are men. Now go stand by those bodies."

Startled by the command both men hesitated.

"You're disobeying a lawful command." Hawk said.

I'll shoot you where you got-damn stand."

As they moved toward the pile Hawk turned back to Crossley.

"Carry your punk ass back where you came from" he said and bounded down the steps to confront Danny and Rooster.

"You think you runnin' shit around here?" he asked.

Neither man answered.

"I'm just sayin'" He pointed the Glock at the stack of bodies.

Cause *that's* what that idea looks like."

Without warning, a blow in the mouth rocked Rooster off his feet. Just as quickly the butt of the Glock smashed Danny in the forehead. In a blink both men sprawled backward onto the pile of corpses.

Recoiling as much from abhorrence as the fear of being next in the stack, they clambered back to their feet.

Hawk put the Glock back in his pants.

There'll be consequences for this shit, he said.

But first things first.

I got shovels for you."

He made sure Booker and Kellogg witnessed the start of the grave detail. He knew they wouldn't stay until the end.

As Kellogg made his way off stage Hawk casually murmured,

"Make sure the President knows these men are buried here."

23
REVOLUTION

Hawk stood in the center of the room staring balefully at the three men seated in hardwood chairs against the wall.

All the other furniture in the room had been shunted aside leaving a clearing where Hawk stood.

Rooster, Danny and Crossley waited sullenly for whatever came next.

"Alright" Hawk finally declared,

Let's get this over with. Rooster, you're up."

Rooster got up and walked to the middle of the room.

He stopped in front of Hawk and took a deep breath. Hawk gave a quick nod and Rooster threw a vicious right hook that caught him just above the temple.

Hawk rocked backward but quickly righted himself.

He rubbed the side of his head and knew it would swell later. Rooster turned around and walked back to his seat.

Danny dismissively waved his hand when Hawk called him up.

"Forget it" he said.

Hawk shook his head.

Danny knew he had to do it. It would be an insult not to.

The punch Danny delivered had been harder than he'd intended. He was tempted to apologize but didn't. Hawk took it better than expected. He was glad he hadn't been knocked out. Nobody listens to a man they just knocked out.

He turned to Crossley.

"Whacha' got son?"

Crossley was the biggest threat of the bunch. He stood a sturdy 6 foot 1 and weighed a hefty 220 pounds. If anybody was going to put him down it would be this guy. He had mixed feelings when Crossley didn't get up but instead slouched back in the chair.

"Fuck you nigga" he said.

"Excuse me?"

Now Crossley stood up. His chest swelled and his fists balled into ham hocks.

"Fuck you nigga, SIR!" he shouted.

A smile crept across Hawk's face.

"That's better" he grinned.

From his vantage point in another corner of the room, Governor Booker spoke up.

"Alright gentlemen. Now that we've gotten our pound of flesh, can we address the remainder of our business?"

In fact the first order of business had already been accomplished. The regular Guard was deployed in Greens Point.

As soon as the old Guard had deployed, a member of the California federal delegation to Corpus Christi had been selected to propose an Amendment to the U.C.C. Constitution allowing the State of California to withdraw from the Church.

The Amendment granting California its independence needed to be approved by 2/3 of the delegates to a Church convention.

The Amendment also needed to be approved by 2/3 of the House of Shepards and 2/3 of the Church High Counsel. If the Amendment passed it would be sent to all Church Deacon boards for consideration.

Next it would need to be accepted by at least 38 of the 50 Church bodies to be adopted.

To protect itself from time consuming legal challenges California included a caveat.

At its own discretion, at a time to be determined, California reserves the right to act 'as if' the amendment had been adopted and declare itself a sovereign nation. To Wit;

The Democratic Socialist Republic of California.

The rebel's staked their immediate safety on the premise that Upper Room concerns over international optics, would prevent them from mounting an unmediated military response.

Political and racial uncertainties throughout the armed forces, would also serve to slow any hasty counter measures.

So it was that the State of California, fearing for the security of its economy and the liberty of its denizens, prepared to leave the union.

These were the circumstances when Hawk and the Governor of California met with the gangsters of Camp Brown.

The entire plan was ludicrous as far as Rooster was concerned. He wanted to know why the Governor would throw in with them under any circumstances.

Booker explained that the present course of action wasn't anything he'd wanted or looked forward to.

"Don't misunderstand" he'd said.

This may very well be the last thing I ever do.

But corny as it may sound, I believe in the principles set forward in the U.S. constitution."

Rooster countered that the constitution was a non-factor when it came to people of color. A point to which Booker'd acquiesced, but maintained,

"We're in a different situation now.

Should we live through it, the new constitution will reflect the ideals of the founders of the new nation."

Danny wanted to know what prevented Hawk from seizing total power if they were actually successful.

Booker admitted he couldn't guarantee anything.

"I judge a man by my sense of his integrity" he said.

That's all I can go by.

Lieutenant Colonel Hawkins doesn't strike me as a man out for himself."

Booker was keen to the fact that times had changed.

The old ways were finished and despite any efforts to the contrary, there was nothing to be done for it.

He'd summed it up by saying,

"Because I can see no peaceful resolution to the troubles we find ourselves in, I and others of like mind, have elected to be proactive in the preservation of Western Democracy.

In the questionable event that we're successful in this endeavor, majority rule would be the outcome we'd expect.

That brings us to you.

Again, should we prevail, to the victor go the spoils.

Those of us in the present majority who hereinafter throw in with you, expect a seat at the new table.

Not at the head of the table, but we still bring a lot, so,"

Hawk wasn't interested in divvying up spoils.

"Ya'll countin' chickens?" he asked incredulously.

He argued their first move had to be keeping the Upper Room from nuking them.

"We've got to leave them a way out" he reasoned.

Something they can accept without losing face or forcing escalation. Otherwise they're turning the beaches to glass."

Booker pronounced the only way to stop them would be to take away their will, and or, ability to respond.

When Rooster asked how they planned to do that, Booker repeated the question back to him.

"We have to figure this out together" he said.

Thanks to the efforts of men like Lt. Col Hawkins and others, we enjoy considerable support within every branch of the armed services. All ranks, all races. At the moment we're so deep under the radar that even we aren't sure of our numbers."

"What about intelligence?" Danny asked.

What're we looking like?"

"That's tricky" Booker answered.

Hawk cut in.

"Coordinating between agencies at this point is non existent" he said.

We know we have support but the differing branches and agencies have no central system of cross communication. They don't know who each other are.

"So there's no one in charge?" Danny asked.

"It's safest to assume we need to establish a network of our own" Booker said.

To date we've not seen any signs of breach.

This isn't a condition we expect will last.

At present we have access to all the considerable conventional resources of the U.C.C. military.

Ironically, your participation in the effort to forestall this assault on democracy is paramount.

It's now or never.

Surreal as it may seem gentlemen, when you gaze around this room, you're looking at the last best hope for the survival of Western Democracy in your lifetime."

The gravity of the statement wasn't fully appreciated by anybody in room.

Everyone knew the odds were long.

The thing was, as far as Blacks and Browns were concerned, there wasn't another viable option.

The way things stacked up, they were damned if they did, damned if they didn't.

To this end Danny had the prescience to amass a matrix of extraordinarily talented geeks. Utilizing his Austin connections along with coders he'd recruited from his Stratfor days, he'd culled together a formidable network of nerds.

His people were savants at circumventing complex security systems and weaponizing code.

While that was all well and good, Rooster wanted the answer to a very simple question.

"What you gone do bout them all them White boys in the military?"

He found Hawk's response less than satisfactory.

"Call off the strike" he said. Get your people to cooperate. I'll take care of my end."

Booker grasped Hawk's hand and prepared to leave.

"Hold on to you hat Hawkins" he advised.

Seeking reassurance as much as offering it, Hawk replied,

"We're doing the right thing."

The remark elicited an upside down smile from Booker.

"Right or wrong" he said, and left it at that.

Then, with a wink that struck Hawk more as whistling past the graveyard than confidence, the Governor left.

———

After watching what he believed to be Hawk's successful handling of the camp uprising, Kellogg returned to Corpus Christi with assurances for Everhart.

At the very moment Kellogg was briefing Everhart, Hawk was sending volunteers into the Los Padre National Forest to find the escapees.

On the day of the break, the escapees had found themselves barreling pell mell toward oblivion. Nobody knew what was coming next, but everybody knew nothing good was waiting at the end of line.

After forcing the engineer to stop the train, the inmates unloaded the supplies that had been intended to sustain them in the fields.

When they were done, they'd wedged a toolbox atop the deadman's switch and sent the locomotive on its way.

There was debate as to whether or not to kill the engineer. The liberal side won out, and more than three hundred men vanished into the woods.

The train had derailed just Northwest of New Guyama, about 75 miles from the camp. Since no bodies had been recovered at the crash site, Hawk knew the escapees were out there somewhere. To prevent anyone else from looking for them, he'd issued a statement declaring that the train had been a run away and all inmates were accounted for.

24
BUFFALO SOLDIERS

The meet with Danny and Rooster had gone better than expected but there were still hurdles to clear.

Hawk wondered if top gang lieutenants would be able to bring the rank and file along with the program.

Bad blood between Black and Hispanic gangs was as old as the gangs themselves.

Socio-economics aside, the basic problem was a macho thing. The two groups just didn't like each other.

Maybe they'd been victims of a divide and conquer strategy, or maybe it was just about the women.

Hawk didn't know the answer, but he knew he had to pull it together.

The bangers weren't trained or disciplined, but their sheer numbers made them a potentially formidable guerrilla force. Provided they didn't kill each other first.

He thought about the thousands of additional bangers languishing in Central American prisons. El Salvador's prisons were at 325 percent capacity; Guatemala's were 251 percent; Mexico's were 126 percent.

He was concerned that the Hispanic numbers could shift the balance of power but he couldn't worry about that now.

The night of the breakout somebody'd opened the pod doors.

Hawk suspected some of the guards had been threatened or at least bribed. He'd look into staff later, but right now he needed to stay ahead of Corpus Christi.

The organized calisthenics had to go. Dominos and hoops had to come back. Things had to return to normal, but normal in prison was chaotic.

Dressed in camp issue, Wesley Painter loitered at the edge of the Black section of the yard watching the Hispanics shoot hoops.

After a few minutes an errant ball rolled his way.

The ball hadn't quite reached the invisible race dividing line before he scooped it up. Instead of throwing it back, he walked away toward the Black workout area.

At first the Hispanics only yelled at him. But then he shouted insults at them. As the exchange escalated Painter taunted, "You want it? Come get it" and tossed the ball away. That's all it took.

This time when the shot callers went to the hole the tremendous show of force Hawk brought to bare kept protests muted.

As soon as he could, Hawk made his way to the segregation unit. When the tiny cell door opened Danny didn't bother to look up.

"You stuff me in this lunch box and got the nerve to ask for a favor? he said.

We already had a deal."

"Yeah we still have a deal" Hawk affirmed.

But it ain't good enough. We have to do more than just start eating again. If this is going to work everybody can't keep doing their own thing. We have to work together."

"I told you to get your people organized and you ignored me" Danny said. Now you asking me to go begging".

"I was wrong" Hawk admitted.

I didn't see this coming and now I'm playing catch up.

But that doesn't change the fact that you're the only man who can fix this.

Your people know you have the honorary rose and Reyes' blessing."

Danny offered a disgruntled grimace in reply.

Hawk was undeterred.

"You cool with everybody" he said.

Nobody has a beef with you. Not Blacks, not Hispanics. Nobody. You're not really even a Carnal, You're like neutral.

If you suggest the co-op, neither side is actually bowing down to the other. You're like Switzerland, a neutral ambassador."

"Bullshit" Danny protested.

I'm Mexican. Period. You're asking Mexicans to humble ourselves to Blacks."

"Not bullshit" Hawk countered.

"I'm Black, and I'm coming to you ain't I?"

Danny wanted to know why the Blacks couldn't propose the peace?

"Blacks ain't got nobody like you" Hawk reasoned.

Nobody neutral. You're looking at the only Black man in the whole system who ain't representin'. Like I said; you kind-a free agent. Blacks ain't got nobody like that."

Danny mocked the argument.

"So I'm special?"

His smirk caused Hawk to drop all pretense at diplomacy.

"No other way around it" he insisted.

We either hang together or hang separately."

Danny's face contorted.

"I know you didn't?" He let the sentence trail off.

"Yeah" Hawk snapped.

Cause it's true. Weren't you the one tellin' me about missing nuts? Bottom line, the government will probably kill us both anyway, but why should we help them."

A moment passed before Danny exhaled hard.

"We agree" he said.

But I can't risk a split in my own ranks tryin' to force soldiers to do something they don't want to do."

Hawk's mouth fell open.

"You might know about code but you don't know shit about command. Those are your soldiers. They do what you tell them to. You can't be afraid to tell them."

"I don't know if I want to tell them."

"Yeah well, we ain't got the luxury of time so, I know you'll do the right thing. Without we stick together, we ain't got a chance. You make them see that."

Hawk promised to release Danny from Segregation and called for the guard. He needed to leave before Danny started arguing again.

When he got to Rooster's cell he told the skeptical gangster that he was speaking for Danny.

Rooster was intrigued by Hawk's shift in philosophies.

"Shit nigga" Rooster chided.

I heard you was the biggest uncle Tom ever got off the plantation. How you Nat Turner all-a sudden?"

Hawk took exception to both characterizations.

'Fuck you' he thought but said instead,

"Think what you want. I ain't no Tom, or Nat Turner either.

His eyes turned uncharacteristically dark.

And it ain't all-a sudden."

Rooster's sympathetic nod conveyed his casual acceptance and since all he had to do was agree to peace, he did.

The next morning, with the rest of the camp still locked down, representatives of both gangs met in an isolated conference room.

The identical mix of delegates was equally represented on both sides. Seasoned O.G.'s who'd served more time than some others had lived, sat next to new breeds who were less disciplined, less traditional, but no less ride or die.

Hawk noticed Danny getting a weak reception from the Hispanic delegation. He suspected it was due to Danny's lack of street cred. The bangers knew he spoke for Reyes, but what had Danny personally done?

He could tell by the Black's body language they were getting hincky over the Hispanic's reticence. If the Mexicans didn't trust Danny why should they? Recognizing how fast things could get out of hand, Hawk stood up. Lifting his arms to get their attention, he raised a boisterous,

"Lemme be clear" and brought the meeting to order.

"We not bangin' no more" he declared.

This, what we doin', ain't that.

He was becoming most comfortable with 'Hood' Hawkins.

I'm gonna say this once and I don't expect to speak on it again.

We not Bloods, Crips, Black Guerrilla Family, Mexican Mafia, MS-13, Serranos, Nortenos, none-a-that shit.

The second you sat down at this table you became enemy combatants. That's how the government will see you and that's how you better see yourselves.

Lemme explain something else. While ya'll runnin' round here thinkin' you all gangsta cause you kilt a couple muhfukkas; The real gangstas out there killin' muhfukkas by the boat load; makin' moves on cities, countries.

That little money you killin' each other over?

They the ones print that shit. It's they picture on that shit. They say what it's worth, and they can change it anytime they get ready. Lemme tell what that is.

That's gangsta.

And when *those* muhfukkas hear that *you* muhfukkas have banded together to withstand them; They gonna fall all over themselves laughin'."

He paused, methodically examining their faces before adding,

I see a lot a ya'll prolly agree with them.

Whatever. Don't matter. Cause when they come for one of us, they comin' for all of us. So, far as cooperation go, really ain't no choice.

He scanned the table again this time putting his hand on Danny's shoulder.

Some a ya'll think Danny here a coconut.

Brown on the outside, white on the inside.

Ya'll wanna say he ain't Mexican enough to speak for you.

Ain't that a bitch.

Do you know who you dealin' with?

You dealin' with racists. To a racist, ain't no difference between a pale-skinned, college educated Mexican, and a black-ass drop out Mexican.

They don't care whether you speak Spanish or if you can't talk at all. To them you all Mexican. Whether you come from Guatemala or El Salvador, you Mexican. And Mexicans ain't shit.

That same bullshit go down with Black folk too. Some-a us talk about bein' Oreos as opposed to 'real' niggas. It's bullshit. It's called divide and conquer.

Set the Blacks against the Mexicans, the Mexicans against the Blacks, the Blacks against the Blacks and so on.

But don't fool yourself; To have any chance what-so-ever of getting through this, we gone need White folk help."

A muffled, "Still Tomin'" came from somewhere in the room.

Refusing the challenge Hawk said,

"Don't get it twisted.

They ain't fightin' for us. They fightin' for theyself. They're puttin' everything on the line for what they believe in, cause that's what they do.

What about you?

And ask yourself this. How anybody else gonna trust us, if we can't trust each other?

Now if, Reyes thought Danny here was the right man for the job, who say they know better? Show of hands."

When no hands moved Hawk abruptly announced,

"We puttin' a stop to this bullshit right now."

Pointing to a young Hispanic he snapped.

Step over here mister."

The heavily tatted kid got up and stood next to Hawk.

He pointed to a Black gangster and waved him to his other side.

Turning to the Hispanic, Hawk asked his name.

"Nestor" the kid answered.

Tyrone answered before Hawk could ask.

"Okay Nestor, if Tyrone here say you ain't shit, does that make you ain't shit?"

Nestor squared his shoulders.

"Hell no."

"Exactly" Hawk agreed turning to Tyrone.

Tyrone, if Nestor here say he fucked yo momma, what you gone do?"

Tyrone ignored the faint chuckles that rippled around the table, crossed his arms over his chest and tilted his head back.

"I'm a fuck him up" he assured the room.

Hawk raised his hand to silence the laughter.

"Cause he said he fucked yo momma?"

"That's right."

"But he ain't fuck yo momma did he?"

"Hell no!"

"So, you know he ain't fuck yo momma but you still ready to die?"

Tyrone stood firm.

"He disrespected me."

A murmur of consensus prompted Hawk to interject.

"So when your momma get the call bout you dead, she alright with it cause, why again?"

Momentarily stymied Tyrone mumbled,

"He can't disrespect me like that".

The hollowness of the words forced Tyrone's eyes to the floor.

As the two men returned to their seats Hawk's dialect changed.

"Men. We have a situation set inside a circumstance.

I'm addressing you as men" he said looking to the Hispanics.

Not boarder bandits or river niggas."

He turned to the Blacks,

Or chain draggers or yard apes.

Men.

Because that's what you are.

Rule number one. Know who you are; Collectively and individually. Don't matter what nobody else says. The only one who gets to define who you are is you.

Understand something else. We're not heroes. We're not delusional. We're just not taking this shit any longer. But the thing we have to understand most of all is this. We're in this thing together."

He paused to let the men take stock of one another.

Your job is to earn the respect of the man sitting across from you.

In the meantime we will treat our brothers in arms as though our lives depended on them."

The air was suddenly heavy and Hawk moved to lighten the mood.

"Cheer up fellas" he quipped.

The way I see it, we have some hell-a-advantages.

First, we been overlooked and underestimated.

Plus we got the element of surprise on our side."

Suddenly his mood changed again and he somberly added,

"I'm not going to bullshit you" he said.

We can't win no all out shooting war.

But if it comes down to it, we can raise enough hell to force em' to the negotiating table. But no matter what happens, this second class human shit is over with.

By the time this is done a lot a us'll most likely be dead. Depending on how things shake out, whoever's left gonna either be a slave or a Buffalo soldier."

He thought their blank stares stemmed from their contemplation of death. Then Rooster asked what a Buffalo Soldier was.

"Oh shit" Hawk grinned.

Well fellas, lemme tell you a little story."

Addressing the chorus of dismay that swept around the room, he chided,

"It ain't like ya'll goin' anywhere."

A subtle pride slipped into his tone when he began reciting the tale like an old western campfire story.

In September 1867, Private John Randall, troop G, of the all Black 10th cavalry Regiment, out of Fort Leavenworth Kansas, was assigned to escort two big wig civilians on a hunting trip.'

Hawk peered stonily at the Black men around the table.

'Cause Private John Randall was a helluva marksman.

Good at his job.

Anyway, they out on the Kansas plains doing they thing when

all-a sudden, outta nowhere, a band of Cheyenne swoop down on 'em.

Had to been bout seventy of 'em.

Randall and them was caught totally off guard and before they even know what's happening; BAM! Both civilian's dead n' George Washington.

So now ole' Randell get ta rippin' and runnin', first this way then that, all the time firin' his rifle like a Gatlin gun, when Boo-ya, his horse get shot right out from under him.

Now he's in the dirt, scrapping an scrambling in the dust trying to get to some kind-a cover. Somehow he managed to wriggle up in a washout under some railroad tracks.

For more than an hour them Cheyenne charged him over and over. They threw everything they had at him.

Boy had blood and sweat dripping and flyin' everywhere but he tied off his wounds and kept on fighting.

By the time help finally arrived, ole Randall had killed 13 Cheyenne.

The Cheyenne had shot the boy once in the shoulder and wounded him 11 times by lance. When asked about the dark skinned warrior, the Cheyenne said,

'The more you hurt him the madder he got.'

When asked to describe him they said he was

'Black as coal with thick shaggy hair, and fought like a cornered buffalo.'

By the time Hawk finished the story you could have lit a fire by the light in Rooster's eyes.

"That John Randall a seriously practical man" he blurted.

Buffalo me up like a <u>muh-thee-FUK-ka</u>".

Something about Rooster's unbridled enthusiasm was contagious. The Hispanics caught it right away.

Maybe it was because they'd soon be blood brothers in a very real sense. Maybe it was the hope that sometimes, under the right circumstances, you could actually beat the odds.

He didn't know the reason, but in some transitional way a camaraderie that had seemed impossible a minute ago, was now permeating the room.

"Hey Warden" Nestor suddenly piped up.

"This Marty" he said pointing to another young banger who lounged back in his chair.

The kid smiled and waved.

Marty like cars" Nestor declared.

"Yeah?" Hawk replied.

Not wanting to alienate his new alliances but also not wanting to be overly familiar he spoke flatly.

"Sounds like a conversation for a different time."

"Okay" Nestor laughed.

But since we all buddy buddy now I just thought you might wanna meet the guy who stole your Cobra."

Marty sprang up from the chair.

Imitating a burnout he screeched,
"Eeeerrrrrup!"
Shifting air-gears he whooped it up,
Whoooo-ooodin."
The room erupted.
Hawk called for food.

———

Danny admitted he'd been responsible for the pod doors being open. Some of the guard's, whose families had indeed been threatened, had done it.

Danny's sphere of influence proved larger than Hawk had realized.

Even without the full support of the rank and file, he'd been able to coordinate an impressive operation.

But why had Reyes so readily given Danny carte blanche over this most potent force in the penal system?

"We discussed what was happening and what needed to happen in response" Danny explained.

We came up with some ideas. He's doing life, wants his name to live forever."

Hawk asked about the group's goals.

"Long range; To build a base across all the Americas, strong enough to protect poor people's interests over the entire continent.

But where we're at now is a reactionary response to what's going on here. We couldn't wait, we had to do something now".

"And that is?"

"You do what you know. Reyes knows how to street fight.

I know how to weaponize code. He had the muscle, I have the technical expertise. Like I said, we didn't choose the time, it chose us. Ours is a defensive posture."

"What's the plan?"

"To organize and unite working people".

"No. That's the goal. What's the plan?"

"Old school street guerrilla tactics. General strikes, paper terrorism."

"How do you deal with the military?"

"Hit and run. Small groups. Scattered cells. We aren't looking for overnight success. Like I said, we have to start where we are."

25
LET'S TALK WAR

Guillory and Kellogg had been waiting in the Billy Graham hospitality lounge, in the Legends of Heaven building, for over an hour. They'd been summoned by Everhart but he had more pressing business first. Lately there'd been an erosion of his deference to their judgement. He was starting to take control. So they waited.

They'd come to the realization that they'd created a Frankenstein and now they were worried about its behavior.

Out of public view, Everhart had taken to occasionally dressing in flowing white robes, sometimes sitting for hours silently staring out over the bays. On occasion he'd repeat unintelligible mantras in an endless loop.

There was no thought of the Vice President stepping in.

As a figure head he was completely unacceptable. He was a mousy reserved man who lacked the savior faire necessary to induce the desired public idolatry. So, despite the President's behavior, keeping the main thing the main thing, was the main thing.

As between the two of them, Guillory was decidedly less enthusiastic about the proposed way forward than was Kellogg.

Guillory would rather stick to the tried and true methods of wielding power; Indoctrination, tradition, hope and fear. These were the instruments that won hearts and minds. He didn't need to go to war to establish his objectives.

The only army he needed was the Keepers. Given enough time, he could establish Orders of the Guardian Keep garrisons anywhere in the world. Their command of local armies and militias would be sufficient to establish trade and maintain order. Given enough resources, he could persuade most situations without resorting to violence at all. He didn't see the wisdom in all out warfare.

On the other hand, Kellogg's arguments had been the most persuasive with the cartel. Islam needed to be dealt with.

But while Kellogg wanted more commitments from European allies, Everhart, who cryptically referenced the power of the Arc of the Covenant, wasn't averse to unilateral action.

World domination not withstanding, they were most anxious to suppress evidence of Everhart's increasingly emerging Messiah complex. Lately he'd taken to closing his remarks with the benediction, "I hear your prayers."

The senior advisors were loath to keep such phrases out of the public discourse. The problem was, neither man knew how best to broach the subject. They never knew anymore how Everhart would react. In as much-as his demeanor differed drastically from one persona to the next, it was a toss up as to who showed up at any given moment.

While his advisors waited, Everhart prepared for his next appointment. Presently he heard the familiar whirring of the elevator as the floor slid back and Doctor Zera Oma-Dera, stepped crisply off the lift.

Doctor Oma-Dera was Everhart's strikingly attractive, incredibly capable, Senior Advisor, and the only Black on his staff.

She was also the head of the Evangelical Church of the Congo.

The Congo Church had long been a proponent of U.S. Administrative policy in Africa and Everhart intended to keep it that way.

Doctor Oma-Dera's late husband had been the previous head of the church, and when he'd died she'd stepped in. Everhart had likewise inherited her.

They'd first met in Alexandria Virginia, at a place called 'The Cedars'.

The Cedars is a mansion owned by a powerful C street fellowship with the ironic nickname of, 'The Family'.

It's a place where heads of state and prominent politicians meet to discuss how they can best be of mutual benefit.

The Congo Christians numbered over 63 million and Everhart saw them as a strategic as well as enriching asset. Their entire value was reflected in Doctor Oma Dera's comportment. She was stately, sanguine and disarming.

Her fealty was crucial to Everhart's plans. When the war came, he intended to use her sub-Saharan Christians, to counter balance North Africa's Muslims.

The undertaking to establish the Congo church stretched back to 1909. It was just after the end of the reign of King Leopold II when Swiss missionaries first arrived.

The newly named Belgian Congo, had theretofore been known as, The Congo Free State.

In the late 1800's, at a symposium known as the 'Berlin Conference', European powers had 'given' the Congo Basin to a private concern run by Leopold II of Belgium.

The territory under Leopold's control exceeded a million square miles. Yet rather than control the Congo as a colony, Leopold solely owned his 'property' outright.

These were his very own personal niggers. He did whatever he wanted with them and answered to no one.

Between 1891 and 1906, he forced the entire population into slave labour. To impose his will, Leopold formed a private paramilitary group of Black turncoats called, "The Force Publique."

The Force recruited mercenaries from as far away as Liberia, and Zanzibar. Chief among the recruits were the dreaded Zappo-Zaps, the most feared tribe in the Congo. They merited the title because the Zappo-Zaps were cannibals.

Leopold understood that nothing so concentrated the mind, as the prospect of becoming lunch.

After Leopold died, Finnish and Swedish missionaries also swooped into the area. Together with the Swiss, they persuaded the natives to accept the doctrines that would eventually transform their primitive wasteland from a backward culture of the past into a backward culture of the future.

A culture whose natural resources would be fully utilized in the service of the Lord.

Doctor Oma-Dera had been indispensable in promoting the agenda of the United Congregations of Christland in the World Communion of Reformed Churches. However, none of the churches had a clue as to Everhart's real intentions.

In his deepening psychosis, Everhart saw the world as being under the authority of a single theocracy.

A theocracy that he would head as,

'First Lord Supreme of the Devine Realm of Christ'.

He saw himself as 'The ruler of Heaven on earth'.

In this world order, the sole purpose of Africans would be to serve Whites.

Under his administration the gigantic, mineral rich land mass of Africa would be transformed into the industrial, agricultural, breadbasket of the world.

He expected resistance. He looked forward to it. He'd make Leopold look like a pauper.

This philosophy didn't extend to Doctor Oma-Dera of course.

She was different. She was someone upon whose personal services he could depend.

As she approached, he rose from his chair and deftly unbuckled his belt.

"Good morning Doctor Oma-Dera" he said while unceremoniously unzipping his pants.

"Good morning Mr. President" she answered as his trousers slid to the floor.

Doctor Oma-Dera came behind the desk as Everhart lowered his boxers.

Dropping to her knees, she brushed the curls of her thick hair from her eyes and opened the desk's lower drawer.

Reaching inside, she slid aside a false bottom and retrieved a small blue velvet box.

She opened it, pulled out a custom made glass hypodermic needle and stood up. Edric turned his back and leaned over the desk.

Doctor Oma-Dera filled the syringe with a clear liquid drawn from a small vial she pulled from her bag. Cupping a pink butt cheek in her smooth mahogany hand, she pushed the needle into the tissue slowly injecting the substance.

After a moment Everhart's head dipped slowly downward. His eyes fluttered and closed as a warm euphoria crept leisurely through his body. Eventually Doctor Oma-Dera's voice floated in his ears.

"How's the Wellness bill coming?" she asked.

Everhart sighed lightly before answering.

"Almost done crafting the language" he half whispered.

He pulled his pants up and flopped back in his chair.

"Should be introduced next week."

Despite its name, the Wellness bill was actually deregulation legislation intended to relax restrictions on designer drugs.

Doctor Oma-Dera put the blue velvet box back in its place.

"Will that be all sir?"

Everhart smiled his approval as she shook her hair once more and adjusted her clothing.

"Yes, thank you" he smiled.

I don't know what I'd do without you."

"Nonsense" she replied sweetly,

It's just a little pick me up. You're a busy man."

And then, like switching on a light, Everhart popped to.

His composure firmly in tact he asked a nonplussed Doctor Oma-Dera to please,

"Call Guillory and tell him to come up."

On the way to the Upper Room a disgruntled Kellogg visibly winced at the idea of Doctor Oma-Dera. Nothing was more antithetical to his universe than a Black woman with political influence. The more Guillory apologized for her, the more upset Kellogg got.

"Be realistic" Guillory coaxed.

Who can communicate with Africans better than she can? She speaks English, French, Lingala, Swahili. She's respected. She's a doctor after all."

None of which mattered to Kellogg who groused,

"The day I need a Nigger bitch to help me keep other niggers in line is the day I hang myself."

Everhart was adjusting his tie when the cabinet members stepped off the lift.

"How're the oil reserves looking?" he asked by way of greeting.

Guillory instinctively deferred to Kellogg.

"We need to secure the California coast and develop the arctic possibilities before we can go full steam."

"What's the time frame?"

"That's kind-a up to you sir."

"If I green light you right now?"

"From an oil point of view sir?"

"Is there another?"

"No disrespect sir. Lot of moving parts. Lots of logistics to consider. The oil is the main thing but"

"Bullshit" Everhart declared.

"Oil's the whole thing. There're no moving parts without it."

Guillory felt Everhart was moving too fast. He'd begun insisting on his own agenda over the plans of his erstwhile puppet masters.

In an attempt to slow Everhart down, Guillory had convinced the

President that as legal counsel, Boatwright should attend the meeting.

Guillory knew Everhart wasn't a fan and only abided Boatwright because of Guillory's insistence. Everhart however would only allow Boatwright to participate in the meeting via video monitor.

Boatwright's legal mind served Everhart well when used in the service of his legislative machinations, but his opposition arguments had cost him the President's favor.

Yet the true nature of Everhart's displeasure with Boatwright stemmed from Boatwright's refusal to placate his God complex.

"The first thing the Russians will do is start exploration of the Lomonosov ridge" Everhart contended.

The rights to the continental crust in the Arctic ocean were in dispute and Boatwright interjected.

"That's going to create a problem with the Canadians" he said.

Everhart insisted the Canadians wouldn't interfere.

"How can you be sure?" Boatwright persisted.

Kellogg wasn't about to let some button down ambulance chaser interfere with his plans and interceded.

"Let 'em try" he said of the Canadians.

What're they gonna do? They got no real army and I'm certainly not going to help them fight the Russians.

Meanwhile we got Conoco, BP and the rest, pledging their Alaska wells. What's all the fuss? We sew up reserves and get down to business."

Because he'd been kept out of the loop, Boatwright wasn't sure what he was listening to.

From a primal standpoint he understood Kellogg's bloodlust.

Apart from his genuine empathy for Everhart's Muslim position, Kellogg was, at his core, a quintessential guts and glory warrior.

Any excuse for war was good enough for him. But that didn't explain everything. He was a wild hair but he wasn't a fool.

Neither was Guillory. But not being privy to the arcane societies' motives, Boatwright didn't understand why these guys were going along with Everhart's nonsense.

The administration's immediate game plan was simple. First, through apparent war games, they'd position the navy to blockade the Gulf. Operatives would then launch a missile offensive against Tel Aviv from inside the Golan Heights.

The mission objective would be to cause maximum human casualties in order to create the greatest outrage.

Initially no group would take credit for the attack, but soon, allied Intel would 'discover' an Islamic Jihad cell to be responsible.

Boatwright knew the Israelis would strike the Heights long before any intel reports came back. He questioned how they'd be dissuaded from retaliating against innocent people.

"You're kidding" Kellogg said.

Nothing's going to stop them."

"And that's okay?"

"Omelets, eggs" Kellogg dead panned.

But don't worry, We'll turn their attention to Tehran soon enough."

"Frame Tehran."

"Jesus man, are you listening?"

Kellogg explained that once Israel got hold of the fake intelligence reports, they'd go after Tehran, and the UCC would back them.

When told of a preemptive black ops blitz on Hezbollah, Hamas and PIJ cells, in advance of the Tehran strike, Boatwright wondered if he wasn't the victim of an executive level prank.

"You're not thinking of striking inside Lebanon?" he'd asked incredulously.

"Wherever they're at sonny" Kellogg answered.

Wherever they're at".

"And when it's learned that Tehran didn't actually attack Tel Aviv?" Boatwright asked.

Kellogg rolled his eyes.

"Whose side are you on?" he asked.

Boatwright persisted.

"We can't kill all the Muslims in existence you know.

No matter what we do there will always be Muslims. We could end up with a worse situation than we have now."

That's when Everhart casually revealed that he'd recently received a visitation from the spirit of the Chinese God, Tianzhu.

According to Everhart, he'd had a vision wherein Tianzhu had challenged him for the spiritual supremacy of the world.

He went on to say that a great battle had ensued between the hosts of good, and the hordes of evil, and that he'd almost died in the struggle.

At the height of the battle the Yellow deity had finally succeeded in dividing Yahweh's armies. He had them on the brink of defeat and just as he was about to deliver the death blow, a multitude of angels suddenly arrived from the West and by righteousness, brought an end to the conflict.

With the battle at an impasse, Tianzhu consented to Everhart's having supreme spiritual reign over the West, while Tianzhu, would have dominion over Allah and the whole of Asia.

The muffled confusion that followed prompted Everhart to clarify.

"Until such time as Jesus returns" he declared,

I will stand in His earthly stead. I have been granted every authority over all those who prostrate themselves before Mecca. Those Muslims who come under my authority will be bound over to Tianzhu, who well understands how to deal with them."

Nobody knew what to say, and in an effort to return the conversation to a semblance of sanity Boatwright overtly ignored the declaration by asking,

"Who fills the vacuum when Tehran falls?"

"The Saudis" Everhart answered, seemingly befuddled by the naiveté of the question.

"With Tehran out of the way Riyadh instantly becomes the center of Islamic power."

Anxious to keep the conversation in the realm of reality Boatwright asked why the faithful would follow the edicts of the Saudi royal family rather than the Imams.

"Imams shemoms," Everhart mocked.

When the faithful's bellies get empty they'll follow the Saudis to the table. In the end they'll worship their bellies above all. And the better for me, because the Saudi's don't have the bomb."

Boatwright suggested they game it out.

"What about the Egyptian Coptics and other Christians in the area?" He asked.

"What about them?"

Boatwright was convinced that local Arab Governments would put extreme pressure on the Christians.

'If that happened' he reasoned, 'Christians here at home would want revenge.'

"Are we going to side with Muslims over there against Christians here" he asked?

"Hell man they're just sand niggers" Everhart said.

A lot of our local niggers here call themselves Christians too. We treat them like shit don't we?

You don't hear any hue and cry on their behalf do you?

But as for the foreign Christians, we'll ransom them out. Pay the Arabs to carve out an autonomous territory somewhere. But no matter what happens, the dark Christians will stay where they are."

Everhart reiterated the Far East's sovereignty over the Near and Middle East. It went without saying that all those of African and Hispanic descent would be in capitulation to the West.

"As far as I'm concerned, Syrians, Libyans, Coptics, Jews, whatever, doesn't matter. At the end of the day, whether they're Uyghers or take a knee-gers, every tongue will confess, me."

Everhart looked to Kellogg for confirmation and quickly got it but Guillory merely smiled benevolently and lowered his head.

Suddenly Everhart asked Guillory,

"Who do people say that I am?"

The question stung. Guillory knew what was coming next.

Still, he gave the expected answer by quoting Mark 8:27

"Some say Elijah, some say,"

Before he could finish, Everhart interjected.

"Who do you say that I am?"

Just as he feared.

Guillory'd always been evasive concerning his benefactor's allusions to omnipotence.

He'd merely been conciliatory to the extent that he'd smile and nod whenever Everhart referenced his deity.

But now he'd been asked point blank whether he agreed with Everhart's claims of divinity.

Guillory knew that any answer short of complete fealty would be disastrous.

Everhart's behavior may have been aberrant but he had the survival instincts of a medieval monarch. Never mind that Guillory'd helped him rise to the pinnacle of political power. The mere suspicion of disloyalty would be his end.

As Everhart's gaze burrowed deeper into his head, Guillory rifled the pages of his vast diplomatic manual.

This time his usually eloquent tongue abandoned him. Realizing that further hesitation would be construed as dithering, Guillory heard himself say,

"God."

26

HALF MOON BAY

Originally from the southwest Texas border town of El Paso, Adelina Flora Bella De La Cruz came to Los Angeles after graduating 5th in her class at South Texas College of Law.

She was a circumspect sort who kept mostly to herself. The popular girls at Coronado High, where she'd excelled in debate competitions, considered her odd.

Not because she was an egg head, but because most girls as pretty as she was, tended to be more socially active.

The truth was she had big tits. But contrary to contemporary standards, she was unconventionally modest. Basically she wasn't comfortable with the kind of attention she got. She'd rather be acknowledged for her mind than other attributes.

Her mother Marta, was the mental mold from which Adelina was cast. Though smallish in stature, Marta was a giant on the inside. She was tranquil in demeanor but emitted a self-assured spirit that served as a natural attraction to others.

She'd been a midwife who'd run her own birthing center, catering mostly to women who traveled from Mexico.

Back then patrons arrived daily at the small red brick storefront on Texas Avenue. They got to her doors any way they could. Some came by car and some crossed the Paso del Norte bridge on foot. Others floated across the Rio Grande on inner-tubes. In those days clients actually did show up on the doorsteps with their clothes still wet.

Although the birthing center was only a mile from the U.S. border, it represented eons from life in Mexico. For $700 Marta Maria Ramirez de la Cruz could ensure that the babies born in her clinic would be U.S. citizens.

Adelina was an only child but she didn't fit the spoiled brat stereotype. She'd spent countless hours at the center doing menial tasks without complaint. She took a particular solace in helping to keep order. It was her peculiar way of keeping her emotions in check. Even as a young girl she'd worried for the client's futures.

It was during those formative years that she'd learned how the real world worked.

There was nothing extraordinary about her family.

They were a typical hard working average household.

She was a daddy's girl and her parents were responsible people who went to work everyday.

Saturday play, Sunday church.

Then one day all that changed.

Her father, Mauricio Ramos de la Cruz, was a six foot tall, man's man with a lean muscular build. Adelina got her height from him. He was generally an even tempered, straight shooter who always let you know where he stood.

Mauricio worked for a wealthy family that counted rental properties among its many holdings. The family had real estate investments locally and in nearby Otero County, New Mexico. His job was general maintenance. It was a position well suited to his can do personality.

When Mauricio headed north up highway 54 that morning, his only concern was what he'd have for lunch.

He'd made the 25 mile trip to Alamogordo New Mexico, just outside Holloman Air Force Base, dozens of times. He was headed to one of the buildings that provided cheap housing for locals and airmen who wanted to live off base.

Despite the fact that it was a consistent money maker, the owners never kept this particular building up to code.

'Maybe that's what made it profitable' Mauricio thought as he pulled the Chevy pickup into the parking lot.

Today he'd perform his least favorite task.

Pulling a large burlap sack from a stack beneath a tool box, he stared at the insecticides, herbicides and other pest control products lining the truck bed.

There wouldn't be any spraying today. Today he'd collect the proceeds from the rat traps.

If there was anything Mauricio hated, it was rats. He lifted an aluminum baseball bat from the truck bed and started toward the building.

The basement was eerily dark even after he'd switched on the overhead light. He'd barely gotten to the bottom of the stairwell before he heard a muffled rustling.

He tightened his grip on the bat as he squinted around for the source of the noise. Something moved in the corner of his eye and a woman suddenly shrieked. Before he knew it a man leapt out of the shadows and lurched at him.

Mauricio instinctively swung the bat. It rang with the same metallic clank he'd heard a million times as a kid on the playground. It didn't surprise him that the guy went down. It did surprise him that he was naked.

Then the woman appeared. She was naked too. It was obvious from the trauma in her eyes that she'd been raped. She clutched a dingy cotton dress against her frail body as she stared at her fallen attacker. All Mauricio could tell about the man on the floor was that he was Mexican and that he was dead.

As blood pooled around the guy's head the woman looked to

Mauricio. When their anxious eyes met it seemed forever passed between them before she bolted up the stairs and disappeared.

The police weren't skeptical of Mauricio's account of events. They believed him when he claimed self defense.

They weren't concerned over the whereabouts of any alleged rape victim. After all it was just Mexican on Mexican crime.

The authorities were ready to tie a bow around the whole thing when the worm took an unexpected turn.

The dead guy turned out to be a rogue border patrol agent who was moonlighting as a coyote.

Further investigation revealed the building was a safe house. Once the property was tied to human trafficking, the owners were determined to shut the investigation down.

To eliminate their exposure they'd sacrificed Mauricio. Rather than rally to the defense of their longtime employee, they instead used their influence to redirect the investigation.

Convicted of murder in the first degree, Mauricio Ramos de la Cruz was sentenced to life in prison.

In the years following her father's conviction Adelina'd fought tirelessly to clear him but nobody would take the case. Her best hope had been 'The Innocence Project', but they maintained there was no legal argument to be made.

In order to prove Mauricio's innocence they'd have to prove massive conspiracy on the part of both state and county officials.

Initially Adelina had hoped to find a job in the Department of Justice. Naivety bolstered her hopes that haunting the halls of fair play would somehow yield a champion who would advocate for her cause.

In short order she was broke, defeated and ready to go home. Then providence intervened.

Through an unlikely series of events, the doors of the Federal Bureau of Prisons sprung open for her.

Although grateful for the job, she viewed the bureau as merely an avenue to gaining freedom for her dad.

Her dream scenario was to get him a new trial. At the very least she hoped for a sentence reduction. In the meantime she'd work to improve prison conditions.

At least that had been the plan.

But today Adelina's concerns went beyond Mauricio.

At the oddest times she'd found herself uncomfortably invested in this man she called Jesse in the comfort of her mind.

Recently she'd noticed a definite change in him.

Instead of his usually upbeat self, he'd become subdued and stand-off-ish. He brooded over muffled phone calls and disappeared for hours into the segregation pods. He hadn't made her privy to his thoughts but she was acutely aware of his physical comings and goings.

Ever since that seminole moment in the office, when he'd all but swooned at her feet, he'd inexplicably avoided her.

If circumstance demanded he talk to her, he'd avert his eyes. She wondered why. Laying in bed, staring at the ceiling, she dwelt on him again.

She didn't know what to do with her feelings.

Did she want him to be interested in her? Was she interested in him? What if she was? What if he wasn't?

It didn't matter. She wasn't going to get involved in an office romance.

But other events at the office had also stoked her imagination. Lately she wasn't sure what to make of what she'd been seeing.

Communications from military types had been coming in from everywhere. Some were active duty, some retired. The messages were always short. Major so and so says congrats. Captain such and such sends his regards.

She'd heard it said jokingly that all Black people knew each other. By virtue of the notification deluge, it seemed to her that all Black military officers actually did.

He'd told her about accepting the Adjunct General position as a way of explaining all the contact. Maybe she'd have picked up on things quicker if she hadn't been otherwise distracted.

Mauricio's health was failing and she was afraid he wasn't getting the medical attention he needed. The notion that he might actually die in prison terrified her. The last time she'd spoken to him he'd promised he was fine and changed the subject by asking if she was seeing anybody.

She wouldn't have broached the subject of Jesse even if they had been seeing each other.

Mauricio wasn't exactly racist but he didn't think much of Black's in general. She'd heard his opinions enough to know as much. Mauricio thought Blacks were losers.

'They're always blaming Gringos for their problems' he'd say.

'They don't stick together. They been in the U.S. for hundreds of years and they still haven't made anything of themselves.

The few properties he'd tended that were occupied by Blacks were always in poor condition. They weren't only run down but were carelessly squalid.

To Mauricio, Blacks had no pride in their surroundings.

No sense of personal responsibility. But most of all he condemned their treatment of woman.

'They think all women are bitches' he'd say.

He summed it up to lack of character. She could already hear him.

'How could you be in love with a Mayate?'

In love.

It was the first time she'd allowed herself to think it.

She'd never been in love before. She'd had phases of infatuation with a couple of boys at school, and even a professor or two. But nothing that remotely approached love. This wasn't that. This was different.

But lately it hadn't been easy to be around him. She'd pretended not to notice the tension between them. She knew he felt something for her but instead of letting her in, he was keeping her out. She didn't have a lot of experience with men, but certainly nobody'd ever spurned her.

Was his distance partly responsible for her intrigue?

There wasn't a lot to do on a Saturday morning in the unincorporated area of Santa Barbra county where she lived. To clear her mind she decided to take a day trip up the coast. The smell of a salty breeze and the sun on her face would be good for her. Half Moon Bay seemed like just the thing.

Years ago, when the coastal community was known as Spanish-town, one of her ancestors had owned property there. The relative had received a small parcel of land from Tiburcio Vásquez, after Vasquez's successful bid to win the Mexican land grant of 1839.

The parcel eventually ended up in the hands of another relative, one Frank Torres, who'd built an infamous speakeasy on the property in the 1920's. She'd wanted to go there ever since she'd first heard the family whispers as a child.

Today would be the day.

Half Moon Bay was about 300 miles up the coast, approximately a four hour drive. If she left now she could be there by early afternoon.

As soon as the overnight bag hit the VW Beetle's backseat, she dropped the top and headed north on California highway 1.

Cruising along the coast listening to the radio, feeling the wind whipping through her hair, she felt oddly proud of herself.

Normally she wasn't so impulsive. It felt good to just do something without over thinking it. She'd been right about the wind and sun.

She hadn't bothered to book a room. She'd find a hotel when she got there. Judging from the town's website, there was sure to be a quaint beach front inn readily available at walk in.

She leaned back, admiring the contrast of the pillowy white clouds against the cerulean sky. Her mind drifted with them as they floated almost touchable over the sapphire waves.

The miles evaporated into the rhythms streaming through the

bluetooth, and before she knew it, the imposing facade of Hearst Castle was emerging in the distance.

The closer she got, the more she marveled at the grandeur of Casa Grande's magnificent towers.

Hearst had spent considerable time and money modeling the castle's architecture after the Renaissance style of the church at Ronda in Southern Spain.

He'd be happy to know she approved.

'What must it be like to have that kind of money' she thought.

She knew she'd never know.

The landmark slowly faded away in her rearview mirror as she got that much closer to her destination.

When she'd checked into the Harbor View Inn, she'd merely wanted to see the room. She hadn't meant to fall asleep.

She wondered how long she'd slept. Moving to the window she pushed aside the curtains and looked down on the waves lapping gently against the sands below. The hour surprised her. The sun would be setting soon.

It seemed like only minutes ago she'd been having lunch at Miramar Beach restaurant. Like a lot of the buildings in the old coastal town, it'd been built in the early 1900s. When she'd commented on its charm, the waitress told her that back in the day, it lured a more salacious crowd.

The Ocean Beach Tavern, as it was known in the 1920s, had been designed as a prohibition roadhouse.

One of its custom features was that it was built with revolving kitchen cabinets in order to conceal the alcohol. When Adelina expressed intrigue, the waitress winked and told her about the 'ten small rooms upstairs, each with just a bed and private bathroom.'

As it turned out the quaint little town had quite a seedy past. By the 1930s San Mateo was known as the most corrupt county in California.

Back then bootleggers off loaded Canadian whisky from ships anchored 12 miles out to sea in international waters. They'd bring the contraband to shore on small boats and drag it up the cliffs. Sometimes, if things got too hinky, they'd bury it right on the beach. From there it made its way another 20 miles or so up the coast to San Francisco.

The area built a fluid underground economy based on the trade. In those days home stills were as common place as door knockers, and some earned ready cash selling gasoline and sugar to those who wanted to make their own 'coffin varnish'.

If she was going to be fresh for work on Monday she needed to be on the road by tomorrow afternoon at the latest. She'd better see whatever sites she could now. The weather was turning chilly and she pulled the fine knit royal blue shawl snuggly about her shoulders on the way to the car.

The top didn't go up at first but a few frantic taps on the button and it reluctantly chattered alive.

When she parked on the causeway, she found the nearly 400 slips at Pillar Point Harbor, filled almost to capacity.

The jumble of masts bobbing randomly into the twilight looked to Adelina for all the world like giant ornate toothpicks jabbing at the sky.

The beautifully constructed breakwaters kept the harbor unusually tranquil. The placid waters provided a welcome safe haven for fat sea lions lazing on the docks.

Strolling between the rows of pleasure cruisers and fishing boats, inhaling the sights and smells of the harbor, she spotted a trawler painted with the words, Dungeness Crabs.

Atop the bluffs in the misty distance she could make out the outline of the Moss Beach Distillery.

The second she walked through its doors she could feel it.

The establishment that Frank Torres built back in '27 still wreaked of subterfuge and romance.

She spied an empty red leather tufted stool at the end of the bar and wondered if she looked like a wanton woman when she slid onto it.

The dinner crowd hadn't started yet and the place didn't resemble anything like when it crawled with local politicians and Hollywood stars.

There were no knees up revelers dancing to live music, no lewd laughter or cigar smoke.

It was no longer 'Frank's Place' but it still perpetuated an air of mystique.

She ordered Dungeness Crab with a glass of Riesling, and as she waited she noticed the bartender staring at her.

Her first impression was that he was being weird. When she saw him about to approach she was ready to nip his advance in the bud when he said,

"Haven't seen you for a while."

"I'm afraid you're mistaken" she replied as he broke into a wide grin.

"Just kidding" he said.

It's your outfit."

The barkeep answered her puzzled expression.

"Haven't you heard about our famous Blue Lady ghost?"

Adelina looked down at her clothes. She hadn't intended to wear matching colors it had just happened that way.

While serving the wine and crab, the barkeep recounted a tale of star crossed lovers who'd met at the bar years ago.

'One night a beautiful young woman had come to the bar in search of an evening of entertainment. During the course of the night she'd become infatuated with the bar's handsome piano player. Even though she was married, the woman became a fixture at the bar and the pair soon became an item.

Every time she showed up she would be dressed all in blue.

Over time their affair became an open secret and ultimately her husband found out.'

Frank's Place stood on a cliff above a secluded cove. When the fog rolled in, the cove's tiny beach provided the perfect place to off load illegal booze.

It was on this beach while she was walking with her lover, that the Blue Lady's husband stabbed her to death.

"To this day" the barkeep said,

The Blue Lady could still be seen roaming the beach and roadhouse."

The shocked expression on Adelina's face coaxed another smile from the bartender.

He didn't know it, but at that moment Adelina believed she'd just seen a ghost of her own.

In the mirror above the bar, she'd seen the reflection of a man coming through the doorway.

She'd spun around in time to see Jesse and a woman she didn't recognize, making their way to a table.

Stunned, she waited until their heads were huddled in conversation before slipping out unnoticed.

27

ZERA OMA DERA

Seeing Jesse with another woman had flipped a switch inside her, and somewhere between Half Moon Bay and her apartment, Adelina made a decision.

She was proud of her virginity, mainly because she'd fought so hard to keep it.

She hadn't remained celibate because she was a prude, she'd abstained because she didn't want to end up like so many of the women who'd come to the birthing center.

All things considered she found the risk reward ratio of casual sex to be out of balance. On a strictly pragmatic level it seemed the best way to keep her options open, was to keep her legs closed.

This frame of mind had saddled her with a modest reputation that was far from the peculiar truth.

In fact, she was the mental polar opposite of a sexual goody two shoes. Adelina Flora Bella de la Cruz had a vivid imagination and she used it in most curious ways.

Adelina lived out her sex life in erotica fantasy worlds.

Her intimate reverie consisted of internet porn, randy romance novels, and the aforementioned imagination.

What began as a mere release, eventually evolved into a type of ritual. By this time in her life she'd become adept at channeling a variety of sexual energies of various appetites.

Her routine was almost ceremonial.

After work she'd head for the local marijuana dispensary. Anyone who thought they knew her would have been stunned to learn she was an avid Rastafarian; Weedily speaking.

The supermarket magazine rack provided the necessary paperbacks. After picking the title that most struck her fancy, she'd choose a wine to compliment her imagined scenario. Red and dry if she were going dark, or light and fruity if the context were more whimsical.

She'd remove her shoes and bra when she walked in the door. While drawing a bath she'd light several aromatic candles and set Spotify to an easy listening instrumental station.

After her bath she'd wrap herself in a towel, sit on the side of the bed and roll a blunt. When she'd found a suitable porn site, she'd mute the audio and play the images in the background while reading, toking and sipping wine.

She'd meticulously create the world her characters came from and the events that had led them to their present situation.

She gave them ambitions outside of the roles they played on the pages. She knew what they smelled like, the feel of the sweat against their bodies.

Slowly, organically, she'd bring the selected storyline to its logical climax. Sometimes she talked aloud.

Did she love him? That wasn't the point. Sometimes you just want what you want when you want it.

She wasn't going to wait any longer. She'd waited long enough. Waited to be chosen, for the right circumstance, until next time. That must have been what people meant when they talked about ladies in waiting.

Her mindset also wasn't at all what she'd expected.

She'd always imagined her first time as a painting, passionately stroked from all the colors on love's palette.

But driving home that day she'd realized something. The only thing she'd really been waiting for was the right guy.

He was surprised when he'd opened the door.

She hadn't called.

Without a word she'd pressed herself against him, pulling his head down and rolling her tongue against the roof of his mouth.

Jesse didn't try to make sense of it. He was more interested in the what than the why. But even when he did try to speak, she'd placed a finger against his lips and shook her head. When she'd pushed him on the bed and stepped out of her coat, she was already naked.

He looked completely stupid, bewildered by the fantasy playing out in front of him. She was even more beautiful than he'd imagined. The perfection of her form would have made the renaissance masters question their abilities.

Brushing the pillows from the bed, she glanced around the trailer. No paperback vamp personality came immediately to mind as Jesse fumbled with his zipper.

Things were moving so fast it was hard for him to keep up. He peeled off his pants and flung them on the floor.

She immediately laid on top of him finding him warm and solid to the touch, like the handle of a cast iron skillet. When she curled into him he found her mouth and softly suckled her tongue.

Soon enough his hand slid along her inner-thigh and she'd rolled onto her back. Prickly tingles tinged the outer edges of her nerves as she opened her eyes and looked on his face. His eyes were closed but she sensed he felt something beyond desire.

She held her breath as he traced his fingers along the contours of her back. When he gently stroked the hair at the nape of her neck, she took a deep breath and nestled her face into his chest. He smelled like outdoors, funky and sweet. When she opened her legs to receive him the pain she'd been warned against proved no barrier to her surrender.

Moving her hips in rhythm with their breathing, she clung around his limbs like ivy on the school-house wall.

For her muse she'd settled on the neophyte determined huntress that she was. She closed her eyes, and abandoned herself to the ebb and flow of the agony and the ecstasy.

The energy wasn't at all what she'd imagined, not withstanding all the imagining she'd done. Nothing she'd read or seen had prepared her for the real thing. She'd seen a million people fuck. This wasn't that.

His muffled intermittent utterances gave her a feeling of tremendous power. Simultaneously, the strength of his arms around her made her feel safe and protected. With his cheek molded into hers, Jesse settled into an almost hypnotic rhythm.

Soon the churning locomotion began stirring emotions in her that she hadn't known existed. He wasn't just penetrating her yani, he was probing her soul.

The grip on her thighs suddenly tightened. When he sucked his breath she opened her eyes in time to see the ugly grimace of love play across his face.

When he'd grabbed the back of her neck, she'd locked her legs and held him down until he stopped convulsing.

He finally exhaled and collapsed like a deflating ballon. When he'd rolled onto his back she'd lain on his chest listening to his heartbeat. Laying in silence she suddenly wanted to call her mother.

———

Adelina had been right.

Jesse'd gone to Half Moon Bay precisely because it was so far off the beaten path. He had indeed thought he wouldn't be seen.

But contrary to what she'd believed, he wasn't involved in any secret affair or dalliance. His meeting with Doctor Zera Oma Dera, had been strictly business.

While the President held Doctor Oma Dera in his closest confidence, if she had her way, the French, Germans and Brits who lorded it over the Africans, would all be speaking Lingala instead of the other way around.

Doctor Oma Dera had been bitterly opposed to the Mugabe government that essentially restored Belgium rule to the Congo. She resented the United States of America because the C.I.A. had been the primary facilitator of the Mugabe regime change that had killed Lumumba and installed another puppet government.

While on the surface, she toted C street's water, her personal agenda ran one hundred and eighty degrees counter to appearances.

She lamented the fact that the nuclear weapons formerly held by South Africa, had been dismantled by the outgoing government. But WMDs were a concern for another time. Right now, in order to ensure basic self determination, communities needed to be able to defend themselves at the most basic level.

That had been the reason for the meeting with Hawk.

There would be no division of North and Sub-Saharan Africans to extent that she could help it.

She was most intent on circumventing the United Nations treaty that decreed against any African nation, with the exception of South Africa, from manufacturing weapons.

She'd approached Hawk after being alerted by MTC Egypt operatives who were associated with the Church's prisoner outreach program.

That initial meeting had led to Dr. Oma Dera's present concentration on Armscor, a South African weapons manufacturer headquartered in the Philippians.

For decades Armscor had supplied weapons to any African warlord or chieftain who could pay for them.

Those people, in servitude of the shiny object, had helped to continue White domination in their given areas of influence. Dr.

Oma Dera was determined that those warlords, Armsco, and companies like them, should pay for their troubles.

The plan was simple. Flip the script.

Whereas previously, weapons originating from European manufacturers had been sold as tools of suppression; they would now be used as instruments of liberation.

She'd been skeptical at first. She'd thought the logistics of delivering tons of weapons and ordinance to Initiative recruits would be insurmountable. However, the simplicity of Hawk's response had both surprised and relieved her.

'We'll submit official UCC requisite P.O.s to ARMSCOR, Raytheon, Boeing, Colt etcetera, through regular channels as always' he'd explained.

'We have people at every station along the way. There's no reason for anyone to suspect anything out of the ordinary. By the time they catch on we'll be armed to the teeth.'

Danny's operatives would handle the necessaries in Central America.

One of the Latin objectives was to amass as many Hispanics at the California and Arizona borders as possible. They would serve as unassailable reserves should they be needed in a ground assault.

As long as they were on Mexican soil, UCC forces were powerless to do anything against them. Theoretically.

Because they didn't have access to official Central American military documents, they'd use the best counterfeiters in the federal prison system to create them.

The military and Central American National Police and Army arsenals would serve as the main arteries through which the weapons would flow. They'd do what they'd always done. Arms would be shipped to, then siphoned from, National police and army stores, as usual.

In order for Danny to be successful, the Central American gangs, officials and others would certainly need to be paid. Where would the money come from?

The office of engraving and printing was responsible for printing paper money. Hawk would use them.

Rather than have co-conspirators in the engraving department steal original currency plates, or run extra batches of Notes, Hawk chose instead to have other official documents printed.

He used Treasury Department letterhead documents to order billions of dollars' worth of UCC Bank Notes, from an outfit called, Crane Currency.

Headquartered in Dalton Massachusetts, Crane is the official supplier of Bank Notes to many countries. To that end, the insurgents used the engraving department's unique attributes to also print official looking orders for billions in currency Notes for the Bank of Columbia.

The Notes would be printed at Crane's facilities in Hal Fa Malta, but instead of being delivered to its customer's respective Central Banks, Hawk arranged, for a fee, to have emissaries take delivery directly from the facility.

As it pertained to arms, Hawk was especially concerned for tele-scoped cased weapons.

These lightweight, high caliber machine guns with precision sights, would provide the high degree of firepower, accuracy and mobility required for the guerrilla tactics the operation called for.

He focused on two makers of the weapons; Textron Systems, a manufacturer based in Providence Rhode Island, and CTAI, an English, French joint venture, based in Borges France.

He determined to submit P.O.s to the makers of these weapons first. He'd get as many of these guns as possible while he could.

Doctor Oma Dera was nothing if not passionate. For her, the operation wasn't merely political, it was personal.

As much as she despised the Brits and Christlanders, Doctor Oma Dera reserved her deepest loathing for the French.

She hated them for enslaving the Vietnamese. She hated them for what they'd done in Haiti, Senegal, Morocco, Tunisia, Algiers, Mali.

She hated them for holding more than 70 percent Muslim prisoners in French prisons.

Her hatred of the French was most likely a simple personal preference, since the British, under Rhodes, were arguably the worst African genocide offenders in history.

But Doctor Oma Dera believed that ultimately all these atrocities would work to her advantage.

The French Algerian Muslims and West African Blacks who lived in the slums north of Paris, were already active in the French Intifada. They were sure to be critical assets when the time came.

But Adelina didn't know about any of that when she dropped her bags in the back of the Beetle and left Camp Brown forever.

28

AMAZIGH SCIENTIFIC TEMPLE

Kellogg had been in position to pounce on the West Adams community when he received word that the crowds had suddenly dispersed.

His opportunity to seize the area had been snatched away and he needed to know why. The answer came in the form of T. Edmond Longstreet.

Intelligence reports revealed that the on-air personality led a double life.

In addition to his identity as a nationally syndicated radio host, Longstreet was also known in some circles as Issac El Bey, Director of the Amazigh Scientific Temple, a Black sovereign citizen organization.

Adherents to the Temple were practitioners of a unique form of the Muslim doctrine.

They claimed to be descendants of the original inhabitants, of both the Americas, and the nation of Morocco.

They further contended that in 1776, when American colonists won independence from England, they hadn't considered that the land they occupied was already owned, and was not theirs to claim.

The legality of the United States' claim to this land, let alone UCC's, wasn't recognized by members of the Temple.

Members further insisted that Morocco had been first to recognize the independence of the United States, and that Sultan Sidi Mohammed Ben Abdullah, had issued a declaration in 1777, allowing American ships access to Moroccan ports.

Accordingly, a Treaty of peace and friendship was signed in Marrakech in 1787 and ratified in 1836.

Under provisions of the treaty, Amazigh-Americans had special rights warranting that;

No Amazigh citizen could be made a slave in the United States.

The Temple considered the U.S. Government to have violated that provision.

Temple dogma found a receptive audience in U.S. prisons and jails where most of its new adherents already practiced some form of the Islamic faith.

Adding to Kellogg's intrigue was evidence suggesting T. Edmond Longstreet might also be the main spook behind Ghost Posse.

The fact that leftist Muslims had influenced Christland public policy was galling enough in itself; but the fact that common street thugs had also played a part, was beyond Kellogg's shallow pale.

'Who were these niggers and why were other niggers listening to them?'

The West coast had to be taught a lesson.

———

Under cover of darkness, streaming bands of marauding choppers and hogs made their way along southland freeways into South Los Angeles.

In the relative quiet of the predawn hours, more than 200 outlaw bikers rumbled along Florence avenue toward the infamous intersection with Normandy.

The mechanical calvary arrived bent on destruction and armed to their meth rotted teeth.

Kellogg had equipped the marauders with prepacked, man mobile, anti-tank weapons, along with instructions that Black lives definitely did not matter.

This particular intersection represented ground zero as regarded Black defiance. By desecrating it Kellogg was giving the middle finger to any recognition of Black self determination.

The short commercial stretch of Florence just west of Normandy, consisted of three churches, an AutoZone, party supply, liquor and a hardware store. All of which were reduced to embers, soot and cinders after the bikers discharged a blinding display of combustion on them.

While the disintegration of the wood framed structures produced a spectacular conflagration against the moonless sky, it was the Chevron and 76 stations at the infamous intersection proper, that reacted most sensationally to the high impact, super-plastic anti-tank warheads.

To equate the night sky with the fourth of July would be to severely under appreciate the state of the biker's patriotism.

In the afterglow of roiling flames, billowing smoke and chaos, the bikers switched off their headlights, broke into smaller groups and scattered onto various of the five different freeways that crossed Florence avenue.

Police response time was slow.

29
PARIS

Sliding into the train's tidy utilitarian seat, T. Edmond breathed an inward sigh of relief.

Making it through the airport hadn't been as bad as he'd thought it might be. He'd flown Air France rather than a U.S. carrier to appear less touristy. At least that's what he'd hoped.

He was traveling on a passport that identified him as Welton Thomas, a HBCU athletic recruiter out of Atlanta

He told the inquiring customs agent he was in town to interview Black French athletes for a pilot student exchange program.

He'd taken a chance when he'd left Los Angeles. He didn't know if he was being surveilled but he behaved as though he was. When Florence and Normandy blew up he read the writing on the wall. But he wasn't running away.

The Regional Express trains ran conveniently out of Charles DeGaul aeroport's Terminal 2, straight into the heart of Paris. The half hour trip from CDG to the Bossier station barely gave him time to catch his breath. Rising out of his seat as the train slowed to a stop he briefly considered walking the rest of the way to the hotel. But when he'd reached the street he'd changed his mind. It'd been a while since he'd been in the city. The walk was further than he remembered.

"21 rue Saint Didier"

he said to the taxi driver who barely acknowledged him as he took his bag. As the taxi made its way toward a trendy part of town he concentrated on the task ahead.

While waiting for housekeeping to finish preparing his room, T. Edmond decided on a late breakfast.

Squeezing between the tightly arranged tables in the tiny subterranean hotel cafe, he chose a seat in the corner of a mini booth.

The counter girl casually called to him in French that he should order before sitting down. Placing a hand on her hip she slumped to one side and waited for him to comply.

T. Edmond instantly knew she was screwing with him.

Parisians harbored a thinly veiled contempt for Americans traveling abroad. Why would she speak French to him unless she thought he was a local. But locals didn't stay at touristy hotels. Especially Blacks.

It was commonly understood that most Americans, regardless of color, seldom bothered to learn a second language. They expected that the entire world should speak English instead. By addressing Longstreet in French she was pointing up his arrogance as well as his ignorance.

He pretended not to notice her fluster when he ordered croissants, concentrated orange juice, cheese, and coffee in fluent French.

Hotel Etoile Trocadero provided clean, comfortable rooms at an affordable rate. Although a bit smallish by U.S. standards, it had well maintained bathrooms with ample hot water. Nothing more was needed.

Looking through the insulated windows separating him from the useless Juliette balcony, he watched the pedestrian's savior faire play out on the streets below.

Their taut expressions reminded him of a child's reaction to biting into a lemon unawares. The Brits may have kept a stiff upper lip but the French kept a turned up nose.

At 2:30pm the room phone buzzed. He didn't answer.

The call was his signal to head out.

They met outside the "Cite", a metro station in front of the Conciergerie, a mammoth building that had formally been a medieval prison. The structure was located on the west end of the Île de la Cité, literally 'Island of the City'.

T. Edmond found the setting ironic in that the descendants of French conquests, would this day, plot against them in the shadow of one of their most revered Revolutionary symbols.

T. Edmond's surprised expression gave rise to a smile from the man who'd come to greet him.

When the man put aside his newspaper, T. Edmond had recognized the green and white banner with the crescent and star right away.

"You weren't expecting an Algerian?" the man said.

The majority of Africans living in Paris came from the Maghreb, a sub-region of North Africa that includes Algeria and Morocco. There were 30,000 Algerians and 21,000 Moroccans in Paris. But since he'd come here representing the Temple, he'd expected a Moroccan to meet him.

Amazighs are the original Amazighen people of Morocco, from the time before the Arabs arrived.

The Indigenous land of Imazighen is a region called Tamazgha. It encompasses Morocco, and Algeria among other places, but most people know the Amazigh people as Moroccans.

They rejected the name Berber, given to them by the Arabs, because it derived from the word barbarian.

Amazigh was the name the indigenous people called themselves prior to being discovered.

After World War I, some Muslims from Algeria and Morocco surreptitiously adopted a North African identity only after arriving in

Paris, and this identity was sometimes bitterly contested, inciting conflict between the Algerians and Moroccans.

But lately things had changed.

Even though Algerians were technically French citizens, they were perceived as not being French due to racial and religious reasons.

Islam was now seen by the French as the biggest threat to their security in the last 100 years. French society's negative treatment of Islam and social discrimination of dark-skinned immigrants had caused some French Muslims to set aside old differences and unite against oppression.

"People are coming together to say we've had enough" the Algerian said.

We are so poor. We live in ghettos without hope. Everyone lives in fear."

The man, who'd identified himself only as Zuthamalin, didn't appear to be unusually angry or bitter.

He seemed to be exactly what he said he was.

Fed up.

Fed up with being perceived by Parisians as criminal, believed by them to be 'sly' and given to random violence.

In order to show their new found solidarity, the Temple Moroccans had allowed an Algerian to receive T. Edmond. That was the atmosphere into which T. Edmond and Zuthamalin traveled by tram.

They were headed to Clichy-sous-Bois, the dark side of the City of Light. Once there they would attend a summit of Maghreb and sub-Saharan Africans who were meeting to discuss how they intended to proceed.

Back in 2005, the area had broken out in riots after the death of two young Black boys who had been escaping a police control.

Eventually the unrest spread to every major urban area in France.

T. Edmond was here to support the French Intifada and the Temple in rekindling those embers.

This new organization would be one that didn't officially exist.

They had no symbols or slogans. There would be no officers, or members. It would be 'fight club' for self determination.

Their survival depended on silence. Only long trusted associates were permitted certain knowledge.

Even so, T. Edmond was keenly aware that he was always only a snitch away from death.

Be that as it may, there was no turning back.

This new extension to the T4 rail line he was riding, that had finally provided a direct route from the city into the community, wouldn't be enough to buy off the grievances of the malcontents.

30
BACK TO THE HOOD

The breaking dawn revealed military personnel and light armored vehicles streaming up Adams Blvd at Crenshaw. Hawk stood behind the M2 Browning machine gun mounted on the front of the M1127 Reconnaissance Vehicle as he led the procession through deserted streets.

At the intersection of La Brea and Adams Blvd, he raised his hand and gave a signal.

Several armored squads broke formation and scurried off through side streets. While there were no all White armored squads, there were a few all Black squads.

The National Guard had sealed off an area of approximately 9 square miles, ranging from CA I-110 at downtown Los Angeles in the East, to the 405 freeway and Culver City in the West. From South Central in the North, to Watts and Compton in the South, the Black and Hispanic communities had been completely surrounded.

Suddenly, neighborhood service garages and warehouses had personnel carriers and armored vehicles jamming their driveways. Troops kicked in storefront doors and wrestled proprietors into the streets while they ransacked their shops.

Gangbangers and civilians alike, unceremoniously assumed the position alongside major thoroughfares.

Sirens wailed below as Kiowa Warrior attack helicopters circled overhead.

Network news copters kept their distance as they recorded everything that happened.

When Blacks learned that White bikers had destroyed Florence and Normandy, plans were immediately made to retaliate.

When word reached Hawk, he recognized the eventual outcome of any mass action taken by untrained Black masses.

He'd coordinated with Booker to institute a pre-emptive strike in response to what Governor Booker had purposely characterized as terrorist threats.

The LAPD had been held back from participating in the police actions while Governor Booker's hand picked State police, assisted Hawk in carrying out the operation.

Citizens watched as businesses throughout the area were rousted. Furnishings and hardware were tossed helter skelter into the streets.

Hawk implemented a dusk to dawn curfew and by early evening Corpus Christi was basking in cable news footage of empty Los Angeles ghetto streets, under government control.

What wasn't visible in the news footage were the copious amounts of ordinance and weaponry left behind in the communities by the Black soldiers.

Neighborhood warehouses, garages and storage facilities, were turned into armories created to defend against future marauding bands of supremacists.

The times were uncertain but one thing was sure.

When Kellogg and his thugs came back, he'd have a fight on his hands.

31
FOR THE GLORY OF GOD

The huge uptick in Latin American gang activity had inspired Everhart anew. If things went according to plan, he'd force Hispanics into acting against their own best interests in spite of themselves.

In as much-as the Catholic church had tremendous influence in the regions he was interested in, Everhart would bring his concerns directly to the Holy See.

Try as he might, Guillory couldn't dissuade the increasingly megalomaniacal President from his intentions.

Part of Everhart's stratagem was the benefit as regarded the recent passing of a preeminent Cardinal.

Amid centuries old frescoes depicting the life of Saint Martial, 'The Apostle of the Gauls', Edric Everhart soberly presented his proposal to his host.

"Let me be plain" he said without deference.

These are disconcerting times. So much so, that in order to preserve the present world order, I find it necessary to open the door on what has become, The New Crusade."

Guillory, wary of Everhart's tone, to say nothing of the Pope's sensitivity to the reference, 'New Crusade', cautiously interceded.

"Your Grace, If I may."

Employing his most melodious timbre he invoked the passing of the Cardinal.

We offer our deepest sympathies for the loss of your beloved compatriot. Trusted colleagues appear few and far between."

Pope John nodded his acceptance of the condolences, but Everhart's cryptic prologue not withstanding, he wasn't exactly sure why the Americans were there.

Pope John wasn't the least interested in aligning himself with any UCC policies. He had his own agenda. An agenda steeped in centuries of political machinations that far outstripped the concerns of the impious idiot standing before him.

"It's true" the Pope said.

Gathering his robes gingerly between swollen twisted fingers, he leaned slightly forward in his seat.

Slowly adjusting himself, careful not to activate the prickly needles of arthritic pain, he agreed.

"A strong right arm is almost impossible to find" he said then changed the subject.

"But what of this crusade?"

At the risk of incurring his boss's ire, Guillory interceded again. Knowing that he and the Pope shared an understanding that Everhart would neither suspect or comprehend, Guillory explained.

"Seeing as how the Christian faith is beset by enemies on all sides, we're most desirous to be secure in the knowledge, that the reigns of the Catholic church are held firmly in the hands of a warrior king.

We simply seek assurances that you are that king."

The Palace of the Popes sits on Vatican Hill, in the city of Avignon, in the south of France.

Completed in the mid thirteenth century, it's the largest medieval Gothic building in Europe.

The palace was established as the church's alternate seat of power in 1309, when the French Pope Clement V, who'd been installed by French King Phillip the Faire, had been run out of Rome after the arrests of the Knights Templar.

It's been used at the churches' discretion ever since.

The present Pontiff, in deference to his heritage, and in order to escape the Byzantium politics of Vatican City, had opted to return the seat of power to France.

Inside the newly renovated Saint-Martial chapel, on the second level of the Saint-Jean tower, Everhart and Guillory sought to persuade the French Pope, John XXVII.

At the American President's insistence all nonessential personnel had been dismissed. There were only the three of them in the chapel.

The Pope showed no exception to having his leadership questioned.

Guillory, even though he was the Provincial Superior of the Society of Jesus in North America, and served as Head of the Assisstancy to the Superior General of the Jesuits in Rome, was still the number three man in the room.

Accordingly, the Pope addressed his remarks to Everhart.

"These are indeed unstable times Mister President" he said.

Careful to convey neutrality, he continued circumspect.

As I find your prelude more than a little intriguing, I'm compelled to question exactly why it is you requested this audience?"

Everhart instinctively employed his famous smile.

"As Father Guillory must have stated in our petition, we merely wish to enlist Your Excellency's support in our efforts to quell the growing Muslim scourge."

The Pontiff nodded accommodatingly, almost whimsically.

"No" he said.

I don't recall anyone mentioning that."

Everhart stared blankly without reply, prompting the Holy Father to ask.

"And how do you propose I support you?"

Everhart's response was instant.

"We would be most appreciative if Your Excellency should issue a Bull" he said.

Decreeing, in the name, and for the sake of the cross,

that all able-bodied Central American Catholics take up arms against the Islamic apostates in defense of the faith."

The ludicrous nature of the request caused the Pope to giggle, which he unsuccessfully tried to cover with a pitiful cough.

When Everhart's lips thinned in response the Pope inveighed,

"My God man, you're certainly not serious.

The diocese will never go along."

"They will if you tell them to" Everhart said.

Pope John wasn't surprised by the American President's desire for war, but that he believed he'd have the Holy Father's compliance, indeed *was* a surprise.

The Pope had no incentive or desire to promote any interests other than his own. He'd not be distracted from his considerations by this ephemeral aberration.

He decided to humor the President, the sooner to be rid of him.

"Let's suppose there's merit to your quest" he said.

How, in detail, would you have my help?"

Again Everhart was ready with his reply.

"Send emissaries into Central America.

Instruct them to teach a new doctrine.

The 'Defend The Cross' doctrine. The basis of which is;

'The Muslims are coming to kill you.'

Use local labor throughout the territories to construct facilities to house and train local recruits for combat.

Pay the workers and recruits a generous advance to get them started and a fair weekly wage thereafter.

Any you can't recruit, conscript. I want entire towns and villages involved. Men women and children. Everybody. Invite activist priests to be observers."

This time the Pope spoke to Guillory.

"You're aware the activists are Jesuits" he said,

intimating that the order, which in Latin America had prima facie become quasi-revolutionary, would never agree to any such action.

"We know who they are" Guillory droned, his tone absent its usual agreeable tenor.

Sensing the Americans would have their say, the Pope resigned to listen, but asked,

"And who's to pay for this?"

"You will" Everhart answered,

his demeanor again devoid of any semblance of subservience.

And you must repeat, repeat, repeat, that the faithful are in for the fight of their lives."

He thrust a finger forward.

Make them understand that everything they love; Everything they believe in; From the way they pray, to the way they name their babies, is going to be stripped away from them. Make them trust and believe that the Muslims intend to slit their throats, drink their blood and feed their children to the pigs."

The Pope listened in silent disbelief as Everhart took a deep breath.

You promise them the eternal rewards of heaven, and anything else you can think of that will get them to take up arms in defense of the Cross.

Especially any gang members.

Swear to grant absolution to the great grandchildren of any thug, dope dealer, armed robber or murderer who dies or kills in the fight for Jesus.

And buy something special, anything pretty, for the women. Give them every reason to trust you."

"And if they resist?" The Pope asked.

"Immediate Excommunication for the lot.

And if that doesn't make them reconsider, assemble them in the fields for official dismissal. Once they're neatly in formation, a couple of Black Hawks, some heavy artillery and ground fire should provide the desired result."

The statement was too much for the old Pope who couldn't restrain himself.

"Sheer madness" he blurted.

You can't just slaughter the fruit of the field."

"Not all of them" Everhart replied.

Just the ones who don't fall in line."

John XXVII's gaze ping-ponged between the Americans.

"That's the craziest thing I've ever heard" he managed.

Latin America is the last field of harvest for the church. Besides being morally bankrupt it would be financial suicide. I can't now, or ever, agree to anything as implausibly insane as what you propose".

The continued references to insanity troubled Guillory, yet there wasn't a hint of hostility in Everhart's tone when he replied.

"I don't think you understand" he said.

This isn't a request.

Let's not pretend the church is above politics. They didn't call Pius Xll Hitler's Pope for nothing.

Besides, how is what I propose any different from Croatian Franciscan Friars murdering over a million Jews?"

Before the Pope could respond, Everhart added,

But I will ask this.

What if the Muslims were to mount an invasion against your precious Latin America?

Who's to say if that couldn't happen?

The Iranians have the bomb.

Do the El Salvadorians have one?"

The Pope blinked.

No?

Then let me pose one last little detail. What good are your stupid peasants, or you for that matter, should the Muslims become the superior world power?"

Pope John XXVII remained silent.

Last, last thing, Everhart continued.

You're going to appoint Father Guillory to the late Cardinal Buntsinger's seat as Secretary of the Vatican State."

The declaration stunned the Pope. The position was a heartbeat from the Papacy.

"I'll do no such thing" he protested.

The Conclave of Cardinals will never sanction it. What you propose carries the stench of the deepest bowels of hell".

Everhart smiled.

"Bowels of hell" he repeated. Not worried.

The General Congregations of the Society of Jesus will deal with the Cardinals. Make no mistake;

These Islamic rug riders intend to destroy all Christians. They don't distinguish between Catholics and Protestants. The same as we don't make distinctions between Sunni and Shite.

They'll chop your head off faster than Marie Antoinette's. Now you listen to me you superfluous relic; You're to command every French, English, Italian, whatever Brown, White, grandmother who ever laid a finger on a rosary, to plead the tears of Mary for their families to obey the Pope and consecrate themselves to the fight."

"And if I refuse?" the Pope asked.

A look of quiet resolve emerged in Everhart's eyes.

"I needn't remind you" he said,

That lurking in every corner of every parish, there are lowly, ambitious priests, who are at this very moment salivating to become Bishops.

And Bishops who will stop at nothing to become Archbishops."

Pope John cast a spurious eye toward Guillory before finishing Everhart's sequence.

"And Cardinals who would be Pope" he said.

What can you offer me that I don't already have?"

Everhart met the Pope's gaze with sublime clarity and replied,

"A future."

32
QUEEN OF DIAMONDS KING OF SPADES

Bombs had been going off all over Paris for weeks.

The French Intifada took credit for the blasts but made no public demands.

As the frequency and randomness of attacks grew, every European person of color became a suspected terrorist.

When a synchronized assault by allied Sub Saharan, North African, European and Latin forces, simultaneously blitzed multinational corporations, arms manufactures and mining camps across continents, everyone was caught flat footed.

Utilizing weapons purloined and procured with the counterfeit UCC purchase orders, heavily armed confederates overran unsuspecting, ill prepared, security forces on a variety of fronts.

No one had anticipated the Revolutionaries who'd sprung, fully formed, from the head of Europe's Black frustration. Nobody knew what they wanted.

The group's manifesto was a curious document promoting the broad and vague objective of dismantling global White oppression.

By providence, the rebel's cause was aided by happenstance.

The Turks, unexpectedly joined the efforts against the French.

The Turks weren't siding with the Intifada so much as advancing their own agenda. But again, the enemy of my enemy.

Having thus coaxed the European theatre onto a forward trajectory, the Initiative moved with all speed to direct its attention to Anglos and Germans in Africa. The rebels were insulted that German was still spoken in Namibia, and injured by African countries still under British rule or occupation.

The fact that Caucasian hegemony was still accepted by African nations, was repugnant and totally unacceptable to them.

For the first time in modern history, global zeitgeist was leaning in their favor. Justice was in vogue but they had no illusions about the carnality that would follow.

As always, the bottom line would be the bottom line.

———

De Beers Diamonds, the British multinational mining company founded by super colonizer Cecil John Rhodes, was a prime target.

Rhodes hailed from privileged beginnings in Hertfordshire England, and as a young man was sent by his family to South Africa in the hope that the climate would improve his poor health.

It's not clear how much the climate helped him in so much as he died relatively young at the age of 48. But before he died Rhodes had established the eponymous nation of Rhodesia, the largest diamond mining company in the world, the most renowned academic scholarship in history, and the colony he headed for 6 years in the 1890's would eventually become the nation of South Africa.

During his short lifetime, Rhodes had also been responsible for the deaths of over 60 million Africans.

Add to the fact that Elizabeth, Queen of the British Empire, through the efforts of Rhodes and others like him, had amassed a personal fortune of more than 150 billion dollars. Not only did she subsist on an annual stipend of 107 million dollars, and live in a 5-billion-dollar house, but she did it while almost 80 percent of the

Congo, on whose backs she'd profited, subsisted on less than 2 dollars a day.

The 'Initiative' intended to change that.

The Queen's diamond income is separate and apart from the revenue stream generated from the so called 'Gold Coast'.

Although the name stemmed from the European traders who flocked to the area in pursuit of the prized mineral, the coast got its start in slave trading.

The four national territories in West Africa that make up the area are controlled by the British crown. Chief among the region's major assets is Mponeng.

At a depth of almost 2 and half miles, Mponeng, is the deepest gold mine in the world.

Located near the town of Carletonville, South Africa, it became a target for takeover. The Initiative didn't care solely for the gold. Their aim was to control all the mineral rights in Africa.

Because of the history of sellouts among Africans, Initiative members adhered to an uncompromising protocol. Anyone revealed to be an informant would die on the spot and their families would be erased from memory.

There were no White operatives in the African theatre by design. The order was to kill on contact any European who presented themselves as a friend.

Likewise the Chinese. Whereas the Chinese had considerable economic interests in many strategic regions of the continent, and offered terms for access that were better than the Europeans, their ultimate objectives were the same.

The Chinese government is atheist. It was universally understood that if left to their own devices, over time, the Chinese would exterminate the entire Uygher Muslim population.

The Initiative understood full well that Black liberation was not in the best interest of the Chinese.

The best hope for their future was for Africans to control Africa.

Although the Queen of Diamonds held a strong hand, the Initiative held all the Spades.

And while the diamonds were flush, the Spades possessed an abundantly full house.

In order to achieve their objectives, the Initiative was prepared to throw as many coals on the fire as necessary. In a war of attrition, they liked their chances.

Their tactics varied according to necessity.

The aim of engagement in the African theatre was three fold. One, take over precious metal and mineral mining operations. Two, capture, and if necessary, destroy manufacturing plants. Three, completely disrupt the status quo through general strikes.

Gold mining magnate Ernst Schnitzel was their first kidnap victim.

Considered one of the biggest Goldfish in the pond, Schnitzel was grabbed in full view of patrons attending his annual, "Learn 2 Think" charity fundraiser.

Black-tie attendees to the event, were stunned when insurgents burst into the ballroom and snatched Schnitzel off the stage of the private club he attended.

De Beers Diamond head Robert Carver, was next. After his abduction, high level executives made themselves scarcer than kosher bacon.

When thousands of armed natives overran diamond and gold mining camps, security forces had been caught literally off guard. Most commonly, because they never remotely suspected any such thing as a mass revolt to take place. The sheer number of natives completely overwhelmed security forces who generally surrendered after offering only tepid resistance.

Oil fields and textile plants experienced similar fates. African operatives working inside targeted objectives easily out maneuvered their underestimating overseers, allowing the Initiative unfettered access to facilities.

Following the initial breaching of a target, compliance by Black employees was self administered. Africans who didn't want to take part simply walked away.

Diamonds held a special interest for the Initiative.

A distinctive feature of the world diamond market is its high monopolization.

The largest mining companies, De Beers among them, take out 70% of all the world's diamonds.

Based on industry estimates, the global demand for diamonds would soon exceed the volumes of proposal.

Based on the forecast, diamond production would also decrease due to lack of new deposits. All of which meant prices would skyrocket.

Matters worsened when it was discovered that the mines and oil fields had been booby trapped. Knowing the Initiative could destroy entire operations with the push of a button, put pressure on magnates and heads of state to negotiate.

33
ANTWERP

The lion woke up and roared.

Rooster's hand tightened around the grip of his pistol.

He hoped he wouldn't have to shoot.

He had to hurry. It would be light soon.

After opening the gates on the display, he slipped away to the next exhibit. The elephants and gorillas were already in play by the time he set the last fire.

By the light of flickering flames he could see the silhouettes of his cohorts making their way to a garbage truck waiting in the tramway. He dreaded having to say much since they didn't speak the same language.

Posing as transport agents, Rooster and four confederates had arrived in Belgium the day before. They'd delivered wild okapis to the Antwerp zoo as part of a program that began in the 1900's to enlighten the Belgiums to the wonders of their conquest.

The hybrid offspring of giraffes and zebras were native to the Northern rainforests of the Congo. Doctor Oma Dera had provided the animals and man power for the mission, but it was up to Rooster to see it through.

After delivering the animals, mission members hid inside the zoo and waited. The wait was over

Rooster slid behind the wheel of the truck. He took the half eaten sandwich off the dash and laid it between his legs.

Listening to his Congolese crew speak French pissed him off. He was suffering from culture shock. Since he'd arrived in Europe, he'd concluded that language was a form of branding. 'These niggas belong to whatever country's language they speak' he'd thought. Until that moment, he'd never considered the implications of his speaking English.

But now that he was about to kick Leopold and Rhodes in the nuts, he felt better.

When the city's first responders reached the blazing zoo, elephants, lions and primates met them at the gates.

As emergency vehicles made their way through the confusion, Rooster drove past them to Meir--Leysstraat, the gateway to central Antwerp.

From here, the capitol lay at his feet.

The city of Antwerp is small and dense. Everything from the Neoclassical Vlaamse Opera, to the National Bank of Belgium, all lay within a few blocks proximity.

A crew member motioned Rooster to stop. The squad scrambled out and ran to the back of the hydraulic lift as Rooster raised the compactor plate.

Hidden in the hopper were scooters and shoulder mounted, anti-aircraft missile launchers.

The Congolese shouldered their weapons and quickly scooted off toward The Antwerp Royal Palace.

Rooster headed to a target of his own.

The National Bank of Belgium had no protection from outside attack, making its Neo-Renaissance towers and spires, easy targets.

Rooster drove into the park across from the bank and got out of the truck. He admired the bank's rococo aesthetics as he raised the preloaded Stinger missile launcher and fired.

The first fragmentation warhead hit the bank's mansard roof, raising ballooning flames that reminded him of a mega version of the Swiss cheese barbecue massacre.

The 2nd and 3rd strikes hit the ground floor, eventually reducing the block long structure to a smoldering baroque ash pit.

Antwerp's diamond district is in a zone known as the square mile. Rooster thought of it simply as a target rich environment.

Hundreds of retail and jeweler shops lined the narrow streets. Thousands more diamond cutters, polishers and crossworkers, who operated the machinery, made their living here.

Four local exchanges employed additional hundreds of brokers and merchants. While gold trading had been suspended, diamond trading had not. Computers were responsible for most of the trading and most of those computers were inside these buildings. They wouldn't survive.

By the time Rooster reached the district, the Congolese had already destroyed the Mansion of the Palace and the headquarters of the Diamond High Council.

These district buildings weren't like those downtown.

The flat faced facades showed none of the flashiness associated with those places. These were plain structures whose security systems were formidable at worst, impregnable at best.

Police, along with dozens of CCTV cameras and armed soldiers, usually protected the area, but tonight they were off chasing elephants and putting out fires.

And while the building's security systems could stop people, they couldn't stop rockets.

The Congolese continued to rain rockets over the entire area as Rooster pulled the truck into a parking lot behind the Cathedral of Our Lady.

Minutes later, after exhausting their ordnance, the raiders streamed up.

They dumped the scooters, jumped inside the hopper and hunkered down. Hawk pulled out onto the street amid sirens, rubble, fire and smoke.

Suddenly the Belgium Federal Police swarmed up and a Command vehicle cut Rooster off. The Commander stuck his head out the window and gave Rooster a long stink eye.

Rooster raised the sandwich from his lap, took a bite and shrugged as if to say, 'Can you believe this?'

A moment passed before the Commander ducked back in the car and sped away.

A few minutes later the truck pulled behind the Consulate General de la Republica Democratique de Congo.

Not long afterwards, 5 Congolese diplomats, entered Antwerp Central Station. Immune from detention, they ignored the stares of security forces, as they boarded a train bound for the Hague.

34

BAR SINISTER

Hawk sat handcuffed in the back of a black sedan. He had no idea where he was headed and none of the other men in the car were talking. If facial expression connoted empathy, the large man sitting beside him might as well have been a robot.

Hawk was unfamiliar with London but he knew he wasn't in the city anymore. Before long the car veered off the pavement and onto a gravel road. After a few bumpy minutes they arrived at the rear entrance of an abandoned industrial complex. In the dark Hawk couldn't make out what it had been used for.

But whatever its purpose, as soon as the three-car caravan descended the underground driveway, a shroud of dread draped over him.

Once inside he was led into an elevator that went down several more levels. He had to be at least six floors below ground when the elevator doors opened. He could see down a narrow hallway to a door that opened into a small, windowless room that was basically a dungeon.

He was chained to an iron ring embedded in the concrete floor where he was made to sit. Other than a desk, two chairs and a toilet, the room was empty.

For whatever reason, his captors had elected to interrogate him in the most inconvenient of settings.

"Cooperate" the chubby suspendered agent repeated.

While admonishing Hawk of the futility of his plot, he referenced a list of names. They were Black and Hispanic military officers all. He tried to convince Hawk that some of the names were already cooperating with the government.

Was it a bluff? Did it matter? They couldn't kill or arrest every person of color in the armed forces. Some of their sympathizers were White. How could they know? They had to be frantic.

Through hours of questioning, the interrogator, despite not advancing his agenda, somehow managed to continuously wear a quirky smile.

But there was nothing smiley about the man who sat in the corner. It was the same man who'd sat beside Hawk in the car. He hadn't spoken a word then and nothing had changed since. He sat for hours, silent as a holy night.

His sullen expression comprised a prominent jawline accompanied by deep set eyes that connoted instant frostbite. On the rare occasion that Hawk glanced up, he noticed the guy never moved. He was like a stone sentry, focused only on him. Hawk was convinced this would be the man who'd kill him.

Even though the silent centurion never uttered a sound, Hawk gleaned from the interrogating officer's soliloquy that mute guy was Co-intel.

He must be one of Kellogg's boys Hawk surmised. If he'd been a Keeper, Hawk figured he would've been tortured by now. Not that torture was off the table. He just figured a Keeper would've started there.

After hours of questioning and no sleep, Hawk would only give his name and title.

"Lt. Colonel Jesse Everette Hawkins, retired, Director of United Congregations of Christland Bureau of Prisons" was all he'd say.

He wasn't sure how much they already knew but It didn't matter. Nothing he could say would save him. He wondered why they hadn't physically harmed him. Did they need him to look healthy for proof of life? He wasn't sure but he knew they had no reason to let him live and every reason to kill him. He also knew they couldn't afford to make him a martyr.

He'd have to disappear.

While his captors were deciding his fate Hawk's self-talk became so loud it drowned out everything else.

His thoughts looped over and over, reliving every detail that had led to the present moment.

He'd been asleep when the phone rang.

Everhart himself had been on the line. He'd instructed Hawk to meet with the head of MTC's British counterpart, MTCNovo.

The United Kingdom was expanding their operation and he'd been tapped to oversee UCC interests in the new enterprise.

A car arrived almost before he could notify anyone about what was happening. In retrospect he should've known better.

The Director of Operations for MTCNovo was a man named Alzo Kromos. Hawk was to assist him in the building of a compound capable of housing 15,000 men, complete with all the labor related ancillaries.

From the moment Hawk arrived at Heathrow International, Alzo saw to it that his accommodations were first class. A driver had taken him straight away to Hotel 41, an establishment named for its address at 41 Buckingham Palace Road, said to be the finest hotel in London.

This was tall cotton for a guy who lived in a trailer and worked out of a bungalow. Things went downhill from there.

The MTCNovo executive committee was conveniently headquartered in London North West, just opposite the Waterloo train station. Hawk's train was just arriving when Alzo rang in on the cell.

The fifth floor office suites where they were to meet, were booked on-line, utilizing hot desking schedules.

Alzo explained that due to an error, the space where they were to meet had been double booked and was already occupied. He was moving the meeting to a nearby pub.

Sounding haltingly embarrassed by the rookie snafu, he'd apologized saying 'It's but a hair's breadth away.'

The pub appeared much as Hawk had imagined; Rich, dark and leathery, with reams of what he supposed was mahogany. Beveled mirrors lined the walls behind extensive bars, where art deco sconces diffused a muted ambiance for an equally muted clientele'.

Upon seeing Alzo, the Maitre D' smiled broadly, greeting him with what appeared to be genuine warmth. It seemed to Hawk that the prisoner privateer was a regular here.

He followed behind Alzo as they were ushered to a sedate private room at the rear of the establishment. As they sat down and the Maitre D' turned to leave, Alzo told him that his assistant was on her way, and to please show her back when she arrived.

A grin of surety accompanied Alzo's next suggestion to Hawk.

"You have to try the roast beef and Yorkshire pudding"

he declared.

He'd praised the latter as being literally fit for a Queen as it was in fact rumored that Her Majesty routinely dispatched couriers to the establishment to retrieve it.

The niceties having been dispensed with, Alzo proceeded to get down to business. He was in the midst of explaining that MTCNovo's London Community Rehabilitation Company, managed the majority of offenders on probation in the city, when the waiter arrived.

Alzo interrupted him before he could recite the specials and ordered steak and kidney pie. Hawk adhered to the recommended roast beef and Yorkshire pudding.

After ordering, Hawk had briefly excused himself, and had just returned from the water closet when the private room door opened.

At first Hawk thought he was seeing things, but then Alzo said the most impossible thing,

"Ah, there you are Miss de la Cruz. Thank you for being so prompt."

Hawk felt like he'd stepped into an astral portal.

Alzo accepted the small medicine vial Adelina handed him and smiled to Hawk,

"I'm supposed to take these with meals" he said of the pills he sprinkled in his hand.

Hawk was stunned mute while Adelina appeared no better able to collect herself.

Mistaking their reaction for instant thunder, Alzo started to introduce them. Jesse cut him off.

"Miss de la Cruz used to work for me" he said.

Adelina offered only an uncomfortable smile in response.

"Well, small world" Alzo exclaimed and invited her to join them.

She hurriedly declined, explaining that she had a doctor's appointment.

"Perhaps some other time then" Alzo said.

Unaware of their true history he was more than happy to release her from the situation.

She didn't wait for Hawk to say anything.

"It was nice to see you Director" she'd said as she lowered her gaze, turned and hurried out the door.

At the time he'd wanted to go after her. Now he knew it wouldn't have mattered. It was shortly after she'd left that the team of arresting agents showed up.

'Why here, why now?' Hawk wondered as he sat staring again at the concrete floor.

He figured Everhart must have wanted to lure him as far from California as possible before springing the trap.

But what about Adelina?

He'd never understood why she'd left Camp Brown the way she had. He didn't pretend to understand women but he had no clue as to what had happened between them.

Did she supply the names on the list in exchange for her father's freedom?

The agents suddenly left the room.

Something told him the next time the door opened, things would go badly.

Despite his troubles sheer exhaustion forced him to sleep.

Later that night, as he responded to the call of nature he heard a familiar voice in the dark.

"You know you didn't have to do any of this" the voice said.

All you had to do was wait."

It was Everhart. He'd come in the middle of the night solely to taunt him. He delivered his needling with sarcastic delight.

"If you'd a played your cards right" he said,

I'd-a made you Arch-Bishop of Niggerdonia."

"You can't make me anything" Hawk asserted.

His voice sounded stronger than he actually felt.

What did it matter what he said now?

"Of course I can" Everhart answered.

I made you Head of the federal bureau of prisons didn't I?"

"So I could build my own cages."

"A bit ungrateful aren't we?

Those prisons were to be your niggerdoms.

And a fine Arch-Bishop you'd have made too.

Arch-Bishop Uncle Jesse.

I'm so disappointed that you spoiled my plans for you.

When you died I would have had you beatified.

All history would have remembered you as

Holy Saint Nappy.

Patron Saint of pitiful niggers."

Everhart cupped his hands together. Clasping his chest he looked upward and made a mocking sad face.

"I can see it now" he said.

When ghost niggers showed up at the pearly gates,

ole Saint Peter would look at them and say,

'Hey you ghost niggers, where do you think you're goin?'

'They'd say'

'Weez gone to heh'um,'

'You know you can't come in this way Saint Pete would say. Ya'll go on round back.'

"And when they get back there you tell them,

'Okay you charcoal monkey looking angels, get yo ashy asses on in here and serve them White angels.'

By Golly boy, I was going to put your face on a box of government grits."

"Fuck you."

"Oh don't be angry.

If anyone should be angry it should be me.

After all, you betrayed me, trying to take my throne."

Everhart's head shook.

But it's not your fault. There's nothing you could have done to change things."

He indicated the chains around Hawk's wrists.

All of this was preordained in a time long before you".

"I don't know what that means" Hawk said.

"No? Let me explain."

As Everhart spoke he slowly lifted his arms above his head and swooshed them apart with a flourish, as though he were parting a stage curtain.

"I am come into the world as a force majeure" he said.

Every thing I do, every thought I have, is an act of God.

I am the Alpha and the Omega, the Jasper and the Sardis stone. The first and the last. I cause the moon to phase and the sun to rise.

I am, have been, and will always be, the beginning and the end of this, and all other worlds to come.

And by me, know you this;

Before I made you Director of federal prisons, I made you a nigger. And I made you a nigger for one reason and one reason only;

To serve and obey your masters.

Not to talk back, not to think, but solely and simply to serve and obey.

Do you understand now?"

Stunned by the revelation that Everhart actually believed what he was saying, Hawk answered with prudence,

"Yeah I do."

But Everhart wasn't done.

"You have some nerve.

You got a lot of people's hopes up."

He suddenly danced a silly jig.

'Weez gone fine-ly be free.'

"What are your people supposed to do now?

You let down your entire race."

Everhart put on an exaggerated pouty expression.

"Did you really believe you'd be that one in a billion nigger who would lead your people to the promised land?"

It wasn't until Everhart asked,

"What made you think I'd ever give you your freedom?"

That Hawk spoke up.

"My freedom isn't yours to give" he said. We were never headed to the promised land. We had always lived in the promised land. We weren't the Hebrew children. We have always been Pharaoh.

"You uppity, arrogant, too big for your britches jig-a-boo. You're nothing. Nobody'd even know you existed if it weren't for me. I created you."

Hawk abandoned caution.

"Yeah you did" he said.

Because every god needs a devil."

"Yes" Everhart agreed.

You are the devil, and devils must be destroyed."

Then, as suddenly as he'd appeared, Everhart abruptly disappeared into the hallway. As he closed the door he said,

"That's what avenging angels are for."

Later, creaking hinges alerted Hawk to another presence in the room.

When a shadow blacker than the surrounding darkness passed over him Hawk bolted upright.

As he stared into the death mask of the giant's face he knew this was it.

As the agent released the shackles from the floor Hawk could see another man lurking in the hallway.

A quick glance confirmed he was armed. Hawk slowly got to his feet. Other than smelling like chitlins and sauerkraut, he felt no ill effects from the time he'd spent chained to the floor. Physically he was numb. Emotionally he was disconnected.

Somehow, as he was led into the deafening silence of the hallway, Hawk found himself accepting his fate. He was reminded of Sergeant William Nesbitt, a Black soldier, who, along with twelve of his men, had been hanged by the U.S. Army. To a man they'd carried out Nesbitt's final command.

"Not a word out of any of you men now."

That'd be how he'd play it too.

Hawk and the Giant followed closely behind the henchman as they could barely see in the dark. They entered a door that opened on a narrow musty tunnel lined with plumbing and electrical conduits. There was barely room for Hawk to stand and the giant seemed to duck walk as they made their way by flashlight toward what seemed like a dead end.

That's when the henchman reached inside his jacket and Hawk prepared to die.

To his relief the henchmen pulled out a cell phone and punched in some numbers. After a moment, a shaft of light beamed down when a manhole cover was removed from above.

Utilizing the rebar steel rungs embedded in the passage walls, the henchman led the way up. When Hawk reached the top, he was hoisted out by ready hands.

He found himself in an alley where he and the colossus were hustled into the back of a waiting car. The henchman slid in front and no sooner had the car launched forward than the giant leaned over and grabbed Hawk by the wrists.

With a twist of his hand he unlocked Hawk's cuffs and leaned back staring straight ahead.

Even though his hands were free, Hawk didn't move as he waited for the next shoe to drop.

It was a short wait.

Not only could the Leviathan talk, but what he said restored Hawk's faith in the species.

"Boatwright's your inside man" he began.

The comment didn't register at first. Even after Hawk was sure he'd heard correctly, he was still confused.

"I thought you were going to kill me" he said.

The pronouncement was more question than statement. Goliath closed his eyes, exhaling deeply before replying.

"For all intents and purposes you *are* dead.

You can never show your face in the UCC again."

"What's actually happening here?"

The agent, who gave his name as Howard Janus, told Hawk that Boatwright had an epiphany.

As a result, he'd concluded he could no longer support the administration's agenda.

"No shit" Hawk jeered,

But he hasn't quit has he? Why not?"

"Everybody knows he's crazy" Janus declared of Everhart.

They're bending over backward to keep it from the public, but it's common knowledge in New Jerusalem.

Boatwright's staying in place because Guillory told him to."

According to Janus, Everhart used his old Fort Jesus compound as his new camp David. He'd been hosting his cabinet on a week long retreat when things took a turn.

The problem began when instead of being present at scheduled discussions, Everhart kept disappearing.

Nobody knew where he went. Then one afternoon Guillory was giving Boatwright a tour of the grounds when they came upon a clearing. In the clearing was a stately, but as yet unfinished, stone building.

'There's something here you need to see' Guillory'd said, and they'd gone inside.

The building was 60,000 square feet of finely detailed workmanship, but construction on the entire second level still remained in the framing stage. The building was intended for church leadership functions and the dimensions of the structure bore witness to the elder's regard for themselves.

After touring the ground level Grand Gathering Rooms, with their crystal chandeliers, granite fireplaces and handwoven tapestries, Guillory showed him something else. In one of the hallways he'd located a particular newel post.

When rotated, the post opened a secret panel in the wall. The opening revealed a flight of stairs that led down to a ornately carved heavy wooden door.

Guillory told Boatwright, that behind the door was a room originally intended to serve as the church's Holy of Holies.

He explained that before Everhart could finish it, he'd been called away; First to D.C. then Corpus Christi.

When Guillory had quietly cracked the door open, Boatwright heard Everhart's voice.

A heavy mist of incense smoke made it hard to see in the low light. The room was approximately 40 feet by 40 feet and although they were underground, the ceilings were vaulted. It was easy to see why.

At the center of the room, standing atop a six foot high,

rectangular marble base, was a 14 foot tall, solid gold statue of the Greek god, Apollo.

Boatwright had watched as Everhart, unaware, raised his right arm, turned his palm toward the golden idol, and spoke to it.

'Lord Apollo, son of Zeus' he'd said.

Protecter of our sacred cause which surpasses all others; Hear me, Edric, son of destiny and your most divine brother.

If, before me, have come my fathers, baring all manner of sacrifice, in other places, I pray today that you will count it unto me and grant me favor.

To this day you have delivered me from the faithlessness of my enemies. I pray you deliver me now from those who would see me the footstool of the fetid Muslim abomination.

I petition you before all the heavens and earth, to hear my supplication.

I beseech you by the thunder bolt of Zeus to bring shame upon those who seek to overtake me.

Grant me dominance over them that I might grind their bones to dust beneath my feet for the magnification of your glory.

Come now into my strength and bring with you victory.'

In witness of Boatwright's horrified expression, Guillory'd closed the door.

'You needed to know' he'd said.

For Boatwright, it had been like seeing a UFO.

Before he could say anything Guillory said,

'The only thing keeping this ship of state off the rocks is me. Fortunately for us, most people are idiots.

He's a face they know. They trust. We can't rock the boat yet. We've got to hold it together until we can unify the people behind us'.

That's when Guillory told him to remember his oath. So he did. According to Boatwright, Guillory was most desperate to keep Everhart's mental condition secret."

"That was a year ago?" Hawk asked.

"Maybe a little more" Janus replied.

"Well he's a lot worse now."

Hawk watched the signs of civilization fade away as the outlaying lights disappeared in the distance. They were traveling further into the countryside but he didn't bother to ask where they were going. Nothing he could do about it.

Eventually the environment started to look like places he'd seen in crop circle photos. Lots of tall grassy fields and not much else. When they'd traveled long enough that he was fairly certain he'd actually live, Hawk relaxed enough to ask Janus why he was sticking his neck out.

Surprisingly, Janus smiled.

"I'm not doing anything for you" he said.

What I do, I do for me.

He paused then added,

It's true you know.

You really can't judge a book by its cover."

Janus explained that he was the illegitimate issue of an affair between a Black housekeeper, and a powerful industrialist.

While he'd managed to build an upwardly mobile career, he'd had to do it without the help of his father, who'd refused to acknowledge his existence.

When he'd been pre-school age, his mother had moved them to another state. Then, when he was around six, she'd gotten sick and he'd gone into foster care. After she died, the family who adopted him raised him as White.

Years later, while researching court records, he discovered that contrary to what he'd been told, his mother hadn't died from any illness. Rather, after having sued his father for DNA tests and child support, she was subsequently found dead on her kitchen floor.

The cause of death was ruled a homicide but the case was still unsolved.

The really creepy thing to Hawk was the eerie fact that, the agent's and the President's mothers had both been murdered.

Janus knew what it felt like to have the rug pulled out and blinders stripped off. Even though he was co-intel and knew that things were seldom what they seemed, learning the truth about himself changed him. Just like Hawk, he felt he'd just been playing a role in a show he'd always believed was real life.

He decided he wasn't in favor of a system that protected men like his father and murdered people like his mother.

Janus said that he'd followed Hawk's Initiative in his counter intelligence role and that there were others who privately empathized with the Initiative.

The way he put it was,

'Blacks are passing for White in every branch, at every level, of government, industry, science and the armed forces.

We can affect the outcome of anything, at anytime, anywhere. We're hiding in plain sight. We're invisible.'

If Janus reported Hawk dead, and his superiors found out differently; Good-bye Janus.

Given the option, he'd defected.

A helicopter took them to a secluded airfield where a private plane flew the dead men to Los Angeles.

On the way Hawk learned it was Wesley who'd ratted him out.

After the leaders of the West Adams incident had been identified, White troops at the San Luis Obispo Academy revolted.

They'd surprised and shanghaied high ranking Blacks and held them hostage. Wesley was a prisoner.

Booker was still Governor, but Kellogg would use Hawk's sedition as rational for seizing California.

To prevent that from happening, Booker sent delegates to Corpus Christi to start the secession process.

———

Fort Huachuca, in Cochise County, Southeast corner of the Church of Arizona, is home base to UCC Army Network Enterprise Technology.

It's the Pacific region headquarters of the Army's Management Command. The base is commanded by Major General Mary Barnett, who's responsibilities include providing oversight for 12 garrisons in 5 different countries.

The Fort is an integral part of the Army command central nervous system. 7000 military personnel, 6000 civilian employees and 10,000 military family members called the base home. On any given work day there were up to 25,000 people living or working here.

Not only was the Fort the site of the Christland Army Intelligence Center, and the Military Auxiliary Radio System, but it also housed the original official home of the Buffalo Soldiers.

The Fort had been the training ground for Black troops when the army was segregated. In 1916 the fort was Commanded by Charles Young, the first Black to be promoted to the rank of Colonel.

Hawk was here to discuss the renovation and preservation of the first Black Officer's club in the U.S. Army.

The famous officer's club had been built from the ground up specifically for Black's. It was erected at the start of World War II and had since fallen into disrepair. As representative of the Black military historical society, Hawk was here to discuss renovation costs.

He made sure his presence wouldn't go unnoticed by notifying the National Register of Historic Places before the meeting.

Everhart wouldn't have broadcast the fact that Hawk had escaped rendition, but he'd know the second Hawk's head popped up.

Hawk was counting on it.

The Adjunct General of the California National Guard arrived precisely on time. For once his punctuality wasn't designed to discredit negative stereotypes. No sooner had he and his detail sat down, before he could properly greet the Commander and staff, the conference room doors crashed open.

35
DONKEY KONG

At gun point Hawk placed his lap top on the conference table. The tension was raised by the ringing of the Commander's phone. It was Governor Booker.

Booker told the Major General that California had seceded from the church, and Hawk was now a citizen, and Secretary of Defense, of the sovereign nation of the Democratic Socialist Republic of California. As such, Hawk wasn't subject to UCC authority.

"And who are you?" The Commander demanded.

Their king?"

The Major General promptly refused to recognize the new Nation State and ordered her police to proceed.

"Wait" Booker warned as Hawk typed on his keyboard.

Hawk directed the room's attention to a wall monitor, where a live aerial view of war ships at sea appeared.

"You're watching live streaming from a drone flying over Carrier Strike Group 5, steaming out of Tokyo Bay" Hawk explained.

The Strike Group Flagship was the Nimitz-class aircraft carrier UCCS Ronald Reagan, which also embarked Carrier Air Wing Five and its nine squadrons.

CSG 5 also included three Ticonderoga-class cruisers and Destroyer Squadron Fifteen, which was responsible for seven assigned Arleigh Burke-class destroyers.

As the only continuously forward deployed carrier strike group in the Navy, the staff maintained responsibilities over all Carrier Strike Groups, cruisers, destroyers, and frigates operating in the Seventh Fleet area.

"This drone lifted off the deck of the Reagan" Hawk announced.

"Pay close attention to Port-side aft" he said, as he tapped a command on the computer.

The camera zoomed in tight on the carrier as a puff of white smoke suddenly appeared at the ship's stern a few feet beneath the flight deck.

Debris scattered into the ocean.

The damage was insignificant but the fact that it happened at all stunned the room.

But when Hawk recited,

"From sabers to satellites"

Major General Barnett noticeably winced.

Hawk was quoting the Fort's motto. He was letting the Commander know that he had access to base satellite systems.

"We're everywhere" he said.

Turning to the MP's he ordered the Major General to,

"Tell these men I'm in command now."

Nobody moved. Hawk turned back to the C.O.

"You'll be hearing from the President any moment.

You'll need to brief him on the Fort's, my, capabilities.

He should know I can sink any ship, whether on or under the sea. I can destroy any nuclear powered, and or armed, vessel.

I can disable power grids, water supplies, telecommunications, anywhere on land or in space, and we're just getting started."

The Major General's phone rang. It was Everhart.

She put him on the monitor.

The President of the United Congregations of Christland was livid.

"Lazarus!" he boomed.

As your commander in Chief I order you to stand down."

For a moment Hawk didn't say anything. Then he stood up.

"I'm afraid you're misinformed Mister President" he said.

I don't take orders anymore.

I give them.

Twenty minutes ago 300 men emerged from the San Padre national forests and descended on Vandenberg. Insurgents inside the base threw open the gates and welcomed them in."

Everhart turned to Kellogg who glumly nodded.

"Every UCC institution across the board is compromised" Hawk declared.

Every branch, every department.

You have planes in the air, ships at sea, troops in the field, and you have no idea which is friend or foe."

Hawk cut an eye at the Major General.

"Command never saw it coming.

Hawk's intentional nonchalance served its intended purpose of rubbing Everhart's nose in it.

"It's only one base" Everhart said.

"No, no" Hawk answered softly.

He sat back down.

"You're not listening" he said. We have this base too, and if you'll hold on a minute, I'll help you understand a few more things."

"You're in over your head Sambo " Everhart yelled.

He would have gone on but Hawk interrupted him.

"You're still not listening" he said.

What are you going to do? Lock us all up?

We control the prisons. We count 2.3 million prisoners, in 2000 of your state and federal institutions among our number.

That's not even counting city jails. We've been bringing arms into facilities for weeks. I got 750,000 violent offenders, locked up across the UCC, who can't wait to do their patriotic duty.

Don't forget Black and Mexican police. State, Federal. Local. Your street cops can't trust their partners, watch commanders, lieutenants, on up. You see where I'm going?"

Hawk tapped on the keyboard again and a visual of the nuclear power plant at San Onofre, in Southern California popped up.

The plant is part of Marine Corp Base Camp Pendleton. The pixels in the monitor scrambled and when they reassembled Danny's image came into focus.

"Nice power plant you got there" he said.

Be a shame if something happened to it."

"Listen up" he said.

There're worms in the operating systems. When activated, they'll instruct the wet storage cooling systems to shut down."

Danny clicked something.

"Check it out."

Seconds later sirens went off at the reactor site.

"Figured you'd need proof" Danny said.

If the rods overheat, the radiation will blah blah blah.

The 40 thousand or so people, at and around Pendleton, will be first to go. The continuing contamination will, repeat blah times ten."

Hawk instructed Danny to shut the worm down.

"This preemptive strike is solely to ensure the safety and liberty of our citizens as we transition into our destiny" Hawk said.

It's meant to demonstrate that Blackness has metastasized throughout Whiteness. You might see it as an inoperable systemic malignancy that's impossible to root out.

Again; we're everywhere.

We don't want trouble. I implore you. Stand down."

· · ·

Everhart was under tremendous pressure. European allies, reeling from collapsing world markets, coupled with domestic unrest and failing economies, were demanding he back off his policies.

Simultaneously, major multi and transnational corporations, were suing his government for reimbursements of executive ransoms, violations of trade agreements, loss of goods and services and diminished market values.

Every night was international 'proof of life' news hour, for some abducted power broker somewhere in the world. Sabotage and piracy had interrupted sea lanes to the extent that ports worldwide were strangled with stranded cargo.

Air transports were under enormous pressure as most flights were grounded due to threats and the fact that insurance policies were impossible to buy. This time it was Hawk who said,

"This is not a drill".

You either Black out news reports about this and we go on like it never happened, or we fight it out right now.

Either way, we're done with the 2nd class human bullshit. We got nukes and nothing to lose."

"That's crazy" Everhart injected.

"Who'd know better than you" Hawk replied.

He instantly regretted it. This wasn't the time to poke the bear.

Kellogg pointed out that,

"Even if you're actually willing to destroy the planet you don't have the codes"

"Don't need em" Hawk said.

I have enough conventional weapons to bomb the nukes in their silos. At that point they become mega dirty bombs at minimum."

"That's suicide" Everhart said.

"Yes. Yes, it is."

But what happens if I surrender?

You gonna just pat me on the head and tell me not to do it again? So, damned if I do, you know.

But, you gotta ask yourself,

What happens in the aftermath Benito?"

When satellite images suddenly showed major personnel buildup at the Arizona and California borders, Kellogg's craggy voice draggled into the room.

"If those jumping beans cross over, I'm turnin' em' into refried tamales by morning" he gargled.

"No you won't" Hawk replied.

Our constitution guarantees any Hispanic who fights for the sovereignty of the Democratic Socialist Republic of California, immediate citizenship. You fire on them, it's an act of war."

"I don't give a single shit about you or your jungle constitution" Kellogg said.

Them bastards cross and I'm fuckin' them up."

"Well" Hawk sighed,

Then I guess there'll be a whole lotta fuckin' goin' on."

Hawk looked back at the MP's still training their weapons and again ordered them to stand down.

"Go on" he said.

At ease."

The Major General's tacit nod gave permission for them to obey.

"Have a seat until you're debriefed" Hawk said

then turned back to the President.

You wanted your White States, now you have them.

You win.

Leave the DSRC to our own devices and we'll leave you to yours.

Either take yes for an answer, recognize our sovereignty or call my bluff."

36
NEW AKEBU-LAN

Christlanders never knew how close they'd come to civil war. Not only had the Initiative stymied Everhart's ability to forcefully retaliate, but representatives of The Democratic Socialist Republic of California, brought suit in the Hague against the United Congregations of Christland, for human and civil rights violations.

For good measure they'd also demanded World Bank senior management positions, with voting power equal to other Western nations.

If Everhart engaged any form of aggression, he'd not only be subject to crippling U.N. and N.A.T.O. sanctions, but he yet had the invisible enemy within to contend with. Rather than immediately attack the New Nation, he decided to let things cool down before he'd make a move.

He'd suppressed news of the insurrection completely. Thereafter, as far as the world was concerned, California had experienced an unexpected, yet uneventful, secession from the Church.

. . .

The following weeks saw the dismantling of ghettos and the beginning of the prisoner exchange program.

Because the UCC didn't want The New Nation holding Whites in their prisons they were willing to deal on the issue.

What Hawk at first thought might be a prickly situation began relatively smoothly.

The White troops at San Luis Obispo were first on the list to be dealt with. Hawk agreed to a ten to one trade. For every ten Black prisoners released , he'd release a White in return.

Wesley Painter was still locked up when Hawk arrived at the Academy. He'd found him alone in a cell.

When Painter saw Hawk on the other side of the bars, he rose from the bunk and sank to his knees. Clasping his palms together he'd pleaded,

"They were going to kill me."

Seeing Painter's pitiful eyes silently beg for clemency, Hawk remembered the day they'd met.

How eager Wesley'd been back then. How different he was now.

He also knew how stupid he'd been to trust Wesley simply because he'd been Black.

As he turned to walk away he'd quietly said,

"Then you should have died."

He never saw Painter again. He knew that some traitors on both sides had been executed by their former compatriots.

He didn't give any such order concerning Painter, but he also never questioned his absence.

Aside from moving the capitol to Oakland, civilian life in California went on much as before. Citizens were simply more free to go about their business without being molested by their government.

But the economy teetered on disaster.

The UCC refused trade with the New Nation and treaties with other nations were slow to develop. The country's natural resources, sea ports and its border with Canada would keep goods moving somewhat but in order to flourish they needed much more economic activity.

To establish their enterprise they'd need to secure backing for the purposed system. The structure of said system had to meet not only their standards of viability, but also pass muster with their intended allies.

Coalition committee participants met with former Governor Booker's transition team to sort out governing bodies.

The first order of business was to create districts and regulations pertaining to commerce and representation.

Proposals were advanced to Central American governments proffering that, in exchange for economic development and educational funding, the Central American governments would repatriate their citizens and implement subsidized public programs.

After being promised small parcels of land, government assistance, and freedom from gang terrorism, many people returned home. Many did not.

In the beginning the freshly forming government of the New Nation coalition looked more like a bad TV satire than a serious attempt at administrating.

Big homies walking the administrative halls amid more conventional politicos at times suggested a carnival atmosphere.

But the veteran power brokers served as badly needed mentors and stabilizers to the sincere, if yet untried neophytes.

The few Shot Callers who represented their constituents were eventually content to allow their interests to be represented by professionals who better understood the game.

Both groups learned from the other.

The benefit was an environment of trust built by mutual necessity enhanced by better understanding.

Those military personnel who were represented would form the basis of all security commands, including Intelligence.

Their main task was to Defend the New Nation and resolve security threats. Danny would coordinate with these people.

Bureaucratic organizing was going smoothly when in the middle of staffing reviews, all hell broke loose.

Some Hispanics wanted legislative and administrative priority in the new government predicated on the premise that the New Nation consisted of lands that had initially belonged to their ancestors.

Hawk agreed, but insisted, that while it was true that the Hispanic's land had been stolen, his actual people had been stolen. And since the Hispanics already laid claim to a great deal of land mass in the hemisphere, whereas the Blacks had no land at all, the Black's should therefore have priority.

The Blacks further contended that they had built the foundations of the old nation, the fruits of which they had never been able to fully appreciate, and in the interest of fair play they should therefore have first right to the foundation of the New Nation.

In rebuttal, the Hispanics contended that they were the ones who'd built the west coast foundations and as a result they should have priority.

It was decided to table the question of district boundaries until coalitions could be solidified. Success depended on being able to knit together those factions of White, Black and Hispanics who best represented the will of the majority.

But everybody agreed that the first order of business was to settle the question of how best to exchange the prisoners who still remained in UCC hands.

Talks were also under way to recognize certain predominately Black cities located in UCC states, as dependencies. They would negotiate to free those prisoners as soon as possible, on the chance Everhart balked at the protectorate designation of cities like Atlanta.

Hawk was positioning exchange logistics when he got a text.

"We need to talk" was all it said.

37
DADDY'S HOME

Adelina hadn't known where she was going the day she'd left Camp Brown. She only knew she couldn't be around Jesse. She'd acted out her passion play but didn't see a future with him. He'd made it clear he wouldn't set aside space for her.

She couldn't stick around and she'd needed a job but she didn't want to think about politics or law at the time.

With no definite plan she'd spent a couple of months in the Los Angeles area working at an Amazon distribution center.

It surprised her that the monotony of working the line, had a calming effect.

While mindlessly shuttling boxes repeatedly back and forth, she unconsciously achieved an inner synchronization with the continuous predictable rhythms of the warehouse automation.

The constant whirring and clanking of belts and rollers was mercifully hypnotic.

But she couldn't keep her spirits up and depression was creeping in when she suddenly had to return to El Paso.

Hawk didn't want anything to do with Adelina.

He couldn't believe she'd contacted him.

He didn't want to see her. But he knew he would.

She was even more beautiful than he remembered.

From day one she'd drawn him in like a black hole and seeing her again made him realize that nothing had changed. He hated himself.

The apartment was a fair size.

He figured it was at least four bedrooms.

She'd done alright by carrying Carlsen's water.

Not a word had escaped her lips since she'd let him in.

She'd only mildly tasered him with her amber torchlights before quickly glancing away. He sat on the couch and waited.

He wasn't going to ask questions. She was going to explain everything and he was going to decide whether or not he'd go along with whatever she said.

A rustling in the kitchen caught his ear and before he could ask Adelina answered, "My mother."

He crossed his legs and continued to wait.

He could see she was nervous and it gave him an odd sense of satisfaction.

In response to Hawk's silence Adelina offered that she was waiting for her mother to be out of earshot before she spoke.

"Not that any of what I'm going to say is a secret to her."

Hawk saw a woman disappear down the hall before hearing a door close.

"Can I get you something?" Adelina asked.

The impatience in Hawk's body language told her she'd best get on with it.

"Okay, listen" she began.

I know you think you know things but you don't."

The sound of crying wafted into the room. Adelina's attention shifted.

"Hold on a second she said.

I'll be right back."

As she hurried out of the room she didn't notice Hawk following.

When she entered a bedroom at the end of the hall and turned to close the door, Hawk stepped in the room.

The woman he'd seen earlier was seated on a bed and holding a toddler. Her black and silver hair framed indomitable eyes that held him in place.

A wiry man in his late fifties sat stiffly in a chair by an open window. His sober gaze registered cautious reservation in his examination of Hawk.

Hawk sensed he'd made his entrance ahead of cue.

Adelina pointed in the direction of the woman.

"This is my mother, Marta de La Cruz" she said.

As Hawk nodded he realized that the guy must be,

"My father" Adelina confirmed. Mauricio de la Cruz. Mauricio stood up and extended his hand. The moment Hawk reached out he heard Adelina say,

"And I'd like to introduce you to your daughter".

38
CHANGE GONE COME

The flight from El Paso to New Akebu-Lan (Los Angeles), hadn't allowed Hawk nearly enough time to digest all that he'd learned in the last 24 hours.

Adelina had never been a Carlsen plant and she'd slapped him when he'd inferred that there'd been a nefarious arrangement between them.

"I didn't have allegiance to him" she'd said.

He had allegiance to me."

She told Hawk of Carlsen's time as Warden of Otero and the day prisoners took over one of the dormitories.

They were threatening to overrun the B.I.O.N.I.C. social programs building when the sirens went off.

The riot had been a distraction.

Three tailor shop trustees, had copied guard uniforms and planned to escape inside a Snap on tools truck during the confusion.

But the truck never showed up. There was no plan B.

The convicts were regrouping outside the administration

building when a squad of real guards suddenly burst through the doors.

Warden Carlsen was behind them shouting directives.

The cons were watching the real squad double time toward the dorm when Carlsen spotted them.

Believing they were real guards he'd yelled,

'What the hell are you doing? Get after it.'

Carlsen was a big man and it had taken all three of them to wrestle him down.

Mauricio had been the trustee on trash duty in the administration building when he'd heard the Klaxons. He didn't know why they'd sounded but he knew it wasn't good. He was in Carlsen's office when a ruckus erupted in the hallway. Carlsen was shouting how something wasn't going to work.

The last thing Mauricio wanted was to be caught up in some riot bullshit. When he'd heard Carlsen yelling about state police, he'd wanted to hide but there was nowhere to go.

The voices grew louder.

Carlsen was definitely coming his way.

If it hadn't been for the powerful people involved, nobody would've ever heard about Mauricio's case. But because his trial had been on TV he'd become a minor jailhouse celebrity.

When they'd opened the office door the counterfeit guards recognized him right away.

Mauricio didn't know what their plan was, but he figured they didn't stand a snowball's chance.

More voices alerted everybody that other convicts had found their way to the building. No telling what would happen to Carlsen if they got hold of him.

Thoughts of Attica sprang to mind.

The fake guards pushed past Mauricio and closed the office door. They forced Carlsen to his desk and one of the men picked up a paperweight. He threatened to smash Carlsen's head in if he didn't get them out of here.

Before Mauricio realized it, he'd wedged himself between hostage and captors.

"You can't hurt this man. It's suicide" he said.

Desperation was the room's common denominator.

One of the convicts grabbed Mauricio by the neck. Mauricio fought back and Carlsen tumbled to the floor.

Scrambling quickly, Carlsen reached into his desk drawer and retrieved a gun.

One of the convicts nodded in the direction of the outside voices.

"You can't shoot us all" he said.

Another fake cop opened the door and yelled,

"Over here."

Footsteps immediately Dopplered toward the office.

Carlsen grabbed Mauricio and pressed the gun barrel to his head. He'd threatened to kill him unless the cons backed up.

"Kill him, the one con said. We don't care."

Carlsen leveled the pistol at the con doing the talking.

"Just you then" he said and fired two shots past his ear.

They backed out.

Carlsen slammed the door and pushed the desk against it.

Only luck and the timely arrival of State troopers kept the mob from reconsidering.

When order was eventually restored, Carlsen personally vouched for Mauricio to state investigators. Later, Mauricio was rewarded with a steward of trustees position.

But while his daily conditions improved, his family was having hard times. That's when Carlsen recommended Adelina to the bureau.

After leaving Amazon she'd been living in a small apartment with Marta when out of the blue Carlsen called. He'd offered her an executive assistant position with a huge advance bonus.

She hadn't asked any questions. It had been the answer to prayer. It was a great deal of money for temporary service.

That day in London she'd been as stunned to see Jesse as he'd been to see her. The awkwardness of their last meeting had made it hard for her to know what to say.

When she'd heard about his arrest she'd quit the position and gone home.

She couldn't put her finger on it but she felt she'd been used as some kind of false flag. At the time she'd been furious, but when Mauricio showed up at her door her anger evaporated.

But there'd been no grand conspiracy. Carlsen didn't know anything about her and Hawk's relationship.

When he'd learned he had an inoperable brain tumor Carlsen felt the sudden need for penance.

He'd been the unjust arbitrator of men's fates for decades. Maybe he couldn't make up for all the shit he'd done but it couldn't hurt to try.

Adelina's MTCNovo assignment had been an alms.

Alzo Kronos had been Everhart's cohort in subterfuge not Carlsen. Given the current circumstances Carlsen had seen the writing on the wall and set Mauricio free of his own accord.

Who would challenge him? Who would even care?

Prisoner exchange was the order of the day. There just hadn't been any exchange.

39
SAY IT LOUD

Adelina wanted to work together again.

She made the argument that they'd been a good team and because of recent experiences, she was most suitable to serve in the new justice department.

She explained why she'd left and now that she understood why he'd behaved as he had, she saw no reason why they couldn't pick up where they'd left off.

'Was she a spy?' Hawk wondered.

Despite everything she'd told him, he couldn't help suspecting the worse.

She'd named the baby, Jessica de la Cruz Hawkins.

It was his kid alright. He'd known it as soon as she'd smiled at him with his mother's eyes. But that didn't mean Adelina wasn't using the kid to get close to him for Carlsen's or somebody else's sake.

Was Mauricio even Mauricio? The experiences of recent years had taught him one thing for sure. Anything could happen.

Maybe he thought it best to keep his enemies close, or maybe he just wanted to believe her.

The turn of events served to crystallize Hawk's focus.

He hadn't been back in New Akebu-Lan a week before emissaries were dispatched to African and Hispanic language countries to solicit funding for the treasury.

The goal was to create a currency, based not only on gold, but on all the resources of participating non-white nations.

New Nation district borders were outlined and articles of the constitution started taking shape. A Justice system based on Mayan, ancient Egyptian and a diluted Hammurabi's code of ethics was adopted.

The judicial system was divided into family courts, commercial courts and major criminal courts.

Minor offenses were left to community courts that were overseen by elected neighborhood panels. Defendants represented themselves. Lawyers were only allowed in international and major criminal cases.

Except in extreme cases, all inmates incarcerated by the old administration were released.

A Period of time was set aside for anyone who wanted to leave the New Nation to do so.

Many Whites sold everything and left. Not unexpectedly, some staunch conservative Black Christians wanted to live in the UCC. They claimed it was the only nation suitable for true believers. The UCC refused to accept them.

Except for violent crimes, most convicted offenders were electronically monitored and confined to their own homes. Their needs were seen to entirely by friends and family.

If there was no family, offenders were placed in special community administered public housing. Inmates were exclusively responsible for the upkeep of both themselves and their surroundings.

Sentences would sometimes be followed by a period of community shunning. During this practice no community member was to acknowledge an offender's presence for a specified period of time.

The death penalty was not generally in effect but in certain instances it was allowed; provided a member of the offended family personally carried out the execution. Repeat offenders were subject to banishment by having their citizenship revoked.

Neutral zones, comprised of non-profit land trusts for the purpose of conservation, were also established.

Military courts remained under the uniform code of military justice. Compromises were made regarding military administration.

Outside of New Nation borders, all parties agreed to an uneasy alliance concerning nuclear, space and foreign intel matters. Since Initiative operatives were already embedded in most UCC departments, and Kellogg had no way of immediately determining who or where they were, he'd reluctantly agreed to terms. No-one expected it to last.

But while circumstances were looking up in the DSRC, it wasn't the case in the UCC.

Growing division among Christlanders had resulted in the formation of factions. The church had been united in its fight for White supremacy, but with The Black and Mexican question settled, differences among church members began to emerge.

40

SANTA CLAUS AND
EASTER EGGS

The conservative Christlanders, consisting of Catholics, Southern Baptists and the like, threatened to take control of the government.

The congregations of the more liberal Pentecostals, Unitarians and their ilk, felt they'd be cut out of representation.

If events continued in the direction they were headed, Guillory, would rise higher in authority than even Everhart himself.

Guillory also enjoyed the fierce loyalty of the Keepers, all of which made Everhart reconsider his path forward.

———

Although they were used to Everhart's eccentric behavior, his cabinet sensed they were about to experience something new.

It was customary for the President to have a manic reaction to certain situations, but lately he'd been unusually subdued. After the New Nation's withdrawal, there'd been a sense that he'd need to be restrained.

But no such moment ever arose.

Today he calmly leaned back in his chair, looked out over the bays and announced,

"We're moving forward with a new approach.

I'm going to do something that hasn't been tried in a while. I'm going to level with them."

He went on to propose simultaneously addressing the entire church Live, via satellite.

All other programming would be canceled and at the appointed time, he'd beam in on the entire congregation.

At the appointed time, after introduction by the Deacon of Corpus Christi, he didn't bother with introductory platitudes, but went straight to his point.

The Church harvest rots in the fields all over Iowa, Louisiana, Florida, Kentucky and everywhere else" he began.

"Texas oil stays in the ground because we don't have enough workers to get it out. The pipelines and tankers are dry, because our trading partners offer us third world prices.

Meanwhile, Atlanta, Detroit, Chicago, New York are humming along like the well oiled machines they are.

How do we compete with that? I'll tell you how.

We don't.

We eliminate the competition.

Always remember, that the aforementioned cities are located within the sacred borders of the holy UCC.

The resources used to bring their products to market; From the raw materials, to the roads, rails and bridges they use, are paid for by your tithes. Those profits belong to you. I'm speaking to the inhabitants of the aforementioned cities when I say; These resources shall be redeemed."

Everhart paused to offer a stern profile to the camera before he continued.

"The question is;

How did we get here?"

He reversed profiles.

"I'll tell you how.

Religion.

You heard me.

I didn't say God.

I said religion."

He turned full face to the camera. His bearing became less authoritarian and more professorial.

"Most of us inherited our religion" he said.

It was passed down to us.

Like our names and granddaddy's ears. We are whatever our parents were. They were Baptists so we got baptized and so on.

That's what we believe, but that's not the truth.

The truth is we didn't inherit our religion.

It was taught to us. The same as any other subject is taught. That's why we call it Sunday school.

We learned parables and allegories that convinced us of the righteousness of good and the perils of evil. But the real lesson was, 'indoctrination plus submission equals salvation.'

We were taught that we serve the one and only true God. Obey him and good things will happen.

Turn on Him and bad things will follow.

The reason you're mad is because you played by the rules. You worked hard, you told the truth, you were kind and generous. And you did those things because you believed that if you did them you'd be rewarded. You were good and life was supposed to be good in return.

But as you got older and experienced the real world, you learned a different lesson. You learned that the people you encountered everyday didn't play by the same rules you did. Didn't matter how generous or loyal you were. They took your kindness for weakness and kept asking for more.

No one has been more guilty of this than the church.

After having faithfully delivered your first fruits to the workmen, you now see your own store houses empty. Now you can plainly see how the institutions that offered you Santa Claus and Easter eggs in return for your faithfulness, have been playing you for suckers.

Yes, I'm guilty too. I admit it.

In my defense I can only say that I was fooled just like you were. I taught you the same lessons that I was taught.

I learned as a child, brought up in the church like a lot of you.

But we're not children anymore."

At this point Everhart's professorial tone started to fade, giving rise to more passionate chords.

"The socialists have weaponized your faithfulness against you. They know you've been taught to turn the other cheek. They know you were taught, that in order to lead, you must first be a servant.

So after you took on the responsibility of managing the affairs of the colored people. Teaching them to read, giving them jobs and the opportunity to live in a civilized society, what did they do?

Instead of being grateful, they took your goodwill and turned it against you.

Today, while their industries prosper, you've become the slave and they've become the masters.

What shall you now believe?

Will you continue after promises of pie in the sky by and by, or will you trust in what life is showing you in the here and now?

There is no pie in the sky. This is the sky. This is the pie.

But to enjoy it you have to be willing to die to the old ways and rise again with me in the dawning of the true light.

There's no time left. Let every beating heart out there know and understand;

The end of White rule on earth is not coming.

It's here.

As members of the Greater Church of the United Congregations of Christ, you enjoy a prime seat at the table. Your seat is important. As citizen believers of this great congregation, you enjoy one of the highest standards of living ever achieved by any empire in the history of the world.

Now suddenly, after we've done all the heavy lifting, all the dying and innovating to establish this economy, this continent; these ungrateful, ill advised socialists have come along to lay claim to it."

He'd arrived at the moment. Now he'd go in for the kill.

"Make no mistake; If we don't stop them now we'll never get another chance. Their numbers and treasuries increase by the hour.

But with your support I can solve the situation. It will take strong medicine and once I administer it you will need to withstand the worst criticisms. But let whomever say what they will. They will thank us in the end.

We know there are spies among us, but let any who disagree remember this.

If the heathens get the upper hand, everything we did to them, they're going to do to you.

If you're not with us, you're against us.

There are many Whites living and working in the cities I've mentioned. My advice to them is to leave now.

But if you stay, don't forget;

We will not forgive those who trespass against us.

There is nothing to withstand the wrath of God."

Later, when asked if he was threatening to nationalize non-White industries, Everhart had no comment.

But Everhart had no intention of nationalizing anything. He wasn't interested in Detroit or Atlanta. As far as he was concerned he already had those places.

His gambit depended on the success of Operation Seventh Seal.

His negotiating tool was a crew of Keepers currently manning a Yasen Class, Soviet era attack submarine in the North Pacific.

To evade deep sea sonar sensors, the craft was submerged to a depth of a mere 100 feet. Sitting just beneath the surface, situated between the Hawaiian islands and the California coast, the fully operational warship awaited orders.

He didn't need an entire fleet in order to obtain his objective.

A single sub would suffice for the purpose at hand.

Provided it was the right sub.

Kellogg had Ukrainian operatives buy the sub on the Russian black market. He'd paid several million more than the asking price in order to insure its delivery.

Once the Ukrainians handed over the sub they'd all been murdered. Kellogg believed submarines worked best when they were leak proof.

He'd outfitted the silos to accommodate eight Trident MK5 ballistic missiles and armed them with 10 megaton warheads.

Since one megaton could destroy 4 square miles, 10 would be enough to neutralize major infrastructure while also providing a strident deterrent to resistance.

There would also be enough environment remaining in the aftermath to ensure rebuilding.

With a range of over 3000 miles, the MK5 missiles could easily hit any major city in the New Nation. The missiles could reach their targets in less than 20 minutes. There'd be no time to respond. The sub had the ability to stay submerged for more than 3 months. That was more than enough time for Everhart to put the remainder of his plan into effect.

41
SHEPARD TO THE WOLF

Now that Guillory had taken over the duties of Secretary of the Vatican, Everhart sought to control the office of Superior General of the Society of Jesus.

With Guillory's help there was no reason he couldn't pull it off.

"You have to be Catholic" Boatwright explained as to why Everhart couldn't hold the office.

"Sounds do-able" Everhart replied.

How do we make that happen?"

Boatwright, always the Jesuit, held true to his oath. Until his superiors told him otherwise, he'd do Everhart's bidding.

"You could simply be baptized" he said.

The baptismal certificate will suffice for the purpose. I'm sure allowances can be made under the circumstances, to forego any novitiate period."

Everhart didn't like Boatwright but he had no reason to distrust him. Guillory had never mentioned any crisis of confidence concerning his prodigy. If he was good with Guillory then he was alright. Besides, Everhart could only enlist the aid of his most trusted inner circle to accomplish his ultimate goal. To that end he'd win Boatwright's confidence through favoritism.

He'd promised to make Boatwright Father Provincial over the western congregations as well as install him as Director of the Conservative Christian Party. To lead the party would be an indication of his heir apparent-ship. Implicit in the agreement was Boatwright's future cooperation with Everhart's agenda.

With the regular military compromised, Everhart had no genuine security. So long as the Keepers remained loyal to Guillory, he was at risk. But when the time came, Everhart would remind the highly disciplined Keepers, that they'd sworn an oath to an office, not to a man.

Despite the silent ridicule concerning his transcendental experiences, Everhart had one revelation that couldn't be denied.

He'd come the realization that the world he aspired to was already in effect. The public name was the Universal Church of the Earth. It was none other than the Holy Roman Empire. Guillory had been right all along. He already had everything he needed if he could control it.

Having dispensed with the task of baptism, Everhart next instructed Guillory to initiate protocol for the induction of the Superior General oath of office ceremonies. For that they'd need to go to Rome.

———

The chapel was smaller than he'd expected. In the dim candle lit interior Everhart could barely make out the figures of the three other men present.

Guillory stood before an alter, his face covered by the hood of a floor length robe.

At either of his sides stood a similarly attired monk.

One of the monks held a banner of yellow and white, representing the papal colors. The other held a black banner. The black banner bore a dagger and red cross in the lower corners. Between was a skull and cross bones with the word I.N.R.I.centered above.

Below the skull were written the words.

IUSTUM NECAR REGES IMPIUS.

It is just to annihilate impious Kings, Governments, Rulers.

Everhart was directed to kneel before a Red Cross inlaid on the chapel floor. Guillory then handed him a small black crucifix.

Everhart took the crucifix in his left hand and pressed it to his heart.

At the same time Guillory presented him with a dagger which he took by the blade. He held the point next to the crucifix. Guillory held the hilt.

Therewith, he was instructed in the oath of office which shall not be repeated here.

Suffice it to say that at the oath's conclusion, Everhart had pledged unfailing fealty, to spare neither age, sex, or condition, from burning, hanging, boiling and worse, in obedience to The Bishop of Rome.

The fact that he was in no way at cross purposes with the oath only strengthened Everhart's resolve.

Time was of the essence. It was unusual for a Jesuit to seek higher office in the church. There'd only been one Jesuit Pope in church history.

Pope Francis 1, had been exceptional because the Jesuits were the only order that took an oath of obedience directly to the Vicar of Christ. Therefore a Jesuit Pope would technically report to himself.

'Exactly' Everhart thought.

He needed to move quickly. For the moment the UCC president would simultaneously perform the duties of leader of free world and Father General of the Society of Jesus.

While a whirlwind of protest swirled among world governments concerning Everhart's motives, it was all meaningless.

There was only one man who could withstand him.

For his part, Pope John did what Popes do. He waited. As for now he'd doubled the guard. Otherwise he slept as soundly as ever, because he understood something Everhart didn't. He wasn't only Shepard to the sheep. He was also Shepard to the wolf.

42

YE OF LITTLE FAITH

Of course it's possible" Everhart declared.

Seems like yesterday the Bulgarians damn near pulled it off.

John Paul 1 lasted what? A month?

We've been killing Pope's since first there ever was a church."

Anchored in the eastern Caribbean sea, off the shore of Saint Croix, Everhart regaled his cabinet from the owner's deck of the Super-yacht, Faith.

Kellogg readily added his support.

"Popes?" He said.

Hell, Rome killed the founder.

And Saint Peter too for Christ's sake."

Guillory rolled his minds's eye.

But General Yogi had a point. Guillory understood Kellogg's motivations. He considered the Security Czar's assessment of the situation upon hearing Everhart declare,

"I command the mightiest armies ever to garrison the earth. Not only do I control thousands of nukes, but I'm able, through emissaries, to manipulate the levers of power anywhere in the world."

The gravity of the General's visage exposed his wariness.

Kellogg's influence had waned precipitously since the success of the secession. His loyalty had never been questioned but now that Everhart was Father General and controlled the Keepers, his relevancy might be.

From Kellogg's point of view there was no chance for a military coup. Officers, rank and file, everybody was too divided to be trusted. Kellogg figured his best option had been to keep his head down until he found the most convenient way to plausibly deny killing Everhart.

For now he needed to remain in Everhart's good graces. The opportunity to serve suddenly presented itself when Everhart mused.

"Who will rid me of this meddlesome priest?"

Boatwright was embarrassed by how quickly Kellogg responded.

The speed with which he'd come forward shrieked of desperation. Boatwright saved him.

"This is not a matter for the military" he said.

Concerning affairs of this nature, we have our own way of proceeding."

Everhart agreed. This was what he'd been grooming Boatwright for. With Guillory as Secretary and himself as Father General, he'd eventually control the Vatican. He turned to Kellogg.

"They say I'm crazy" he smiled.

The General's guts wrenched. He didn't know whether to be grieved or relieved when Everhart suggested,

"If I were you, I'd consider baptism."

During the course of the evening Everhart noticed that although the newly selected Secretary hadn't indicated opposition to his plans, he also hadn't shown more than obligatory support.

After the others had retired to their state rooms, Everhart summoned Guillory back to the deck. He'd changed from his custom tailored Seville row suit, into the white robes.

Looking over the rippling moonlit waves, Everhart pointed starboard to a tiny island.

"See that reef?"

Back in the mid 1700's a Dane by the name of Diedrich, established a slave colony there. The place used to be covered with trees. The slaves cut them all down for export. It's called Buck island.

Truth be told, you could call the whole of the Caribbean, Buck island.

The French have their Polynesians and we have our bucks. The UCC Virgin Islands, the Marianas, Guam, Puerto Rico, the whole lot.

He paused for a moment before seemingly changing the subject.

I thought we'd have a little talk before you returned to the Vatican. Are you aware that the Blacks out west are all over social media, printing and distributing various depictions of Jesus as a Black man?"

Guillory braced against his chair.

"I know all about it".

"Then you know why they're doing it."

"Obviously to break the confidence of the congregation by insinuating that they're worshipping a Black man".

"That's right and who the hell cares if they are.

I know I don't.

My only concern is that I represent whoever they end up worshipping.

But here's the important part. The Black Jesus thing is catching on. The good part is that they still believe in Jesus at all.

Imagine they start looking for salvation in themselves. There's billions of them. That's when it's our turn in the barrel. That's when *we* end up on Buck island.

I'm not going to let that happen so pay attention.

Recently, for the first time since its inception, the Catholic church elected a non-European Pope.

How did that happen?"

Guillory didn't hear the question as rhetorical and kept silent as Everhart continued.

At the end of the 2nd world war, every Nazi who could, found his way to Argentina.

They were able to thrive there. They were safe there. They were protected. Some say by emissaries of the church.

Whether or not stolen Nazi gold made its way into Vatican coffers as quid pro quo for this harboring is of no matter to me.

Perhaps it's mere coincidence that this non-European Pontiff who had previously been head of the Argentine Jesuits, ascended the Papal throne. If so, then so. I Don't care.

My only concern is that the next Sovereign of the State of Vatican City, be me.

Tilting the snifter slightly, Everhart poured his favorite cognac.

I hear rumors, he said.

Is it true that the Jesuits adhere to a specific code of instruction, written in a document called the Monita Secreta?"

The question startled Guillory. As was referenced in its title, the book was a secret. Everhart hadn't been steeped even in rudimentary Catholicism, let alone arcane matters like the Monita Secreta. How did he know about such things?

Guillory had to be careful. He didn't know if Everhart was asking based on scuttlebutt or if he had actually read the text in question.

"I assume you mean the instructions concerning securing wealth by any means necessary" he said.

Everhart held the Remy under his nose and inhaled slowly.

"Yes, that's it" he answered.

The doctrine that affirms every treachery so long as the result brings wealth to the order."

"I assure you, guillory insisted. I have no personal knowledge of any such book. I've never seen or read it. As far as I know there is no such document or doctrine. It's a vicious lie meant to discredit the Order."

"Of course it is" Everhart murmured.

If it were true, that would put you in the service of Mammon, and you can't serve two masters can you?"

Guillory struggled to keep his tone measured.

Even though he outranked Everhart in church hierarchy

He knew his place as between the two of them.

"Surely you've no doubt of my fealty Edric."

Everhart leaned over Guillory's shoulder and set a balloon glass of cognac on the table in front of him.

"No Secretary Guillory" he answered cordially.

I have no doubt what-so-ever of your loyalties."

If Guillory had been only a bit more enthusiastic Everhart may have changed his mind. The Secretary had been given a chance to reaffirm his allegiance and he'd come up short.

When Guillory reached for the cognac, Everhart stepped behind his chair and produced a thin braided cord from inside his robes. Before Guillory could raise the glass, Everhart coiled the cord around his neck.

"I know about the crypto-currency in cold storage" he said.

Wrenching the cord tighter while bending closer to Guillory's ear, he whispered.

"I the Lord thy God am a jealous God, thou shall have no other Gods before me. I am the Alpha and the Omega, the Jasper and the Sardis stone, the first and the last."

Guillory's eyes bulged and his tongue protruded between his lips. His soft hands were no deterrent to the garrote cutting into his throat. Soon enough his body went limp and slumped backward in the chair. Everhart placed his hand on Guillory's mouth and spoke aloud as though he were the dead man.

"And he touched my mouth and said:

Behold, this has touched your lips; your guilt is taken away, and your sin atoned for."

Everhart's assurances of his becoming the future Carmerlengo secured Kellogg's cooperation.

Assistant to the Pope was a cherry job, if it ever materialized. But what choice did he really have? He'd created a monster and it was out of control. There had to be others who wanted him dead too but they were all scared to act.

With Guillory dead, Kellogg feared he'd be next. Until he could figure his way out, he was in. While the others slept, he'd chummed the waters around the yacht and silently lowered Guillory's body into the sea. The Caribbean reef sharks did the rest.

43
GO TIME

The untimely death of the Secretary of the Vatican was officially deemed an accident. The press reported the event as;

'While walking alone on the deck of the Faith, Secretary Guillory apparently lost his footing and fell overboard.'

The exact time of the incident was undetermined.

Jody Nugent loaded the last of the equipment into the back of the dilapidated station wagon and started up the access road. He'd take Mustang Island's highway 361 to its intersection with the JFK Causeway and hope for the best.

It had taken Hawk almost a week to find him and time was in short supply. They'd had to work up a plan in a hurry and worst of all, it was impossible to do a trial run.

"You got the altimeter" Jody asked.

Hawk stuck out his left arm displaying the instrument attached to his wrist. They'd gone over everything a million times but they couldn't afford to miss anything.

Hawk checked the device fastened around his other wrist. The small magnetized metal box appeared deceptively non-threatening.

Danny sat silently in the faded vinyl back seat rapping his fingers over the closed lid of his laptop. Everything depended on what happened next.

Jody pulled a map from over the visor and indicated the Naval Air Station runway the President's plane would use.

"They'll fly right to you but you have to be in the air before they take off."

"Let's just hope they leave on time" Hawk said.

"You'll need to get close enough to see inside" Jodi said.

There was more resolve than confidence in Hawk's response.

"I know" he said.

"Okay. Let's go over it again" Jody prompted.

How much flight time do you have?"

"At full power, counting both craft, 12 minutes. Less power, more time. 16 minutes max."

"What's your first move?"

"Launch from the bridge at 08:58 hours.

Ascend to four thousand cherubs."

"Alright, four minutes pass, it's 09:02 hours and he's at your nine at 2000 cherubs, ascending at 200 mph, what's your next move?"

"At that point I start descending.

When he's vectored into the wind, I switch to the jet pack."

"What's your altitude now"?

"Roughly 3500 angels."

"How much jet battery time do you have left"?

"Less than three minutes."

"Okay, he's banking and climbing. What are you doing"?

"I'm dropping in, diving, picking up speed, coming down on the left, ahead of the wing."

"Alright, you're there. What?"

"I trigger the box and peel off."

"Stay out of the wash".

"I'll keep it in mind."

"And if the Naval Station deploys escorts?"

"Radar's never gonna pick me up,

but even if they Alert 5, I'll be out of the sky before they can get off the ground or turn around."

They continued driving toward the bridge at Red Dot Pier, a fishing enclave only a couple of miles southeast of Naval Air Station Corpus Christi.

The Air Station itself was just on the other side of Oso Bay within a mile of Ward Island. Its close proximity to New Jerusalem made it the ideal Presidential departure point.

At 09:00 hours Air Force one was scheduled to take off from there.

Hawk had gotten the call two weeks before. The voice said not to talk but to listen carefully.

In order to install himself as international spiritual strongman, Everhart planned to simultaneously assassinate the Pope and nuke major New Nation cities.

The caller didn't identify himself but Hawk knew who it was.

The Pope would be killed and the uproar would be buried by news of the missile attacks.

Everhart was leaving for Avignon, to attend a memorial service for Guillory. He intended to set his operation in motion when he landed.

Traffic was heavy and Hawk asked Jody to speed up.

Danny wanted to know if Hawk was scared.

"Too late for that" Hawk answered.

Danny checked the time. It was later than he'd thought. They had to launch in the next minute or risk missing their window.

As soon as the bridge's girders came in sight Jody started the station wagon's flashers going. He slowed down and Hawk reached over the seat and grabbed the fiber carbon jet rig.

"You sure the board can handle the extra jet pack weight?" Danny asked.

"We'll know in a minute" Hawk answered as they skidded to a stop.

Hawk pulled on his helmet, opened the door and got out. He strapped on the jet harness as Jody put the car in park and slid out behind him.

Horns blared as the traffic stacked up. After checking the ultra-lite jet wings Hawk climbed on the side of the bridge.

Jody set the Fly Board Air on a girder and snapped the kerosene fuel pack into Hawk's chest plate.

"See you in North Beach" Hawk called as he fired up the turbos and lifted off the bridge.

Jody slid back in the station wagon and gunned it.

The commuters who'd witnessed the scene weren't entirely sure what had just happened.

Hawk continued to ascend while Jody headed to the popular tourist area of North Beach.

If things went well they'd meet there in a few minutes. If not, his thoughts trailed off.

Ascending as fast as he could, Hawk checked the altimeter. He didn't have a lot of options if Air Force One didn't follow the preconceived scenario.

He'd been in the air a couple of minutes scanning the skies but didn't see the airliner. He wondered if his coordinates were off as he went into hover mode. The thin air made it necessary to keep the turbos at maximum RPMs. He couldn't wait too long. The chest tank was emptying fast.

Jody drove purposely down U.S. highway 17 on his way to the 181. He spoke to his cell phone.

"Siri call 'Sky'" he said.

'Calling Sky' the phone replied.

A second later he asked,

"Can you hear me?"

"Affirmative" Hawk answered through the mic in his helmet.

"Do you see him"?

"Negative."

"How much gas you got"?

"Not much."

"Engage the jet pack".

"Too soon."

"Gotta jettison the board" Jody insisted.

"Too soon."

"We talked about this. You see him yet"?

"No."

"I'm pushing the button."

"Wait" Hawk pleaded.

Jody nodded to Danny who pressed a key on the laptop. The kerosene chest tank disconnected from Hawk's breast plate and tumbled toward the bay. The turbos shut down.

"Shit" Hawk huffed as he dumped the Fly Board, laid out horizontally and formed up to fly.

'I'm counting on you jet-pack' he thought as he throttled up. The jets had more than three times the power of the board but he adapted immediately.

He didn't want to take it up to speed and risk running out of power but he had no choice. He had to be at the right speed at the right time.

He'd crossed the Rubicon. From here on it was all a leap of faith.

With still no target in sight Hawk started to worry.

What if the power runs out before I get a shot?

What if there'd been a delay in the departure?

Seconds ticked by.

He was contemplating the real possibility of failure when he saw it.

A thousand feet below on his nine, Air Force One came into view.

If ever a man was born for a moment, it was him for this one.

A common theme ran through his life.

Whenever the issue called for immediate decisive action,

he automatically went to a place that didn't require thought. It wasn't a place of decisions, it was a place of happenings.

At times like these he seemed to be outside of himself, like he'd been wound up and set loose by some unseen hand.

As soon as the plane started banking into the wind Hawk angled to come in above and behind it.

He opened the throttle all the way.

With an assist from the dive he reached a top speed of 217 knots.

As the plane banked and gained altitude, Hawk dropped in and dived alongside the left wing.

Releasing the compressed gas propelled metal box, he instantly twisted into an inverted dive and soared down and away from the banking aircraft.

The box attached itself to the fuselage just below the window line when the jet pack suddenly lost power.

Hawk tucked into a ball and released the harness. Watching the jet pack fall away he counted on the wing suit he still wore to see him the rest of the way to North Beach.

Among the passengers on the plane, only Boatwright knew what was about to happen. He crossed himself and gazed out the window while Everhart and Kellogg yukked it up in the Cathedral lounge.

The metal box that attached itself to the fuselage contained a small explosive charge. Once it discharged it would create a hole just large enough to depressurize the cabin.

The bomb itself was programed to react to outside air pressure. When the pressure dropped to less than 4.0 psi the bomb would trigger. Boatwright knew that wouldn't happen until they reached 35,000 feet. They'd be well over the Gulf of Mexico by then.

Carter closed his eyes and reclined. As he considered the events that had led to this moment he found himself thinking, 'Those whom the gods would destroy.'

What Everhart had never understood; What he'd never considered, was that Carter Boatwright wasn't a Christlander. He wasn't a Republican or anything similar.

Carter Boatwright was a Jesuit. That's all he was.

And as such he'd remained true to his oath.

To be all things to all men.

To be a spy, even among his own brethren.

To sink so low as to be a Jew among Jews,

even going so far as to become a willing corpse in the service of his Pope.

As Air Force One headed southeast over the gulf, Hawk vectored north looking for his landmark.

For every three feet traveled forward, he descended one foot. He wasn't sure exactly how far away his target was.

The UCC Lexington aircraft carrier was anchored at North Beach. The carrier wasn't active anymore. It was now a museum moored just off highway 181. If he could find it, he wouldn't land on it but he'd land near it.

When he'd gotten down to less than a thousand feet he saw it.

As he approached the rendezvous point he ripped the cord and hoped his luck would hold.

These waters were full of jelly fish.

44
DEN YOU MAY

Operation Seventh Seal never happened.

Pope Edric never happened. But they could have.

Hawk realized every day that somewhere, somebody, was formulating machinations designed to advance their own world position to the detriment of his.

His job was to make sure they failed.

But most importantly he meant to ensure that the principles espoused in the New Nation's constitution would survive the human condition.

It wasn't his ambition to create a legacy of succession. Dennis had been right, he didn't want to always have to win. He'd remain in a position of leadership until such time as he felt he could safely transfer power to the people's choice. What he'd do after that remained to be seen.

Given the circumstances of Guillory's death, it was super-ironic that the demise of the President, along with his senior cabinet, would also be reported as a freak accident.

Their deaths were attributed to hypoxia, a condition resulting from the lack of oxygen in body tissues.

As the story went,

'The jumbo jet's air filtration system had malfunctioned, causing the oxygen supply to shut down.

The loss of oxygen had caused the pilots to lose consciousness and fly the plane into the Gulf.

Because there is no pain or discomfort associated with hypoxia, its onset would have gone unnoticed.'

There was no mention of any explosion.

————

The continuity of the UCC government went into flux because the church charter had no articles addressing the chain of succession.

In an attempt to show unity, Nell Everhart, who hadn't been seen publicly in years, made a satellite appearance alongside the UCC Vice President to plead for peace between UCC factions and the DSRC.

————

Leaning on the railing of the wraparound porch, Dennis surveyed the landscape of his 300 acre almond farm.

He watched as the massive crop conditioner machines traveled through rows of trees, clearing and collecting sticks and stones ahead of the tree shakers and harvester equipment that followed.

His product was in high demand with almond milk producers who had no compunction about buying from him despite UCC tariffs.

He stood in the shade of the porch, shielding himself from the hot Fresno sun and let out a heavy sigh.

He'd done all he could to give himself permission to keep living. But no matter how well things went, there were always times when he'd slide into melancholy.

This was one of those times. It wouldn't last long. He'd shake it off but he knew it would come back.

Long days of hard work generally kept his mind occupied and despite everything he'd built a successful business. But although he had plenty material things, nothing would ever fill the sucking hole in his soul.

Hawk had helped get him appointed deputy director of park services. He didn't do much as regarded the office. It was more or less honorary. On the rare occasion that he offered it, his advice was always sound. He didn't need money. Government contracts alone would support the farm until he died. He didn't look for closure.

After his dream about the trains had come true, he'd stayed in the hospital a couple of more days. When he got out Hawk assigned him to a detail that oversaw arriving inmates.

It was an easy gig. He was part of a team that provided guidance to the proper departments when high profile inmates arrived.

He mostly drank sweet tea and perused nudie magazines.

Then one day a particular group of men was brought in. The thing that stood them apart was that they were all Eastern bloc natives.

They'd been intercepted at the Canadian border with two tractor trailers packed to bursting with Mexicans.

They'd been charged with human trafficking.

No one noticed when Dennis entered the segregated pod where the men were being held.

When the sound of sustained gunfire drew security forces to the area, they found Dennis kneeling in the center of a room with his hands behind his head.

Bodies lay strewn all around him, limbs akimbo, like macabre marionettes.

He was never convicted of the crime.

Because the accused smuggler's victims had been Mexican, the matter had been adjudicated in the Mayan courts.

The court found that at the time of the killings, Dennis had been suffering extreme duress.

They ruled that his actions had been engendered by acute grief, and further, that as a former prisoner of war himself, he was not responsible for the flashbacks, that caused his conduct.

The case was dismissed.

There had been no flashbacks and although it was true that he'd been under duress, Dennis knew exactly what he was doing when he'd killed those men.

After his acquittal he'd acquired the farm where he retired and continued to have prophetic dreams.

————

Doctor Zera Oma Dera became the most influential person in Africa.

At the end of hostilities between Initiative fighters and African factional resisters, she was installed as Guardian Mother, of the newly formed Coalition of Pan African Nations.

Her office had the last word regarding any foreign business involvement anywhere on the continent.

Her first order of business was to direct her Department of Continental Resources to establish economic development zones throughout the nations.

Copying the Chinese template, she oversaw the training of millions of Africans in the skills needed to transition from working the fields and mines to working the factories.

Her intercontinental infrastructure programs set the continent on the path to sustained economic stability.

In addition to her economic endeavors Doctor Oma Dera instituted sweeping continental educational programs designed to transform the system from the bottom up.

She continued to be a regular at the Cedars where she tirelessly promoted CPAN.

As Director of the Root Project, an Afro-centric program designed to promote native languages in educational institutions, Odell Giles became the New Nation liaison to the Linguistic Communication Alliance.

The federation of African nations was dedicated to the perpetuation and dissemination of African languages, dialects and culture.

Giles eventually moved to Ethiopia and became fluent in Oromo, Swahili, Kikongo and Tshiluba.

For his contributions to the sovereignty effort Louis Reyes walked out of the penitentiary at Pelican Bay as a full bird Colonel in the New Nation's army.

He was sworn in as Commander of Fort Zapata, a base built for training LatinX and former bangers for the nation's defense.

His soldiers were perennially acknowledged for their exemplary discipline and courage. He remained at the post for the rest of his life.

T. Edmond Longstreet resigned from the Temple.

With the New Nation operating as a sovereign constitutional democracy he had no cause for opposition.

Rather than return to radio he established a production company that promoted major sporting and entertainment events. The receipts funded his Huey P. Newton Foundation. The foundation provided full ride scholarships to students who excelled in the disciplines of law and political science.

Danny Ortega declined further government involvement and instead established the Society for Cyber Solutions. The open source enterprise was comprised of volunteer world renowned scientists who conceived theorems to advance the frontiers of artificial intelligence.

Jesse married Adelina.

The End

www.ingramcontent.com/pod-product-compliance
Lightning Source LLC
Chambersburg PA
CBHW070340010826
48976CB00017B/446